THE ACCIDENTAL SPY

Jacqueline George

Published by:
Q~Press Publishing

- 1 -

"Thank Allah it's Thursday," The Virgin thought to himself as he wiggled his key in the lock of his garden door. He had escaped from the office on the dot of six o'clock and no-one from Almadi or the desert could reach him for a whole luxurious fifteen hours. Fantastic. And Thursday night was party night, because everyone could sleep in tomorrow. The lock continued to resist his probing.

"Goddamn country," he muttered to himself. "Doesn't anything work?"

He heard a click as the lever was pulled back from the inside, and the heavy steel gate swung slowly open. He found himself looking straight at Evelina through the widening gap. Dressed in her white nurse's uniform with the absurd head piece. Evelina looking very wan and uncertain.

"Good grief! What are you doing here? How did you get in?"

"I climbed over the wall. I'm sorry - I didn't know what to do." Her lower lip trembled and The Virgin could see that he was expected to absorb a crisis. He took her in his arms and kicked the gate shut behind him. She buried her face against his neck and sobbed with great heaves of her body. He waited, making soothing noises as if she were an over-grown baby.

Cuddling Evelina had been an exciting fantasy from the day he had first met her. Not that she looked particularly pretty. She was slim and had strong black hair, but most Filipinos could say the same. She had dark, deep eyes; that too was normal. Unlike most of the Filipinos, she had a terrible complexion. Deeply pock-marked, which completely marred any conventional beauty. But who cared? She was lively and cheerful. A natural leader for the rest of the girls and a real ice-cold, heart-breaker for the men. She preferred, as far as The Virgin could make out, not to have a boyfriend at all and he had been forced to look elsewhere. Never mind; it felt pleasant that she had turned to him when she had a problem. Slowly, he eased her up the path to the front door and they stepped out of the sun into the cool darkness of the house. He took her through to the breakfast room and sat her down at the table. He hurried to get an iced coke with a shot of flash to calm her down.

"Come on then," he urged. "Drink this. What's the problem?"

She sipped and sobbed, and sipped again but seemed unable to tell him.

"Is it the other girls? No? Not bad news from home?"

"No - not that. It's Captain Zella."

That bastard Zella. He should have guessed. The petty tyrant who could not handle having total control of so many foreign women. He had a record of trying to blackmail girls by refusing to grant exit visas, and if they did not have his rubber stamp and signature, they could not leave the country for vacation or final exit. God knew if any of them had been foolish enough to give in and let him have what he wanted. They were all smart enough not to go into his office alone.

"What's he done this time? Is he trying to stop your holiday?"

"He caught me in the store room." She covered her face. "He forced me. I shouted but he was too strong. He - he touched me. With his finger." The sobbing came back and she rested her head on her arms. What could The Virgin do? He stood with a hand on her shoulder. "He pushed it in. He hurt me. The bastard! I was virgin, and he's broken me! One of the Sudanese heard me and opened the door, and he ran out. What will I do?"

"Are you alright?"

"No, I'm not alright!" The sharpness in her voice was a good sign.

"How did you get here? Why didn't you go back to your flat?"

"I didn't want anyone to know. I took a taxi and made him drop me over there. He stayed and watched me, so I climbed over the wall. I hate this place!"

"Climbed over the wall? You must have been really cross; have you seen how tall it is? I can just imagine you climbing over in your uniform."

Evelina gave a little squeak. "Yes. And the taxi driver was looking at my legs."

"I'm sure he would have helped you over if you'd asked. It would have made his week. Or may be his year. He's probably sitting in some tea-shop talking about you right now." The thought made her smile. Just a little smile, but it helped.

"So… What are we going to do with you? You want a shower, right? What about clothes?" His ex-wife had left a few things, but she was shorter and fatter. He checked them off mentally; a couple of satiny evening tops, slightly used underwear, a winter coat. Not promising. "Look, I'll leave a pile of things in the bathroom. Some of

Maria's things and a sports suit. A tee shirt. Just help yourself. Take a bath, that's better than a shower if you're upset. I'll put some water on the stove and we'll run a bath."

He remembered a sachet of bath gel, whatever that was, tucked in behind the aspirins and this seemed the occasion to use it. While they waited for the water to boil he ran around collecting bits and pieces from Maria's old room, clothes and cosmetics, his newest tee shirt and his track suit. He left them together with his one fluffy bath towel and called her in.

His wife had refused to eat anything he cooked as a matter of principle, which had suited The Virgin well enough at the time. Unfortunately, it left him sadly out of practice when she threw him onto his own resources, and he had been surviving on microwaved snacks and eating out. Cooking something for a distressed Filipino nurse would be a challenge. He settled on a mild chilli and set a piece of frozen steak in the microwave.

Evelina spent a long time in the bath. He heard her emerge from the bath room to disappear into Maria's room. The sound of the hair-dryer followed. Dinner was already in reasonable shape and he was chopping the tomato salad when Evelina appeared at his elbow. She looked relaxed. The sports suit did not look too ridiculously big and she had made herself up, even painting her finger and toe nails with Maria's varnish.

"Wow! You look pretty. Are you good at rice?" A stupid question to ask a Filipino.

She snorted and went over to the pan. "It's not ready yet - I think it's not right..." He searched for excuses as she tried it with the wooden spoon.

"OK. You go and sit down, and I'll finish. Where's the rice?" With relief The Virgin showed her around. While she was hustling the food along he went in search of the table cloth that should have been in the breakfast room but was not. He ran it to ground neatly folded amongst his winter shirts.

The food tasted good - surprisingly good really. Evelina was hungry enough to eat and seemed to enjoy it. As she finished she looked up with the germ of a smile on her face. "That better?" he asked hopefully.

"Yes. I feel much better now. Not sore at all. There was no bleeding, so perhaps I'm still virgin."

The Virgin was stumped. Medical people seemed to discuss anything anywhere. And as for twenty-eight year old virgin girls, he had no experience at all, no frame of reference. He would not know what to look for if the opportunity had ever presented itself. "Of course you're a virgin," he reassured her. "You didn't make love, so you're a virgin."

"But his finger went inside - I felt it. He must have broken me."

"That's nothing. Plenty of girls don't have anything to break. And you play sports..."

"Not that sort of sport!"

"No, but they say... I'm sure I read that sport could break it in older girls. Anyway, you didn't make love, so you're a virgin. That's all there is to it. And if anyone ever asks, just tell them lots of virgins are like you."

She was not convinced. "I don't believe any girl who says that."

The Virgin was rapidly getting out of his depth. "I'm sure I read it somewhere."

"Oh yes? You didn't just find out by experience?"

Now he was certainly in trouble. He suspected Evelina would not approve of sex without marriage. In fact he was sure she would not, or she would have tried it by now. "Well, no. I never made love with a virgin. I think."

"So all the girls you've had were experienced? Very experienced?"

"There's not that many, honestly." It was true. He had tried counting them once and had not even run out of fingers.

"Poor Virgin," she said sympathetically. "You should get a Polish girl-friend." That was true too. Most of the activity around town centred on the Polish nurses working for the Government. They were a generous, open-hearted bunch who like to dance and party. The trouble was that they were mostly older, divorced or had husbands back in Poland. And some were just too desperate. Well-off Western bachelors with oil-field salaries were prized catches, and the prospect of being grabbed by a large, fortyish Polish mama terrified him. The other major group of nurses, the Filipinos, lived in such a close group that they could not do anything without the entire community knowing. For them gossip and the shame of having an active foreign boy-friend far outweighed the advantages his relative wealth would bring. The Virgin inwardly complained at his lot again.

He tried to change the subject. "What would you like to do now? Go home?"

"Why? Are you busy?"

"Oh no. It's just that I thought... I mean, you've never come here by yourself before."

"But you're different. I don't mind visiting you. Everyone knows you wouldn't do anything bad."

Well, there's an insult, he thought. Am I really such a harmless character? He felt quite crushed. "Would you like to watch a video, then?"

"That would be good. I'll wash up while you shower, and we'll watch a video. You don't mind if I stay tonight? I can use Maria's room."

The Virgin swallowed his fantasies. "Oh no, you're always welcome. I'll look out some sheets for you."

Evelina jumped up and started to tidy the table. "You shower then. Don't worry about the sheets, I already took them." He went off to the shower thinking to himself that she must know the contents of his house better than he did himself. He had loaned his house for parties a couple of times, and left the girls there during the day to get things ready. They must have gone through all his things, every cupboard. He had nowhere to hide anything embarrassing. If he took it to the office his secretary would find it; if he left it at home Nancy the Filipino lady who did his cleaning would soon discover it. Oh well; who cared? They probably thought him a complete screwball. Anyway, he liked nice to have women around the house. It forced him to be a bit neater than his natural inclination. He often found himself giving the house a quick tidy before Nancy came.

When they turned in that night, the click of Evelina turning the key in her bedroom door depressed him. He left his door ajar, just in case she changed her mind.

Next morning was Friday, and The Virgin had only to visit the office for a short time. Almadi did not work on Fridays, so he simply checked the telexes and telephoned Bill over at TAMCO to see what the rigs were doing. A quick chat with the desert to relay the news, and he drove back home for breakfast by nine o'clock. Evelina was waiting for him with breakfast ready to heat. Very civilised. He could grow to like the idea.

"So what would you like to do?" he asked over his fried rice and eggs. "Shall I take you home?"

"You go to the beach today, right? OK. You can take me home after ten o'clock, when the others are at church, and I'll get changed and go with you."

The Virgin was struck dumb. Filipino girls did not go to the beach, especially with foreigners. For a start, they were afraid to go brown. A complexion and skin colour that European girls would murder for, and they wanted to stay as white as possible. And any girl mixing with Europeans on the beach without a substantial Filipino escort would be hopelessly compromised. He hurried to agree.

The gaffir at the gate held them up. It was always difficult to predict what would happen with gaffirs. Some days the gate was pegged wide open and everyone drove in and out while the gaffirs kefalikked with their friends in the gatehouse. Other days the gaffirs guarded the nurse's quarters like a harem. Today was easy; the old man simply wanted a closer look at which nurse was in the car alone with a man. As he bent to peer in, his curiosity was met by a stony-eyed Evelina. She had changed back into her uniform and looked capable of subduing an army of gaffirs. The old man backed off mumbling and went to open the gate.

"We're lucky," ventured The Virgin.

Evelina said nothing, but kept her General's face on until they had passed the gate. "Now they will talk about me," she said peevishly.

"Never mind. It's nice to have a reputation. Better than being boring." She did not seem to agree.

The time of their arrival at the hospital avoided her friends. They pulled up at the staff house and The Virgin waited outside. There had been a time when he had made a determined assault on Evelina and he imagined some signs of interest. She was attractive; lively, cheerful, endlessly competent. A very desirable lady, but he had never made any impression. Everyone must have known he was chasing her; her friends pushed her to him at dances, made a big deal of sitting them together. The truth was that Evelina had always kept him at arm's length, never visited him alone, never sat in his car a moment longer than necessary. He had taken the hint in the end and left her alone - though he never understood just what she had wanted of him.

That was all over now. He had taken a field-break, a couple of weeks touring in Turkey and tried keeping away from her when he returned. That suited her. She just kept on with the old distant friendship and seemed quite happy. It was just as well The Virgin did not take the brush-off too hard. He would have lost a friend if he had. She bounced out of the staff house in baggy tee-shirt and jeans, dropped a bag on the back seat and they set off.

The road to the beach, like all the country around Sabah, was flat and boring. Centuries of damage by wandering goat and sheep flocks had reduced the summer vegetation to unpalatable camel-thorn and clumps of heather-like scrub. The bare bones of the country showed through. In some places the Government had tried to kick-start real agriculture by ripping up the thick rocky pavement that shielded the surface. This left ragged embankments of limestone slabs around the few cultivated areas.

The blacktop headed south, parallel to the coast. As they left town the amount of rubbish lining the road decreased, and soon they saw little beyond dead tyres and the odd junk truck parked in its last resting place at the roadside. The horizon stretched brown and flat to the east but to the west, just beyond the sabkha, lay the Mediterranean. He sometimes thought the Mediterranean was Tabriz's only likeable feature. Complain as much as you liked, Sabah was still a Mediterranean sea-port and rich Europeans paid a fortune just to spend their holidays on the opposite shore of the same sea. The Virgin, on the other hand, was paid for being here and paid fairly well.

The word this week was that everyone would go to fifty-nine kilometres. Foreigners liked to keep together to avoid young local men harassing the ladies, and so they packed on a short stretch of the one thousand kilometres of empty beach. The turning to this week's beach was marked by the remains of an ancient Russian truck and when they reached it, they swung right and dropped off the blacktop. A bumpy track brought them to the edge of the sabkha and the wheel marks fanned out over its sun-baked surface. The Virgin headed for the glare of car windows in the dunes. Keeping his speed up he bounced over the narrow sandy track and came to rest next to a long line of parked vehicles with foreigners' registration plates.

Over the low dune was the sea and a solid wall of beach umbrellas, each pitched just too close to its neighbour to allow an intruder to settle in between. It was a cosmopolitan spot. East Europeans with names like Zdzislaw and Ivan rubbed shoulders with

Alfredo from The Argentine and Bola from Ghana. John could be from UK, or America, or anywhere in the Commonwealth. The Greeks, both the mainland and Cypriot varieties, were present as they had been for at least the last three thousand years. There were even a few Korean construction workers, cut off from the rest by culture and language. They frolicked in the sea, barbecued fish and took photographs, but no one else had any idea what they said to each other.

The Virgin searched for the rest of the Hash and found them around an ancient Toyota four-wheel drive with its cassette player turned well up. A crowd of boisterous, boyish men sizzling in the sun and sipping home-brewed beer. They had a fair sprinkling of girl-friends with them, mostly Hashers in their own right. Heads turned as the two of them walked up and he thought he heard Evelina groan.

"Hey, Virgin! You're late - what's been keeping you? Here - have a beer."

"Don't stop over there - come here - we want to talk with your friend."

"No chance of that. She won't want to talk to you..."

The same old crowd. Good hearted, noisy, like kids out of school. And why not? The wife and family were back home and the men worked here earning the salary to keep them in bread and butter. So why not enjoy life when you could? The disadvantages of Tabriz were enough to make the simplest of pleasures glow. The Virgin headed for the edge of the crowd where the ladies lay working on their suntans. Including Danka, assistant matron in the hospital, a short, plump fire-cracker of a woman with traditional Polish red-tinted curls and badly repaired teeth. Evelina ran for her company and protection.

The Virgin concentrated on erecting the umbrella and spreading the beach mat while the girls chattered. Stripped down to his bathing costume, he went to sit with them.

"I missed an accident yesterday," Evelina told him. "After I'd gone they brought in some burnt soldiers."

"Yes. Bad burns," Danka shook her head with resignation. "Then just we trying to take them from the Army pick-ups, some officers scream up in big Mercedes car and make them all go back in the pick-ups and go away. It is big problem. I don't know where they take them. No other hospital in town. I think those men die soon; some of them. Burns like that very difficult."

"I wonder what the bastards are up to now?" The Virgin mused. "Some-one probably screwed up loading gasoline and they're trying to hide it from Almadi. But if people are dying..."

"Sure. They dying for sure. And Virgin, not normal burning. Big blisters but no black. Steam, maybe, not fire. I don't know, but they dying. Boże. Those poor boys. But what can you do? Not even possible to make them injections."

The Virgin shuddered. He often heard horror stories from the nurses that made his skin crawl. He did not know how they could handle the ugliness of it all. Perhaps having the power to do something about the suffering made it easier. This accident seemed a bit different though. Firstly it was Army, and secondly they were obviously trying to hide something. He wondered what it could be for a moment and then made for the water, leaving Evelina hiding in the shade of the umbrella. She was wearing an incredibly old-fashioned, ruched pink one-piece swimming costume and reading a magazine.

He delivered Evelina back to the hospital before seven next morning. If that did not destroy her reputation, nothing would. He could not understand why she should suddenly want to court the disapproval of her community, but she had just insisted quietly that she wanted to stay another night, and equally quietly locked her door as she went to bed. If she understood what she was doing to The Virgin's nervous system, she did not let it worry her. His frustrations were lost in the start of a new week.

The office was quiet at seven o'clock. Almadi did not start for another hour at least, but the boss had insisted that Sabah should start early enough to get a clear telephone line to the desert. So the first hour of the day was always quiet. Just a quick phone call to pick up any queries and fuel orders, and then he could settle back with a coffee and get on with any thinking work before the rest of the office came in.

The major job on his desk this morning was a job procedure for the RomDril-1 rig drilling just north of Sabah. Having a rig thirty minutes drive away was an unusual luxury. It meant he could get out of the office with a legitimate excuse whenever the work got too tedious. Of course, as a downside he occasionally had to go and sit through operations at inconvenient times, but it was worth it. He liked to play at being a field engineer once in a while.

The job coming up was a 13-3/8" casing cementation. Not difficult, but big. They would set the casing at 1800m, much deeper than normal because TAMCO wanted to drill deep on this hole. The thing about cementing 13-3/8" casings was not that they were technically difficult, but just that they took so much cement. If TAMCO wanted to do a proper job, filling a nominally 17-1/2" diameter hole with steel casing of 13-3/8" outside diameter left a gap between the pipe and the hole wall that could take 5000 sacks of cement to fill. Add in the chemicals - retarder and dispersant - to keep the cement slurry liquid for long enough to pump it into place, and the final bill for the operation would start to get large. Plus the casing hardware, delivery charges and the actual operational costs, and TAMCO would be running for cover. The money would lie in the size of the job rather than its sophistication. The Virgin's task was to persuade TAMCO to write an expensive cementing program while trying at the same time to make 5000 sacks of cement look small. The proposal was going to be a challenge.

The trouble did not usually come from Bill the Drilling Superintendent. He was Canadian and used to doing things properly. Tayfun, the drilling engineer in charge of mud and cementing, was the one who always gave The Virgin nightmares. Time after time he would come up with suggestions drawn from his native Azeri oil-patch, where everything was always rosy and they never had difficult wells. Ask him for a 13-3/8" design and he would come up with a 200 sack plug that would just about hold the casing shoe in place. Blow-outs were something he read about occasionally but never expected to happen to him. The Virgin took care to write an open-ended proposal that did not look too expensive at first sight, but had the potential to grow into a really big operation. Once the concept of a proper job was on the table, it would be so much harder for Tayfun to trim it down without putting his own name to it, and like most of the foreigners in TAMCO, he would rather just let things roll on than sign his name to anything.

The Virgin fired up the office computer and prepared to fit a quart into a pint pot. He was still there when his stomach told him that lunch would be appreciated. If RomDril had not been RomDril, he could have driven to the rig for a meal and a coffee with the company man, but the thought of dry Romanian fried chicken sent him home instead. Micro-waved jacket potato and tinned tuna again. Why not? Add a couple of fresh tomatoes and it was nutritious enough. Anyway, he did not want to eat too much because it was Saturday afternoon, and Saturday meant the Hash.

Five o'clock saw him driving off to Cape Horn, this week's Hash venue. Cape Horn was a minuscule rocky nubbin interrupting the smooth run of sandy beach north of town. For most of the year the Mediterranean lay lifeless around its sandy rocks, and rounding the Horn was a pleasant summer dog-paddle. Now the early autumn days meant cooler weather, and the local fishermen had packed their gear away for the year. The car bounced down the track to an old tyre that some-one had stood on edge against a rock. 'Run #783' was daubed crudely around its walls in pink paint. The others had started to arrive and were hiding in their cars from the watery breeze. Over the next five minutes another dozen cars bumped up to the old tyre, and their occupants got out and began to change. It felt a touch chilly standing around without a track suit and The Virgin thought about running in a sweater. Some vestige of masculine pride prevented him.

The clock soon drove the Master over to the old tyre. He pulled his miniature hunting horn from his track-suit pocket - no false pride there - and blew a raspberry. "Sabah Hash House Harriers, Run Number 783, running on pansy pink - ON-ON!" He ran a token half a dozen strides at the head of the pack and lapsed into a walk. The serious hashers jostled past him and away.

They followed pink splotches of paint daubed on loose pebbles. The marks stood out clearly against the bare sandy earth and cropped vegetation, and the pack was soon well spread out along the trail. Fast runners at the front, the casual hashers walking along behind and every sort of unfit or lazy foreigner straggling between them. The Virgin applied himself to guessing where the trail would be going, and where profitable short cuts might lie. Normally at this venue the trail was a tight loop heading out along the coast and back on the beach (or vice versa). The Virgin could run as far as his energy level would allow and then cut across the loop and sneak home. But the Hare this week was Rubberdy-Dub and he had a reputation for second-guessing even the most determined of short-cutters. Right now his trail led them straight away from the sea and who knew if he would turn left or right? As The Virgin puffed up to the first check it seemed that Rubberdy was living up to his reputation. The front runners had already found and abandoned two false trails and were scattered wide looking for the real one.

The trail zigged and zagged, and headed more or less away from the cars for a depressingly long distance. Difficult checks with easy trails beckoning back down towards the beach - all false. The Virgin's private energy conservation programme would normally have led him off to one side or the other by now in search of some not-too-blatant short-cut. This week he was still undecided which way to turn.

He jogged on into some scrubby trees to yet another check - number 7 painted on the rusting shell of an abandoned refrigerator. He hardly had time to catch his breath when the Hash Horn beeped from somewhere in front and to his left. He slid down a bank into a stony wadi and followed the other slow coaches. He had begun to doubt Rubberdy's sanity when the wadi opened out into a bigger channel and the paint turned right - up towards the jebel and still further away from the sea.

Rubberdy was waiting for them where the main road crossed the wadi. He had somehow borrowed a bus – a fearsome Russian wreck with no glass in its windows and very little of its original blue paint surviving - to drive them back to the cars. No-one but Rubberdy would go to such lengths to fool everyone. Still, it felt good to jolt slowly back to the cars. It felt even nicer to watch all the faint hearts, who had given up early and not reached the bus, having to jog back down to the sea under their own power.

The sun was dropping scarlet into the sea as they drove the short distance to the Bash. A hollow in the sand dunes, out of sight and relatively safe. Eytie Joe had brought a pick-up load of broken pallets from his camp and the boy scouts amongst them got busy lighting a fire. They put the table up and set the Tilley lamp glowing. The pack stood and watched as the amber was decanted into the insulated urn and then crowded around with their plastic cups, faces glowing in the lamp-light as they poured their first drink of the day.

The Virgin felt a tug at his elbow. "You go swimming tonight? I come too." He looked down at Danka.

"Swimming? It's too bloody cold for that. Besides, I don't have my swimming gear."

"Neither I," she announced blandly. "Come on, we go a little away."

Too polite or too lazy to refuse her anything, The Virgin turned to follow. Strange, he thought, why me? There had never been more than shared friends and polite conversation between them, and now she had invited him to skinny-dip in the starlight. What could a gentleman say? She took his arm as they picked their way along the beach.

"Where is Evelina tonight? You not bring her to Hash?"

"No - well - I don't think she'd want to come." He could just imagine the expression on Evelina's face if she had been forced to join in the noisy drinking games for which the Sabah Hash was famous.

"I think she have trouble with Zella."

Now The Virgin understood. Danka was fishing for gossip. "Yes – the bastard caught her in a store-room. He tried to touch her but she screamed and one of the Sudanese came into the room. No harm done, but he really pissed her off."

"I think she hurt him. He not come to hospital today and she cut her nails too short. I think she scratch him and break her nails." Danka would obviously get the full story eventually.

"Good. She should have scratched his eyes out." Indeed, The Virgin wished she had done some real damage.

"And then you take her home, right?"

"Ah, yes. She stayed with me. In the guest room." Danka looked at him in disbelief. "It's true. She slept in the guest room." And locked the door, he might have added, and me with my tongue hanging out in the next room.

Danka chuckled. "Poor Virgin! Never mind - she too dry and bony. Not good in bed." She chuckled again and hung on his arm, a hot, round, inviting dumpling of a girl. "I think she never try a man. And you not want to be the first. Too much trouble I think, and not good fun."

Her closeness and cheerful sexiness had begun to stir The Virgin and he was just wondering if it would be worth getting a bit closer when she turned back. "Good. We go far enough. We swim here." The Bash showed as a faint glow in the dark dunes behind them, and the twilight from the west gave little light to see by. The breeze had died with the sun and the shivering cold had gentled. Danka began to undress.

What could a gentleman do, The Virgin asked himself again? He quickly stripped off, trying not to look too closely at the white form emerging beside him. It was too dark to make out any details but the animal in him was beginning to raise its head. He started for the sea to drown his embarrassment but she called him back. "Wait, wait. We go together."

She was unhooking her bra and then using his arm for balance, she pulled her socks off and dropped them onto the heap of clothes. "Ah. It is too cold. And will be colder when we come out. Oh look!" She chuckled and made a firm grab for him. "Jaki ładny! Is very good. I like him! Come, first we swim." Like a dog on a lead, The Virgin found himself being drawn into the water. It was cold enough to reduce the problem.

Getting out was a cold business. Neither of them had a towel so The Virgin rubbed her down briskly with his tee-shirt and then wrapped the jacket of his track suit about her shoulders. Sitting bare-bottomed on the dry sea grass, he hugged her close and felt his blood start to race again. The craziness had started to run through Danka's veins too and she burrowed into his embrace, offering a kiss. She tasted strong and sexy. Reaching under her legs he lifted her onto his lap without breaking their kiss. His free hand groped inside the track suit jacket to squeeze a heavy breast.

"Stop right there!"

Standing in front of them stood a man with a gun. A soldier. In uniform. Pointing a stubby machine gun at them. His dark green clothing showed almost black, and his face was invisible beneath the peak of his forage cap. Danka gave a gasp and tried to reach for their clothes.

"No! Stop right there. If you keep still nothing will happen."

Danka pushed The Virgin's hand from her jacket and tried to cover herself up. As they sat uncomprehending, more uniformed figures appeared behind the threatening man. Muted comments were made in a language The Virgin did not recognise, and met with quiet laughter. It was not Arabic, and the American-accented English of the man in front of them had given no hint of their origin either.

"What do you want?"

"I want you to stay sitting where you are. Just for a few minutes. Then we'll go."

"I want my clothes," said Danka. Her voice sounded shaky and close to tears. The soldier called to one of the others and their clothes were brought over. Still sitting, they wriggled into them.

"Stop. No shoes. I don't want you to run away. Here, I'll throw your shoes over there, OK?"

That's nice of him, thought The Virgin. At least we're not stranded and if he's taking that much trouble, we're probably safe. "Who are you?"

"Never mind that. Just keep quiet." He called to the soldier who had brought their clothes and gave him the job of guarding them. He walked off along the edge of the water, peering out to sea.

Danka inched closer, and The Virgin put his arm around her. "What do they want?" she asked.

"Not speaking!" Their guard gestured with his gun and they fell silent.

From across the dark water The Virgin became aware of a low grumbling sound. Two of the soldiers slung their weapons over their shoulders and waded into the sea. The one who had first secured them was muttering into a hand-held radio. He seemed to be the officer in charge. Everyone was looking out to sea.

In a rush, two inflatable boats rode into the beach on white foam trails. The officer hurried over to his prisoners and again held them at gunpoint. Behind him, the boats had been spun round and the soldiers were wading out and jumping aboard. With his free hand the officer spoke again into the field radio. For a moment all was still until two more men ran out of the dunes and down to the boats. It all seemed very quiet and professional.

With the two sentries safely aboard, the officer raised his gun to the peak of his cap. "Well, goodnight. I hope you have a very exciting evening." He turned and in moments the two boats were picking up speed, their heavily silenced engines making no more than a subdued puttering sound. The whole episode could only have taken a few minutes.

"Moj Boże!" whispered Danka. "What is happening? Who are they?"

"Not locals, that's for sure. Not Americans either. And very professional." The Virgin thought for a moment. Whatever had happened, he knew he would have been better off not seeing it. Or even being anywhere around. They had just seen a small group of foreign soldiers being covertly extracted from Tabrizi territory. Whatever they had been up to was undoubtedly a lot of trouble for some-one, and life threatened to get very unpleasant for The Virgin if the local security forces got wind of it. And for the Hash and all its members. Half the foreigners in Sabah in sports clothes, men and women together, drinking beer, at night. That was enough of a catalogue of sins in the narrow Muslim mind to put them all away in calaboosh for a few nights at least. Add to that military saboteurs or assassins and they would all be locked up forever. Flight was the surest remedy.

"OK, we'd better get out of here right now. God knows who'll be chasing after that lot, and if they catch us here we'll be shot on sight. If we're lucky. And we'd better tell the Hash. Come on, where are our shoes?"

They fumbled across the dark sand to find their shoes. "I'm very frighted," said Danka. "I think we have big problem."

"Too right! Come on, get moving." They hurriedly brushed the worst of the sand from their feet and started to get into their shoes.

Too late. From behind the dunes came the thumping sound of someone running to the beach. They were just straightening up as another soldier burst onto the sand, gun at the ready.

There did not seem to be much they could do. Their hands went up automatically as the gun swung towards them. The soldier ran past them to the water's edge. He knew he was too late, but he turned anyway and shouted something at them in Arabic.

Danka answered but he did not seem to understand and tried again in English. "You are foreigners? Did you see soldiers here?" He was panting heavily and looked pathetic in his distress.

"They've gone. It must be five minutes ago," The Virgin said.

The soldier cursed and strained to see what was happening across the water. No sound came back to them. He cursed again and sat down on the sand. Obviously things could hardly be worse for him.

"What will you do now?" asked Danka.

He seemed to become aware of them again. With an effort he pulled his thoughts together. "Now I must go from here quickly."

"Can we help?" The Virgin found it hard to recognise his own voice offering help. It was probably just the fact that the soldier was a foreigner subjected to another outrageous twist of fortune. Living as they did in Sabah, all foreigners felt they had some kind of responsibility for their neighbours.

The soldier was rapidly recovering his wits. "You have a car? Yes, of course, you must have a car. Yes please, you can help me to leave here quickly. First I must change into my escape clothes. Please wait." Without delaying further, he started to pull off his boots. Soon he was standing in his underpants.

From one of his belt pouches he pulled a tight roll that he shook out into a djellabiyah and waist coat.

"You're going to wear that?" The Virgin asked. "That's no good if you're travelling with us." There was no alternative; he took off his track suit and offered it to the naked man.

"What about gun?" asked Danka, practicality coming to the rescue.

"Oh no. No guns. We get caught with you and a gun in the car, we're dead. Throw it in the sea."

The soldier agreed. "Yes, OK. Guns make too much trouble. All of this has to go in the sea." Working carefully he filled each boot with sand, and his empty pouch, and wrapped the whole uniform up into a tight bundle in his shirt. "First I put this in the sea, OK?" Without a hint of embarrassment he stripped off his underpants and stepped into the water. The gun he threw as far as he could. The bundle he first soaked to make sure it was going to sink, and then pitched that after it. He came back to the sand brushing as much water as he could from his body.

Their route to the cars took them along the beach and past the Bash. The ceremonies were well under way and voices were raised in a raucous chorus as yet another hasher downed a compulsory drink for some sin, real or invented.

"What is that?" asked the soldier.

"Oh, it's nothing. Just the lads enjoying themselves. What do we call you?" asked The Virgin as they stumbled across the sand towards the cars.

"Ah - Dov Nagel is good now. But in my escape clothes I am Ali Mohammed."

"We will take him to the Bash?" asked Danka.

"Are you crazy? No-one's going to see him. He's going straight to the car and he'll lie down in the back." The Virgin was beginning to think properly now the pressure was on. That just left the Hash to deal with. "Here. Take the car key and go on. I'll have to do something about the Hash."

He stopped and reached out for Danka's arm. "Look - you'd better stay out of this. I'll take him home with me tonight, and do something with him tomorrow. There's no point both of us getting mixed up in this."

Dov agreed. "He's right. It could be dangerous. Just give me somewhere safe tonight, and then tomorrow I will go into town. I know what to do there. I will be in no trouble."

Danka looked at them both and swallowed. "No. I come also. It will be better at checkpoints if you have woman in the car. They not want make too much trouble if I am with you. I come with you tonight. Tomorrow you take me early to Barani to get my uniform and I take taxi to hospital." Neither of the men said any more.

As The Virgin stepped into the firelight, he was welcomed with shouts and sly questions about how Danka was feeling. A foolish smile on his face, he went up to Noddy, standing on an upturned box with his clip-board in hand. He was about to punish The Virgin with a drink or worse for putting sex before beer, but he must have seen something in his eyes because he bent to listen. The Virgin drew him a little away from the Bash.

"Noddy, you've got to listen to me. We've got a real problem here. We've just had a bunch of troops run over us and out to sea in boats."

Noddy would have been an old man anywhere else. Grey of hair and beard, he should have been wearing a jacket and tie to the office in Dublin during the day, and going home to the old suburban wife at night. With nothing more than a trip to the Public Library to brighten things up. Here his wiry legs stuck out of green running shorts and his tee-shirt proclaimed him as a veteran of many hashes. He was not drunk yet, but he had trouble getting his mind around what The Virgin was telling him.

"You mean the Army's on the beach?"

"No, no. Not the local army anyway. These guys were something else completely. Foreigners. Not Americans. Nor Europeans either – well, not north Europeans. I don't know who they were, but they weren't screwing around. They just came running down the beach, held us up with guns, and took off in two inflatables. You've got to get everyone out of here before the locals catch on."

Noddy shook his head, not wanting to believe. "Oh Jesus, Mary and Joseph. There's going to be shit everywhere. Oh Christ. I'll get them moving; come and tell them what happened."

"No, Noddy, I can't. Danka's in trouble, I've got to go to her. Don't tell them everything. Just say we got stopped by a couple of soldiers who are going back for their sergeant. That'll move everyone. Don't say anything about the foreigners, or word will get around and Danka and I are toast. Please! You're the only one who knows."

Noddy could understand the position, and The Virgin knew the man would not talk. "OK," he said, "I'll get them moving. Better have them split up; we don't all want to go in procession. I'll send some left and along the ring road. And I'll wash out the beer cooler. We'd better tip the beer into the sand, dammit." As he returned to the Bash, The Virgin ran for the car.

Dov and Danka were sitting in the darkness. He leapt into the car and started back up the dirt track to the road. Thorn bushes, looking remote and threatening in this new world, swung in and out of his headlights as they jolted along.

"Er - Dov. What documents do you have?"

"I have an Egyptian ID card for Mohammed Ali. Nothing else."

"Right. This is how we'll do it. If we get stopped, it will probably be just to check the vehicle papers, so don't worry. If they get personal, say you're a business man staying in the Bab al Sabah hotel and we're giving you a lift from the Hash. Don't say too much and you'll probably get away with it. If they ask you for more, I don't know what you can say. You're on your own.

"Maybe you'd heard about the Hash from a friend in Cairo who had telephoned some-one to find out the location, so you came by taxi to meet some of the foreign business men. That would do. But you stopped in the wrong place and got there late. We're just giving you a lift back to town. OK?"

Dov listened intently; the threat to his life was very real. "OK. It's thin, but it might keep you two out of trouble. Are they likely to ask?"

"No. It's never happened to me yet. We'll be alright. Relax and enjoy the ride." The Virgin found he could kid himself that everything was fine most of the time, but every now and then an icy hand would reach up out of his stomach and threaten to strangle him. The car bumped onto the blacktop and he headed for town. Dodging the old pick-ups and taxis without lights kept his mind occupied. He began to wonder about his guest.

"What the hell were you guys doing here anyway?" he asked.

Dov thought for a while. " I don't suppose it matters if you know. It will be all around town tomorrow anyway. There was a little Palestinian doctor of chemistry who was making a nuisance of himself. So we shot him." He made it sound quite a natural thing to do.

"Jesus - what sort of nuisance was that?"

"Chemical weapons. He was working up some cheap and nasty production line here. Not a good man at all." Dov sounded calm and unperturbed. Perhaps such things were natural for him.

"But that means they're going to be running all over town looking for you!"

"Don't worry about that. They won't find him until tomorrow at the earliest, if the dogs have left anything. We didn't make any trouble, and he's well hidden now. We just rang his door bell and told him to come along. He thought we were Tabrizi." Horror piled on horror in The Virgin's mind. They had just called the little doctor into their car - did they have a car? Where was it? Where was the doctor?

"You didn't leave him back there did you?" If the body was found near to the Hash, they could expect some very uncomfortable times ahead.

Dov laughed. "No, don't worry. We killed him somewhere along here I think. One of the side tracks on the right, in the reeds at the edge of the swamp. Then we hid him and dropped our van near the pick-up point. I was making sure the van was taken away OK, and the bastards left me behind. Now I have to find my own way home."

"Who are you anyway?"

"Me? Or us? Well, can't you guess? Let's just say we don't have too many Palestinian friends."

They drove on in silence.

It was a good time to drive through the check-points. The assorted soldiers, police and paramilitary security men were all comfortably full of their evening cous-cous, and too concerned with sitting and chatting to their friends to give any trouble. The Virgin was just nodded through, an uninteresting foreigner with his wife and a friend, unable to speak Arabic no doubt and with all his documents in order. Before they got home he had Dov lie down in the back seat and stay there until the car was out of sight in the garage. With their high walls, Arab homes are designed to give their families privacy and Dov could be smuggled inside unseen.

Danka busied herself in the kitchen and The Virgin opened a beer. This brew was not too bad. He was no expert and often produced beer only fit for the Hash, but this time it had turned out well, clear, gassy and full of hops. He decanted it carefully into an iced jug and took it through to the front room. Dov took a sip, and winced. Not a long term Sabah resident and quite unable to appreciate the distinctive flavour.

"What is this? This is from Tabriz?" he asked, making no effort to be polite.

The Virgin shrugged. "I made it. Stay a while and you'll learn to like it. Some people even miss it so much when they go home that they have to take up brewing. Go easy - it's stronger than it seems."

Dov looked unconvinced. "It is a very good reason to leave quickly, I think."

"Boże, piwo!" Danka came in carrying an empty glass. "Na zdrowie!" The first glass disappeared and she poured another.

"Dov is being rude about my beer."

Danka laughed. "He should stay some more longer and run with me to the Hash. Then he will see bad beer. This is very good. We open one more. The spaghetti will be half hour or some more." She settled back in the armchair, unworried.

The Virgin opened the next bottle. He also felt unworried; home seemed safe and the unpleasant side of Tabriz stopped at the gate. He left the jug with the others and went for a shower. Nancy would have some extra washing this week; first Evelina and now two more guests. He would have to look out some more sheets, pillow-cases and towels.

The boiler could only manage a tepid shower and he washed quickly. As he dried himself, he probed his emotions, unable to leave them alone. It was like coming back from the dentist after an extraction and being unable to stop his tongue wandering to the empty hole. He was now a bit-part player on the world stage. Interfering with the Middle Eastern balance of terror and military retaliation. It should have been more remarkable, more frightening. Instead, he was taking a shower and waiting for the spaghetti. Was this what it was always like? Were the racks of violent thrillers at the airport not telling the whole truth? He supposed that, like many other things in the world, the reality was far more ordinary than the telling of it.

They turned in early that night. It would be a six o'clock start next morning and the tension had made them all sleepy. The Virgin lay in his bed with the light turned down, waiting for Danka to finish her shower. It took a long time. He heard the water stop, and then she must have found the hair-dryer. Its low hum was soporific. He was dozing when he heard the bathroom door open. Then the creak of the guest room door and a firm click as it latched shut. He switched the light off.

He rose to Danka's knocking. "Virgin, is nearly six o'clock." He struggled up and cleared the bathroom without really waking. Dov appeared for breakfast unshaven and wearing his djellabiyah. He had a rough length of white cotton wound around his head. Another day's growth of beard and he would look perfect.

"Hey, Mohammed Ali! For Christ's sake, don't stand up like that. You'll look like a soldier in a bed sheet if you don't slow down."

"Yes. You are right. I must think like Mohammed Ali also. But for now, I will be myself." He sat down to toast and coffee.

"Do you have somewhere to go?"

"Do not concern yourself with me. I know what to do in this circumstance. I have instructions." He sounded icy calm.

"How about money? Or anything else? Food?"

"I have with me seventy-two dinars. I think this will be enough. Also some dollars. But you may give me some sandals if you have old ones. Or I will go in bare feet."

The Virgin was taken aback by his poise. Dov found himself alone in enemy territory, many kilometres from the nearest frontier, which in itself was not particularly friendly, and yet he appeared unperturbed. He had been well drilled and prepared for his job. Nothing but the grossest bad luck could stop him now. He went to find some old flip-flops.

Getting Dov out of the house was as easy as getting him in. There were no eyes on the street to see The Virgin drive out with his girl-friend who had just spent a very un-Islamic and probably illegal night in his house. Or so it appeared. In fact, The Virgin had no doubt that at all that some of his neighbours already knew he had taken another whore nurse home, Polish this time. He had only the vaguest impression of what would be going through the local men's repressed minds, the lurid pictures, the insane jealousy of his forbidden life-style. And the women folk would be equally fascinated at the thought of a shameless harlot having sex with who-ever she wanted, right next door to them.

Out on the open road, Dov sat up. The day was still grey but a brave sun gilded the undersides of the clouds. Another fine day in the Mediterranean holiday resort. There was a scatter of traffic on the roads; no-one liked an early start in autumn or winter. They drove towards the old vegetable market where already the Egyptian and Sudanese casual labourers had begun to gather in the hope of a day's work. Dov slipped out at a road junction. A simple 'Shukran - masalama' and he had gone. In the mirror The Virgin saw him start to shuffle along the road in his borrowed flip-flops, no hurry, no destination, just another homeless Egyptian looking for a few cents.

They drove to the apartments at Barani. Tall concrete blocks, straight from the outskirts of Budapest, but planted here in bare earth and surrounded by rubbish and pools of diluted sewage. He delivered Danka to the door under the eyes of a group of her compatriots waiting for the hospital transport. She would make the bus if she hurried.

She closed the door and put her head through the window. "I am sorry, Virgin, but he was alone... Next time I come with you, yes?"

The Virgin was feeling definitely piqued as he drove off. His reputation had suffered again. Evelina would know before coffee break that he had been making love to Danka. He did not know why that should bother him, but it did. And he was not sure that he wanted the consolation prize that Danka had offered. She could be fun sometimes, but she was not The Virgin's dream girl. Too fat, too old, East European dentistry - he did not know what it was, but she did not stir him. He would not make himself too available.

There was a police station-wagon waiting outside his office block, and his stomach turned over. It was full of young policemen wearing black leather jackets. They were chattering animatedly and smoking. He forced himself to look at them without interest as he passed by. There was no response.

He peeped down at the street from his office window. The station wagon was still there, but no-one appeared to be watching. After twenty minutes, two of the policemen got out and started hand-in-hand down the road. The others drove off. He told himself that they had just stopped for a chat and a cigarette together.

Over the next few days, The Virgin began to realise that his initial reaction to the events of Saturday night had been wrong. They had not been ordinary events, and he felt far from ordinary inside. Nothing was happening, but nothing seemed to be the way it had been. At least, he thought nothing was happening. Now every time he passed a police car or was stopped at a road block he had a flashback of what he had seen and done. His waking thoughts were occupied incessantly with wondering if the police and army presence had increased, or if that he just noticing them more.

He heard no news of 'the little doctor'. None in European circles, anyway. He would have liked to ask Abdul in the office but his hints brought out no news. Apparently nothing had been said on the television about commando raids or captured assassins. He found the lack of information coloured everything he did and thought, and he slept badly.

His daily visits to Tayfun to hammer out the details of the 13-3/8" job had become drudgery. Surprisingly, Tayfun's reaction to his lack of interest was to let the design move ahead without too much interference. The Virgin brought him the lab test results on the proposed cement formulation, and he made no request for further testing of cheaper formulations. The job looked set to blossom into something quite substantial.

He ran into Evelina again when he visited a darts match. She played for one of the teams, played competently, and did not seem to mind the drinking that went along with the matches. The Virgin had not joined a team. He could not work up any feeling for the game and the meetings went on very late at night. But darts matches were the next best thing to visiting the pub, and the flash was free. He generally took along a big bottle of coke or lemonade as a mixer so his freeloading was not too obvious.

Evelina looked coldly at him. "Where's Danka?"

"Er - I don't know. She's nothing to do with me." It did not sound convincing and did nothing to soften her look. What was he supposed to tell her? 'She didn't sleep with me. She was with a stray commando we picked up on the beach. In the guest room, just like you were.' Why did he feel embarrassed anyway?

"Look, she's not with me, and she never was. She came home for something to eat and that was it. Nothing else."

"That's not what she said. Anyway, it's good for you to have a Polish girl-friend. I am very pleased. Look, it's my turn now." She turned and went to the dart-board.

He spent most of the evening sitting at the bar talking to Eytie Joe about the days before the Revolution, when Sabah was a tourist resort and the sort of place a man could enjoy himself. It took an elastic imagination to see himself sitting in a pavement cafe with a cold beer, watching the pretty girls go by. That was the place Joe had come to twenty-seven years ago, and he had watched it go down-hill ever since. Of course, there were more roads and buildings now than there had been then, but there were many more people as well. The Revolution had tended to travel first class when it came to building apartment blocks and bridges. They had employed the best European and American engineers and contractors, who built to the highest and most expensive standards. Then the East Europeans came and carried on the work with a little less finesse and for a slightly lower price. Now Sabah was a strange mixture of municipal grandeur and gimcrack private buildings, all inhabited by people who would probably have been happier with something far simpler. The funding for the big construction projects of the 1970's and 1980's had just about run out now and the Western experts had gone with it. The Russians had fallen from political favour and only the ex-satellite countries remained in the game.

Eytie Joe, the local manager of a tiny Italian concern that seemed forever on the edge of bankruptcy, had seen them all come and go. He had made a great deal of money for his home company over the years and if bad times seemed to have fallen now, it did not worry him. The contacts he had built up over the years meant he had first news of any small project where a dollar or two might be made. He made his money from the stage payments that any contract might bring, and hoped that one day some of the two million dollars he was owed in final payments would be paid as a wind-fall. It occurred to The Virgin that if anyone would have heard about 'the little doctor', it would be Eytie Joe.

"Joe, you hear much about the security situation here? Do you think the Great Man is going to survive?"

"Ah, you listen to me. The Great Man is very intelligent, you see. He knows that he must give the ordinary people what it is they want. That is why he is always travelling. He never stays long in one place, you know. It's not because he is afraid of the CIA; no, that is a stupid story. He travels to see the people. Always he is visiting the villages and the people come to him and tell him all their troubles. And he helps them. So outside the big towns, they love him. They don't know any better.

"Also, he does the same with the Army. Always visiting and talking to the officers. He knows what to look for. That is the way he started, right here in Sabah. He and a few friends from the wrong sort of families started the Revolution, and in two weeks the King was living in Switzerland. So he visits and talks to the officers personally, and he knows if they are for him or not. And if he is worried by what he sees, they are taken away and killed. Finish! Just like that. He is a very intelligent man.

"So; nothing happens here. No-one talks about making problems or playing with politics, or they develop a terminal condition very quickly. And they have most of what they want; their macaroni and tomato paste, tea, sugar, they are all very cheap. All they have to do is join The Party, and they can buy food for next to nothing. So they all join; wouldn't you? And now they have their little shops where they can sit with their friends, may be trade a little bit. Perhaps if they have the right friends they can change a few dinars at the official rate and make easy money changing them back. They are happy enough and trying to change anything is quickly fatal, believe me."

"So the Great Man's going to just carry on?"

"Why not? No-one else is going to volunteer. None of the foreign countries care too much as long as he doesn't send too many bombs out to Germany. And the Americans have got bored with him now he's quietened down." He paused to sip his drink and chuckled. "No, no. This is a very good place to do business, if you know how. Always there are new projects coming, not so big now, so my friends and I can do business. They leave me alone, I do nothing except business, there is no problem. When I get tired or want shopping, I catch the plane to Rome, three hours, and go to my headquarters. It is not so bad, but summer is better."

Evelina came to him as he left. "Did you hear that Danka had trouble with the Army yesterday?"

"Jesus! What happened?"

She was gratified by his concern. "They came to the hospital and spoke to her with Captain Zella. She looked very white when they finished with her."

"What did they want?" he asked although he already knew the worst.

"She didn't say. Only that she'd been told not to talk about it. And they took all the papers from the office. All the files, all the patients' records. Even the roster off the wall. It must be impossible in Outpatients now; every case has to be treated like a new patient. I don't suppose the records will ever come back. I hope Danka's alright."

So did The Virgin. Very heartily. He toyed with the idea of driving around to Barani to check what had happened, but it was already late. The chances of being stopped by police were always higher in the evening, and after eleven o'clock, the chances were better than even. He went straight home and lay in bed thinking about how he could get out of the mess that loomed over him. There was no legal way of course. His passport had been impounded by the tax department, a standard practice with office managers and meant to ensure that no foreign companies cheated on their bills to the Government. The earliest he could get the Almadi office to lodge a substitute passport in its place would depend on who in the Almadi office was planning to stay in-country for a while. And then he would have to work up an excuse for getting out quickly, and get a plane ticket sent over.

A quick legal exit was not possible, and he did not know how to start leaving illegally. Being caught anywhere near the frontier without a passport would mean instant imprisonment, and the loss of his job. His boss in Almadi was not an understanding person, so flying over there for a couple of days would not help. Anyway, no-one could help if they were after him. All he could do was deny anything they charged him with. He sketched out a plan for the morning and got some fitful sleep.

After he had made his morning call to the desert, he walked down to the Italian Consulate and left a note for Giovanni the consul. If he did not call in tomorrow, at least some-one would start looking for him. Then around to Barani to see if he could find one of the girls. He waited at the barred door for one of the residents with a key. It had started to rain and the wind blew drops onto his legs as he sheltered in the door-way. He had been waiting for quarter of an hour when the hospital bus lurched up through the puddles and dropped the tired night-shift girls. Hamdullah; Wanda got off and she was always good for a coffee and some gossip.

Not even bothering to check if the lift was working, they started on the climb to the eighth floor. Wanda was a tough child, out in Tabriz to support a family back home in Warsaw. She ushered him into the apartment. It was not a bad place to live. Of course, the promised hospital furniture had never materialised so they only had the few sticks that they could buy cheaply from foreigners going finish. At least Wanda had arrived in one of the older recruiting drives, which meant she had a room of her own. More recent arrivals were two to a room; six people making a home in an apartment that was full with three. She put the coffee on and lit up.

"So, Wanda. How's life? What is happening at the hospital?"

"Boże! Everythings happens. The Army is coming every day to Captain Zella, and Captain Zella is calling people to his room to ask questions. Is a big problem."

"What'd he want?"

"Ach, it is those soldiers who were burnt last week. They want to know who saw them. They know Danka saw and one of the Tabrizi doctors, and two of the Sudanese barella men. Everyone else is saying they not see anything, don't know anything, not like to know anything. Is crazy, that is all. Stupid!"

The Virgin felt his head start to pound. "What's the big problem?"

Wanda shrugged and reached for another cigarette. "Who knows it? Who cares it? Nobody! Is just politics, that is all."

Just politics. The soldiers had been playing around at something, got caught in an explosion of some sort, and now the authorities were trying to hush it up. He could feel a sense of relief reaching down to his toes. "So what's going to happen to Danka?"

"I think nothing. The two Sudanese have been transferred to work in army camp in the desert – may be prison - but nothing happen to Danka. The Polish consul came last night for visit, just to tell she is not alone. Is very good, I think. I never hear that consul can do this. Normally he is too busy with his real diplomatic vodka to do anything good for us."

"I heard they took all the files from the office."

"Yes. This is big problem for Danka. Everything she must do again and you know how it is. No photocopier, no secretary that can type in English or even Arabic. This is the worst problem."

The world was a happy place for The Virgin as he returned to the office. Abdul was in, working on the next charter vessel they expected. As usual, vital documents were scheduled to arrive at the very last minute and the Tabrizi Customs department was not a place where faxes or unstamped copies would be accepted. There was a deputation from one of the trucking co-operatives waiting for him. This time they not only wanted higher rates for transport, but they were insisting on payment in advance as well. The rates they had now were astronomical. It cost thirty percent less to hire a truck to the desert from Cairo than from Sabah, and Cairo was thousands of kilometres further away. It annoyed The Virgin to be forced to use these people at all, but a benevolent Government had granted them a monopoly in one of the Party Congresses and that was that.

The co-operative leaders made real money for doing nothing much. No risk, no responsibility, all they did was submit an invoice on behalf of the truck-owners and then take a cut of it. Fortunately, the little power cells like these co-operative leaders abounded in Tabriz, and they could all persuade a Party Congress to issue a monopoly to do something or other. As no Congress felt bound to check what had been done last time, they issued contradictory local laws. Nobody knew for sure which laws were in force, as old ones were abandoned by neglect rather than decision. All The Virgin could do was play one group off against another and generally try to force prices down. It took more than an hour of polite insistence to make the co-operative see that if they tried to push too hard, they would just lose the work.

Even negotiating with the Co-operative felt good that morning. Visiting Tayfun was no burden either. The cement programme had been signed as recommended and all they had to do now was wait for the rig to drill to casing depth. The Virgin rushed back to the office to give the desert the good news. He had a pagan suspicion it would be unlucky to add up the possible revenue from the job, but it was clearly going to be high. Tayfun had been frightened into cementing the casing right back to surface, so they would need a lot of materials on site. The desert would have to start moving them up right now. He spent the afternoon around at RomDril-1, checking the stock of chemicals and spares, and drinking coffee with Terry Jones the company man. They would have no problems with the cement job that he could see – always provided that the rain stopped. If it did not, the trucks would tear up the red soil and they would have something like Flanders Field to work in. The slick balloon tyres of the desert trucks were no help at all in mud.

He dropped in on Evelina that evening. She was as friendly as she ever and made no acid references to Danka. She had not been called into Captain Zella's office yet, and it looked as if she would be left alone. Captain Zella must feel too embarrassed to face her. A couple of men in plain clothes had visited that morning, but had only stayed a short while. Perhaps they had lost interest. Danka and The Virgin had survived for the moment.

It was not for another two weeks that Tabriz took an interest in The Virgin. He returned to the office after lunch and found Abdul waiting for him at the entrance. "You have visitors. I know one is from Security, and they will not tell me what they want. You must be very careful."

His mouth suddenly felt dry. He had no escape. He went into his office.

Two men were sitting there, one of them behind the desk in The Virgin's chair. In spite of the sign on the door, they had been smoking and there was a full ash-tray on his desk. The man behind the desk jumped to his feet.

"I am sorry. I was using your telephone to call my family." He edged around the desk and gestured The Virgin to his chair. He held out his hand. "I am Major Jamal, and this is Captain Zella." The Virgin shook his hand and tried to get his bearings. Major Jamal was a big man with a grey, military moustache. He wore a tweed jacket, cavalry twill trousers and brilliantly polished brown shoes. His accent sounded upper class English. He was unmistakably Public School and Sandhurst. A pre-Revolutionary soldier. Captain Zella held The Virgin's attention longer. He was a much smaller man, and much more typically Arabic. Dark wavy hair above a high fore-head, straight, prominent nose and a pencil moustache. Sitting on the other side of The Virgin's desk he did not look as dominating as the nurses had painted him. He found himself looking for scratches that Evelina might have left.

Abdul came in to offer coffee, which was a good indication of how he rated their importance. Both men accepted, and it began to seem as if their visit would be held at a social level. They made small talk about the weather and visits to England until the coffee came and then Zella said something to Abdul which made him leave, shutting the door behind him.

The Virgin must have shown his surprise. "I am sorry, Mr Cartwright. It is better that we talk in private," Major Jamal announced. "We have special things to talk of. We want you to do a favour for us." He stopped and looked at Zella who blinked his watery black eyes and brought his chair nearer to the table.

"Mr Cartwright. You are from Britannia, yes? I have your passport." Zella reached into his jacket and pulled out a red British passport. "I can make too much trouble for you."

This should not be possible. The Virgin knew his passport had been given to the tax office and this little creep should not have been able to get his hands on it. He looked at Major Jamal who moved uncomfortably in his chair. Then Zella made a mistake and smiled.

The Virgin felt his blood pressure rise. He addressed himself to the older man, trying to keep the anger out of his voice. "I don't understand. You come into my office to talk privately and ask me to do a favour for you, and the first thing this man does is say he will make trouble for me. Why? If I can help you, maybe I will. But not if he is going to make trouble for me."

"Oh, Mr Cartwright. Do not be angry. We only want to talk business, nothing else." He spoke sharply to Zella who put the passport back into his jacket. "Nothing will happen, believe me. Captain Zella is not in the right way. We can talk business, if you will allow me?"

Trying to pretend that what he had just seen did not worry him, The Virgin bundled his thoughts together. Whatever they were in his office for, it did not seem to be connected with the little doctor. They really did want something from MacAllans, and Zella had just screwed up by threatening him. "He will take my passport back to the tax office?"

"Of course. There is no problem. Believe me, I did not know he had it in his pocket."

Some chance of that, The Virgin thought. Still, he had better co-operate. He really had no option. They were probably looking for a used pick-up and he could just refer them to the desert where they would have to take their chances with the local bosses. Or else they wanted MacAllans to buy an improbably large number of dinars at the black market rate. "What do you need?"

"Captain Zella wants to buy some chemicals - show him."

Again the Captain reached into his pocket and this time pulled out a folded paper. It was a poor quality photocopy from a catalogue. Headed 'Laboratory Reagents - Diffraction', it had half a dozen products listed together with their physical properties. One had been circled. Tetra-ethylene disulphide. It rang no bells. The chemical formula shown was apparently not so very complex, but it meant nothing to him. "What is it? Some kind of solvent?"

"Yes, exactly," the Major said. "A special solvent."

"Well, we don't sell that one. Maybe we have another that will suit you. What are you trying to clean?"

The question seemed to have caught the two men unprepared, and they looked at each other for a moment before Zella said firmly, "We must have this one exactly. No others. They are not the same."

"Well, I'm sorry. We don't have it."

"You do not understand. We must have this one and you will bring for us on your boat. We will pay you to bring it."

They knew about MacAllans' charter vessels. The Virgin began to wonder if this was a business opportunity after all. "How much do you want?"

"We want a minimum of two thousand litres. May be a little more."

"So, if I can find this chemical, how will you pay us? If it's good business, I might be able to help you."

They had the answer to that one. Zella spread his arms. "Anyway you like to be paid. It is not a problem. If you like we can pay in dollars cash. Or in your bank in England."

Was he being offered a private deal? The Virgin had never been offered the opportunity of being corrupt, and had always assumed it only happened to other people. Not that there was any real chance here. The documentation involved in getting anything onto the boat would make it impossible. "My boss will want a letter of credit."

"No problem. Letter of credit, even on a British bank. Just get us this chemical and we will pay you very much."

This was sounding more and more peculiar. No Arab in the world negotiated this way. The price seemed to be irrelevant. It sounded all too fishy. "I'll talk to my boss about it."

"Very good," said Zella. "We will wait. You must tell him we are from Security. Then he will want to co-operate."

"You are from Security?"

"No. We are from the Army. Special Security Operations. Do not worry. If we say we can pay, you can believe. Now, please telephone."

Intrigued, The Virgin reached for the telephone. He dialled and the connection failed. He put the phone on automatic and, as he kept pressing Redial, he read the photocopy. The material was listed as flammable and had a vapour hazard. And heavy; a specific gravity of 1.28. No problem. It could travel as deck cargo if the vapour hazard made it necessary. Two thousand litres was ten drums. Three pallets. A small consignment compared with what they normally handled. Still, he did not want the problems of getting some-one else's chemicals through Customs.

"Could we deliver it FOB?"

"FOB? I do not understand."

"Free on board. It means we ship it to Sabah and you handle the Customs and the rest."

"Of course. As soon as it comes to Sabah, we will send a truck and take it from your boat." Zella made it sound so easy but then, perhaps it would be easy for them. The Virgin shivered at the thought of anyone taking a shipment from the vessel out through the harbour gate without the long, tedious paperwork and negotiation that Abdul did day after day. If they understood what they were talking about, these men had real power.

The telephone clicked into life, and there was Harris barking at the other end. "What's up, Greg? What have you sold this week?"

"I have two gentlemen from Security here. They want to buy some tetra-ethylene disulphide?"

"What the hell's that? Do we sell it?"

"No, we don't. But they want us to get some and sell it to them."

"How are they paying? I'm not taking any Government orders without cash up front."

"Letter of credit."

"Oh yes?" Harris was interested. Letters of credit were as rare as hen's teeth in Tabriz. "Irrevocable, major European bank?"

"Yes. They say we can even have folding dollars, or a bank transfer if we want."

"Who are these guys? How much do they want? They're not just blowing smoke up your backside, are they? Hey, you don't have me on the speaker phone, do you?" Harris knew enough to be polite to customers, if not to his staff.

"They want two thousand litres. Ten drums. It's some kind of solvent so I guess it will be pretty high value."

"OK. You chase it, and get back to me. I'll fix the price. And warn them; I'll want that letter of credit in my hands and verified before I lift a finger. Anything else?"

"No. Nothing else."

"OK. Keep me posted." Harris rang off as he spoke, in keeping with his carefully polished image of being continuously busy.

"Good, gentlemen," The Virgin had begun to enjoy himself. "He says we can do business. But first I must check with the suppliers and then I'll give you a price."

Both of them beamed and Major Jamal took over. "Very good. I'm glad you're able to help. I can give you the address and telephone from the catalogue. I'll telephone you tomorrow."

"Tomorrow? This going to take time. My direct line is cut and you can spend all day waiting for the overseas operator. Make it a week."

"You have a problem with your telephone? What is the number and I'll have it repaired." Major Jamal obviously knew the right people.

"It's not exactly a problem. Just the usual. They forced us to pay ten thousand dollars to have a direct line connected, and after three months they cut it off and said it was Government policy for foreign companies not to have direct lines. I wish it was Government policy to pay back the money."

Major Jamal laughed. "The money, no. That I cannot do. But I can re-connect your line today. You will see. For Military Security, anything is possible."

"And my passport?"

He was all smiles. "Certainly. You can have it now." Zella put it into The Virgin's bewildered hand. "Don't worry about the tax office. I will tell them that it is no problem."

When they had gone, The Virgin sat behind his desk and thought about what he had just heard. Whoever they were, these people obviously had uncommon authority. Just the business of the passport was enough to show that. And as for connecting the international telephone line, if that happened he would know he was in touch with the very top of the Tabrizi power structure.

Abdul came in diffidently. "There is a problem?"

"No. No, thank God. They just want us to ship in some special solvent for them."

"That is all? Those people are very bad, you know. Very, very strong."

"They said they would re-connect our direct line. Do you reckon they could do that?"

Abdul had no doubt at all. "For those men, anything is possible," he said firmly.

An hour later, the telephone beeped and fell silent. Still doubting, he dialled his parents' number in England. On the second attempt he got through. He spoke to another planet. The trees had been stripped bare by an Atlantic storm and there was another waiting its turn in the Western Approaches. His father had just finished stacking a truck-load of firewood behind the garage, and mother had been to the market that morning. He could picture the bitter grey wind blowing across bare fields. What they most wanted to know was when he would be visiting. The Virgin did not want to tell them that his carefully accumulated field-break would be spent in Thailand, sitting under the coconut palms and playing with little brown girls. England in winter offered no competition.

The address Zella had given him was in Poole Harbour, Dorset. Karelia Specialist Chemicals. He decided to fax his request to save being passed from phone to phone until he found some-one he could talk to. The fax went straight through. It was amazing what the Telecom department could do if it felt the need.

The office was quiet now. Abdul finished work at half past two every day and The Virgin spent the rest of the day alone. He decided to run out to RomDril-1. Terry was having trouble planning the displacement of the cement. Any normal rig would have had no problems. MacAllans would pump the cement into the well casing and then the rig pumps would kick in to displace it with mud all the way down the casing and back up the outside. A big job like this one needed the high pump rate that the rig pumps could give. The MacAllans cement unit could only displace in these conditions at around eight barrels a minute, and that would take far too long. There would be a good chance of the cement setting up before it had all been forced out of the casing and back up the annulus between the casing and the hole wall.

The operation should have been straight forward. The only requirement was that the rig should keep a close watch on the volume of mud it pumped so that they pumped the casing contents and no more. RomDril-1 was not a bad rig, bought brand new from the USA only four years previously. The difficulty was that RomDril was still a Romanian government company, and simply would not release hard currency for spare parts. And who would sell to RomDril without hard currency in advance? There were hardly any spares available and RomDril-1's stock of emergency equipment was laughable. So when the mud pump stroke counters had broken down, they stayed that way. They now had no way of measuring pump rates or volumes except by dipping the rig tanks with a measuring tape and calculating volumes.

Terry was trying to get his demands for working equipment over to the tool-pusher, but the man spoke no English. The camp cook, who doubled as interpreter, was doing his best but they all knew it was a hopeless case. RomDril offered low daily rig rates. If you wanted a cheap rig, then you got the cheap service that went along with it. It always cost more in the long run than an American or Canadian drilling rig, but Tabriz was one of the few places in the world where people really believed that you could buy something both good and cheap.

The only solution would be another MacAllans pump unit to double the displacement capacity. Then all Terry had to organise was a four-inch delivery line to send mud over to the cement units from the rig pressurising centrifugals. The Virgin had to promise him a four-inch tapping and butterfly valve so the rig welder could modify their system. The extra unit would add another twenty-five thousand dollars to the job, so the desert would be pleased. He paced out the length of hose they would need. It was a long way from the pressurising pumps to the cement unit on the other side of the location.

He left Terry to yet another rubber chicken dinner and headed for town. The craziness of the evening rush into town was just starting. All the male Sabah residents seemed to meet in town between five and eight o'clock, and the evening roads were bedlam as a result. The Virgin decided it would be safe to visit Danka and find out what had been happening. Danka looked a little embarrassed to see him, but made him welcome none the less.

The Virgin dived straight in. "I heard you've been having trouble with the Army."

" Boże! Every day they are coming and making trouble. Now Doctor Farouk tell them not to come any more. What I tell them? They know that the soldiers did not stay. They taken away before even I could get doctor to examine them. Enough! I not talk any more about them. Have you heard from Dov?"

The Virgin winced and held a finger to his lips. "Forget it! Forget him too. If they ever find out..."

"I not forget him as easily like that. He very good in bed. But now I have my period so I cannot come with you tonight."

The Virgin almost choked on his coffee. All nurses were impossible but this was eccentric at least. "I didn't come for that! I just wanted to see if you were alright. Really."

She gave him a condescending smile. "I know what you like, Virgin. I come with you next week, no trouble. I cook dinner and we watch blue videos and make love on sofa. It will be very good, yes?"

Major Jamal called next day but The Virgin had nothing to tell him. He sent another fax to chase the first. When he opened the office the following morning he was greeted by two faxes. The first was from Karelia Chemicals.

Dear Mr Cartwright,

Thank you for your query. We will be pleased to make a quotation for the requested material, but as we have a limited stock at present we will not be able to give a firm price and delivery date for another two or three days.

Looking forward to contacting you at that time,

The signature was illegible. Oh, well. Major Jamal would have to wait.

The second fax looked far more interesting - from London office. From the Marketing Department.

Regional Marketing Manager will meet with you soonest. Please catch absolutely first flight and telex us exact flight details. Check in at the Rutland Hotel, Portman Place. Bring a suit. Have cleared this with Harris.

Have a good trip,

Heather

Heather was the marketing manager's secretary, and at that instant very high on The Virgin's list of loveable women. Anyone who sent invitations like that had to be wonderful. The question of what the meeting would be about was secondary. If they had wanted any preparation, they would have said so. Perhaps they would transfer him from Tabriz to somewhere exciting. The Virgin told himself he did not mind where they transferred him, as long as the telephones worked.

He set himself to checking off what might be possible. If everything went well, he should be able to catch next morning's flight to Crete. Crete/Athens could be a touch difficult, but it would be easy to reach London once he had made it that far. The first leg was the hardest - getting out of Tabriz. He took his passport from the safe; Hamdullah! At least Almadi had remembered to get him an exit/re-entry visa stamp before they lodged the passport with the tax office. So he could get out of Sabah, if he could find a seat.

Would there be time for Jimmy Risou in Heraklion to issue a PTA and telex it to the Olympic office in Sabah? No foreign company paid for its tickets in dinars, as the official exchange rate meant taking a hit on their dollar balance sheets for enough money to fly around the world first class. Much better to set up an account with a Heraklion agent and pay for the tickets outside. He made for the telex and punched the 120+ code for the operator. The machine spat 'MOM' at him and continued to hum. The Virgin made a coffee while he waited. He was surprised to see his hand shaking as he added the sugar.

The telex did not come to life until he was half-way through his call to the desert. He dropped the telephone and ran for the telex.

He rattled off the standard formula. 'Good morning my friend pls connect me with Greece 20155++'. The telex spat another 'MOM' and went on humming. He felt a sudden urge to urinate but going to the toilet was impossible; he would miss his line for sure if he did. He sat down and started to make a shopping list. Opportunities to shop 'outside' came rarely. He looked forward to going to a supermarket, and to buying clothes that did not fall apart at the first wash.

> Dental floss
> Deodorant
> Warm shirts (2)
> Malt extract and hops
> New shoes
> Guitar strings
> Christmas presents for girlfriends
> Squash balls

What else? Most of his fantasies involved things he could not bring in, like girlie magazines or bacon. Or soft cheese and real wine. Perhaps he could get a digital short-wave radio to pick up the BBC for world news. The one he used now drove him mad with its poor reception. London was not very cheap for electronics compared to Canada or the States, but at least things were available. He was still chewing his pencil half an hour later when the telex restarted ' GO AHEAD AFTER ANSWERBACK YOU ARE CONNECTED' and he was through to Jimmy Risou's office.

Step one completed, The Virgin checked his watch. It was twenty past eight already. If he was lucky, the Olympic office would be open by the time he got there. Rabka, the secretary/book-keeper, was late as usual so if he went out now the office would be empty and the telephone unanswered. Never mind; he stuck a yellow excuse note to the door and locked up.

In the streets the morning rush hour was at its lethargic maximum. Any office that really worked should have started at least half an hour ago but people were still driving to work. He decided to walk; it would probably be quicker and it would give Olympic a chance to open before he arrived.

They had two surprises for him. Firstly Jimmy Risou had already got the PTA through; secondly, someone had made a reservation in his name right through to London and back. He would be there for two days and three nights. It could only have been Heather in the London office taking a chance. A bit silly of her not to mention it in her fax, but who was complaining? Within ten minutes The Virgin had a ticket in his hand and was standing on the pavement feeling disoriented. Things just did not happen that fast in Tabriz.

The rest of the day passed in a similar daze. Harris sounded grudging and warned him not to think of spending any week-ends at home, and to hurry back as soon as he could. Over the telephone Major Jamal seemed to shrug his shoulders and accept the situation with Islamic resignation. Bill Gordon gave him some mail to carry out and asked for some chewing tobacco. He paid a courtesy call on Suleiman Busify, Bill's Tabrizi boss. He was as politely welcoming as always and discreetly kept the conversation away from anything to do with the technical side of drilling. His main concern was a Mothercare catalogue that he hoped The Virgin would be able to pick up from the big store in Oxford Street. All married Tabrizis had very large families and they liked to cherish them.

He found himself at home with everything packed by nine in the evening. He took a long bath to make the time pass and went to bed with a notepad on the bedside table in case he thought of any additions to the Shopping List. Compact discs. Tough running shoes for the winter Hashes. Coffee filters and real coffee. Disposable razors. Something for Evelina to show he still cared, and nothing for Danka to show he did not. He slept badly, waking several times in the small hours to check the clock.

Chaos ruled at the airport. For some reason the check-in never opened until an hour before the plane was due to arrive, by which time most of the passengers were already standing in what passed for the queue. Standing in line was a habit that Tabriz had yet to acquire.

A heavy grill separated the passengers from the empty check-in counter. Around it stood a crowd of the people who were lucky enough or rich enough to travel outside. The young single men with cheap suitcases and ski-coats were going to attend a course of one sort or another. They had won the highest reward a Government employee could hope for. An overseas course was a prize that meant a few giddy months with a dollar salary in countries where alcohol and women were freely available. Many of the courses were funded by clever contractors who had included customised client training in contract bids. No contractor could afford to be too hard on its clients, so schedules were light and assessments generously reflected aspirations rather than achievements. The prize of an overseas course was doled out to people with influence or the right connections and here they were, confused, wide-eyed and frightened.

The rest of the Tabrizis were in small family groups; father with one or two fat wives in head-scarves and just a couple of kids. It was not possible to take the whole tribe along every time, so for children the trips were rationed. The Virgin found himself wondering again exactly what the sleeping arrangements would be. Do they take a room for the kids and a room for the adults? If so, where do the wives sleep? Do they double up with their husband, or does the spare wife stay with the children. Looking at the size of them, he found it hard to imagine that the adults would all fit in a normal double bed. And as for who did what and to whom, it was beyond speculation.

Amongst the crowd, seated on the sidelines, were aged parents travelling overseas for medical treatment not available in Tabriz. The Government was aware of the social importance of such trips and allowed substantial amounts of dinars to be converted into hard currency at the official rate to pay for travel, accommodation and treatment. Every black market dinar, worth about thirty cents on the street, yielded a handsome three American dollars and sixty cents - a twelve hundred per cent profit. True, many of the patients staged miraculous recoveries once they got to Germany, leaving enough unspent dollars to buy a used Mercedes to travel back in, but such was the glue that cemented the middle class into a buffer of support for the Great Man.

The final component of the crowd was a small number of foreigners going home for their rotational breaks. Oil-field workers mostly. Rig hands from the Philippines and Thailand. Staff men from

Canada, assorted professionals from Europe, a contingent of Croats from the refinery. All wore a slightly anxious look; too many people had been turned back from their field break flights at the last minute because one piece of paper or another was not in order.

A movement at the head of the queue meant that the ticket clerk had appeared. Everyone who could take up any slack surged forward. Hands thrust wads of tickets through the grill, demanding attention. Comfortably out of reach, the Greek ticket clerk grimaced and took the first bunch. From then on, things went smoothly. All the tickets that were wait-listed or for other flights he firmly returned. The genuine ones he ticked off the manifest and accepted baggage. Olympic took a flexible attitude to the baggage weight limit; being too firm about charging for excess baggage would mean waiting while extra suitcases were distributed to other passengers, which would amount to the same thing in the end. They were firm about insecurely wrapped baggage or strange shapes, and the ticket clerk would just set the ticket aside until the problem had been solved. The Virgin spent an uncomfortable forty minutes being squeezed up towards the counter before he could check in his nearly empty hold-all.

Boarding pass in hand, the next queue was for immigration. Tabriz was one of the paranoid countries that let no person leave without an exit visa. Immigration and Security appeared to have been trained by the Russians and were Stalinists to a man. Next to the queue for Immigration was another where the exit visa cancellation stamp which had just been put in his passport was checked, presumably for evaporation. Then through a turnstile to Customs where the first step was to queue for another passport check. Every bag was opened for inspection. The Virgin never had figured out exactly what Customs looked for in these inspections of out-going passengers. It was a very democratic operation; everyone was treated equally, locals and foreigners.

The final check was by two men in uniform. They checked passports again and then asked if the passenger had any dollars. No foreigner would carry anything out of Tabriz. They all had credit cards, Eurocheques or travellers cheques. And no local was going to be foolish enough to admit to any unofficial, undocumented dollars. The two men must have found their job unsatisfying. The Virgin collected another stamp on the back of his boarding pass and passed on to the waiting lounge. It was already departure time and half of the passengers had not been processed. He settled down to read his novel.

An hour later, the flight was called and they queued up for the final passport check at the lounge door. By now spirits had begun to bubble, and the expats smiled at each other as the Tabrizis jostled to the front. They were guided to a ramshackle bus without windows and driven a few metres onto the apron where the commuter jet in Olympic colours stood waiting. On the tarmac lay a long line of baggage ready for identification by the passengers and carrying to the loaders. This weak security measure set everyone's minds at rest. Now they were sure their baggage had been put onto the plane.

When the doors closed and the engines wound up, The Virgin relaxed in relief. They were on their way; they had escaped at last. The bureaucratic octopus had failed to strangle them this time. Civilisation was only a short flight away. He watched the brown landscape slip way beneath them and quickly give way to the clear blue of the Mediterranean. He had already made a cultural shift. There would be time for a beer and a sandwich before Crete.

Heraklion had two real sources of income; tourism and Tabriz. If the Tabrizis ever collected their economic wits together, they would have no use for Crete's large body of business people who had one foot in Europe and the other in the Middle East. As it was, the patience and negotiating skills needed to turn a Tabrizi need into good business were not found in Europe proper. A community of intermediaries had grown up, fattening like leeches on their Tabrizi host. In the airport signs in Arabic abounded. A special gift shop and book-store stocked the glitzy clothes and jewellery so dear to the Arab heart. There were Egyptian news magazines and a wide selection of pornographic magazines displaying Arabic ladies of dramatic proportions.

The Virgin went to the transfer desk to confirm his onward booking. The professional smile of the girl at the desk warmed his heart as if it had been meant personally. "Mr Cartwright. Yes, you will be boarding at 10:30, gate number 2. Have you remembered to put your watch back? Do you want a smoking seat?"

A smoking seat would guarantee a maximum of young Tabrizi men drinking as much whisky as they could hold, so he generally preferred to take his chances in the non-smoking area, even if that meant risking the children. But this morning he was feeling benevolent and all was well with the world. "I don't mind. Just put me next to a pretty girl like you."

She dimpled gracefully and looked coyly down. "I will do everything I can. Oh, and the rendezvous point is over there, if you need it."

Strange, he thought, as he carried his boarding pass away. Why should she say that? His route to the coffee bar took him past the rendezvous point and he found himself looking without reason for a familiar face. He decided not to take a beer; it was usually a disappointment after such a long wait and anyway, alcohol and planes tended to give him a head-ache. Coffee and a pastry just to waste time, carefully keeping the receipt for expenses. The book shop was a desert as far as books went. Nothing but the nastiest of American horror and romance in poor quality paper-back bindings. He settled for an up-market girlie magazine and wandered towards his gate.

He found himself in a window seat towards the back of the plane. It did not take him long to get settled; just slide his brief-case under the seat in front and latch his safety belt. The aisle was crowded with people trying to squeeze over-sized hand baggage into the overhead racks and he did not know for some time if the seat beside him would be occupied.

A tall girl emerged from the crush in the aisle and gave him a polite smile. The Virgin sat up in surprise. The girl at the transfer counter seemed to have done her best for him. His flight companion was more than pretty. Glamorous would be a better description. She looked Mediterranean. Long wavy black hair and olive skin. Her eyes were deep and dark, her mouth wide and sensuous. She had a light blazer around her shoulders over a short and simple black dress. Dropping her jacket on the seat, she tried to get her over-night bag into the rack above. There was nothing The Virgin could do to help. He could only watch her lithe figure as she reached up. The dress, already short, rode up towards the limits of decency as she struggled. For a moment she stood still, her arms raised. The Virgin lifted his gaze and found her smiling in amusement at his obvious interest.

"Er... Hi, my name's Greg," he said in his embarrassment, and offered his hand.

"Hi - Elena." She put a long cool hand with painted nails in his as if inviting him to kiss it and slipped into her seat.

In The Virgin's experience, pretty girls had an automatic defence mechanisms to protect themselves against unwanted men. They carried a barrier against the world, ready to be erected against any intruder. He expected Elena to retreat into a magazine and cut him out of her presence. Instead, she initiated a conversation and in a few moments they were chatting like old acquaintants. As the plane took off, she leant over him to the window and her long hair brushed his fore-arm. She smelt exotic.

As soon as they were air-borne, the stewardess wheeled the drinks trolley up to them. Elena ordered a gin and tonic, and The Virgin took a beer to keep her company. She had an open, talkative nature that made her good company. She told him she worked as a ground service supervisor for Olympic in London, and had taken advantage of cheap ticketing to have a few days on the Cretan beaches.

"It's good this time of year. Not too hot and crowded, but you can still go to the beach and get brown." She looked at her legs reflectively. "The other girls are going to be jealous. And you work in Tabriz, right?"

"Is it that obvious?"

"Oh, you get used to people. I used to fly a lot and you soon learn to recognise types. You're not exactly business, you're not holiday and you're flying out of Heraklion. It's easy to guess. You're in oil? A rich oil-man?"

"Wouldn't that be nice? No, just a regular oil-man. I think all the rich ones disappeared in the slump."

"It must be difficult in Tabriz. All the political problems... How do you survive?"

"It's never as bad as it's painted. People get along, and there are no problems inside Tabriz. The Great Man's in charge and that's it. No-one argues. Or not for long, anyway. Still, it's nice to get out once in a while and see the bright lights of London."

"You're going to London too? Connecting flight?"

A thought crossed The Virgin's mind. Just maybe the girl at the transit desk... "Do you have your boarding pass for London?"

"Why? It's here."

"What's your seat number? Mine's 17A."

Elena checked. "17B! How did you guess?"

The Virgin smiled right down to his toes. "It was the girl at the transit desk in Crete. I asked her to put me next to a pretty girl and she said she would do all she could. I shall have to bring her back a present."

Elena raised her glass. "Here's to the little girl in Crete. What will you buy her? I suppose that depends, yes?"

The same thought had popped into The Virgin's mind, and he was sure he was blushing.

She laughed at him. "Well, we had better enjoy ourselves then, don't you think so?" The Virgin did think so, passionately, and raised his glass to hers.

If he added up all the flights he had taken around the world, The Virgin would have to say that this one was the best. They had a party for lunch and emerged in Athens still merry. They enjoyed each other's company in the transit lounge, and were old friends by the time they got on the London flight. Elena dozed on the first part of the flight and The Virgin found himself doing the same. Over France they woke and sat chatting with soft drinks in their hands. It was then that Elena dropped a surprise on him.

"Where are you staying in London?"

"We always use the Rutland in Portman Place. Why?"

"Oh." She seemed put out. "I stay there sometimes. Why don't you change hotels and then I can come too?"

The Virgin was stunned. He opened his mouth to ask why, and shut it again before he could say anything stupid. "Well - sure. Yes, I mean. Yes, please, you'd be welcome."

"Great. Let's go to the Holiday Inn in Marble Arch. It's about the same price. And we'll go out for dinner. Fantastic."

Maybe it was due to Elena's charm, but The Virgin felt quite relaxed and natural about the prospect of an evening in town with her, as if being courted by elegant ladies was quite normal. The satyr in him was definitely not relaxed however, and he found his eyes straying to the tanned thighs beside him.

Heathrow was its normal dull and efficient self. The Virgin enjoyed Immigration. It was nice to hurry through with his European passport while everyone else - even the Americans - had to wait in line. It was doubly nice to be addressed politely as 'Sir' by some-one who was, after all, a civil servant. A far cry from Sabah. Picking up his baggage was more of a problem. Even though the baggage hall did not seem busy, the bags from their flight took a long time to come. And when they did, The Virgin's was not among them.

Elena had her modest suitcase on the trolley but the carousel was clear. The indicator board clattered and went blank. The Virgin and Elena trailed over to the Lost Baggage office. He was filling out the form when a Security man walked into the office carrying the missing hold-all. It looked normal; inside his shirts were undisturbed. He shrugged off the incident and they wheeled the bags out through Customs. Elena took a moment to give her mother a quick call and make a reservation at the hotel, and they took a cab. Normally The Virgin would have travelled by the tube and claimed the cab on expenses, but this time it did not seem appropriate.

The hotel was hidden away off the beginning of the Edgeware Road in a modern but carefully camouflaged building. Inside it was a standard international business hotel, the hush and the service making it familiar to travellers of any origin. His room was reserved, a single of course, and he expected a little embarrassment from the reception clerk when she saw Elena standing behind him but she said nothing. Perhaps reception clerks got used to unacknowledged ladies accompanying their guests. He wished he had had the nerve to ask for a double bed, but with Elena close by he just could not summon up the cheek. The bell-boy ushered them to the lift and stood in front of them as they rode up. Elena reached for his hand and a tingle of anticipation ran up his spine.

The room was predictable. Clean, functional, a little smaller than usual perhaps but that reflected London conditions. Elena walked straight to the window and drew the curtains. She threw her blazer on a chair and stood in front of the mirror for a moment. She flicked her hair back. "God, I look a mess. You get a shower first because I'm going to take a long time." The Virgin would have liked to get close to her right now, but she seemed off-putting. He dug out his sponge bag and made for the bathroom.

If ladies were the thing he liked most in all the world, the second best treat was hot water. The hotel had a good, strong, steaming shower that washed worries and will-power away. He spent longer than usual getting himself presentable. He used the hair-dryer carefully and even had a special evening shave. He dabbed himself with hotel after-shave before emerging dressed only in his towel.

The room had changed in his absence. Elena was standing near the window, smoking a cigarette nervously. The connecting door to the next room was open and in the doorway stood a short, lightly built man with thinning hair. He wore a grey suit.

"Good evening, Mr Cartwright. Please excuse the surprise entry." He reached out for a handshake. "I'm Hobson. Both Miss Anthony and I work for the Foreign Office."

The Virgin was stunned. Uncomprehending, he gave his hand to be shaken and looked to Elena for some kind of explanation.

"I'm sorry, Greg. It's true." She did have the grace to look sorry, and she did not try to meet his eyes. Hobson gestured him through to the neighbouring room and sat him at the small writing table, still dressed only in his bath towel. The Virgin found he was following orders like a sheep. Elena sat on the edge of the nearest bed, clutching her handbag on her lap and looking uncomfortable. Hobson took the other chair and opened a large diary that lay ready in front of him. He reached into his jacket and took out his pen with a flourish.

"Just for the record, Mr Cartwright, you are Gregory James Cartwright and you work for MacAllans International Incorporated in Tabriz? Yes?" He nodded encouragingly at The Virgin and went on. "Good. Now, Mr Cartwright, I'm afraid you have done something - and I'm sure you have a very good reason for it - you have done something that has upset Her Majesty's Government. Upset it a good deal, I would say. To the extent that you could be in very serious trouble." He stopped and waited expectantly. When The Virgin did not respond, he merely waited longer.

The Virgin had to fill the silence. "I don't think you have the right person," was all he could manage.

"Oh, I believe we do. Did you or did you not send this fax?" He took a single sheet from between the pages of his diary and passed it across the table. It was a photocopy of his fax to Karelia. It seemed to have had comments written on it that had subsequently been whited out. "Do you know what tetra-ethylene disulphide is?"

The Virgin was in deep water. "They said it was a solvent. For cleaning something."

Hobson made an ostentatious note in the diary and then looked up. "Tetra-ethylene disulphide is also known as mustard gas."

Holy Shit! He thought of Major Jamal and Captain Zella sitting in his office. Could they really have done something like that? Those dumb Tabrizi bastards had made him order a shipment of poison gas. As if it was available on the open market like candy or cake flour. And for a place like Tabriz, with all its rhetoric about supporting freedom fighters and psychopathic odd-balls from around the world.

The implications of what he had done were staggering. No wonder the alarm bells had rung and Her Majesty's Government was upset. What stupidity! It was beyond belief.

"But it was in the catalogue... These two Tabrizis came into my office. Captain Zella and Major Jamal. They wanted to buy some solvent and they showed me a photocopy of a catalogue."

"That is true. It is in Karelia's catalogue; in very small bottles. For geological laboratories. I believe you will find that it does have a use in the determination of the refractive index of certain minerals. I am told that one places a small drop of the liquid onto a microscope slide touching the mineral you are examining, and a geologist can then compare the refractive index of the mineral to that of the liquid. Its index is uniquely high, apparently. However, it is supplied in tiny quantities. The amount you ordered is more than the free world's consumption for a decade." Hobson deliberately laboured the point, rubbing The Virgin's nose in the mess. There could be no doubt left in his mind that he had some serious trouble.

"I didn't realise," he croaked. And then the obvious question - "What will you do to me?"

"Ah." Hobson sat back. He realised he had won the match and that The Virgin had no illusions left. "To you. Yes, well, I suspect 'with you' might be a better term. Let me tell you first what we have done already.

"Karelia called us as soon as they got your fax - it's their duty, you know, with anything that might fall into the wrong hands. That would have been Monday afternoon, yes, Elena?" She nodded in reply. "Monday afternoon. So the first thing we did was to call your Marketing Manager, a Mr Forbes from Scotland. We would have liked to speak to your Regional Manager but he is from America, and we preferred to keep things in the family, so to speak.

"So; I spoke to Mr Forbes, and he agreed to bring you to London for an interview. That was the first step. Then we dictated a reply for Karelia to send - you got that, I presume? Which only left the business of getting you safely to London. That is where Miss Anthony came into the picture. She made sure of your bookings and arranged to sit with you on the aeroplane. She tells me you have been the complete gentleman. That you made no telephone calls and posted no letters; that you are very polite and did not get upset when we had to delay your bag at Heathrow while we had a quick look through it. I think that's true, Miss Anthony?"

Elena seemed ill at ease with Hobson's pedantic manner, but took the chance to speak up for herself. "Oh, yes. And Greg, I still want to have dinner, only not tonight, you understand?" There was in her eyes an unprofessional appeal to be understood and liked, which The Virgin found comforting.

Hobson started again. "Not tonight. Unfortunately, I'm sure. No. Miss Anthony has been detailed to baby-sit you, and she will continue to help us by doing just that until tomorrow morning when you will have to meet some very important people. What a pity you could not come earlier in the week. Now we will only have Friday in which to finish things off, and the Private Secretary wants to leave early tomorrow. He is riding in Norfolk.

"Never mind. Now tell me; are you inclined to co-operate with us in this matter? I warn you that we can get very nasty if we have to."

Somehow the threat seemed more vicious when it was couched in such an off-hand manner. The Virgin thought for a moment. "Do I have a choice?"

"Well, no. Not really. And it is all in a good cause, you know. Your country needs your help at the moment, so I think you can't really refuse. Good. That's that out of the way. Now, Mr Forbes insists that you call him. He said he would wait at the office until you did. I suggest you call and tell him you have met me, Hobson, and that everything is going well. We will bring you to the office for half an hour in the morning - eleven thirty would be best - and you and he can sort out your business then, if you have any. I will come with you and speak to him, as he seems to need some kind of re-assurance.

"He was very upset when I spoke to him and insisted on going to his superiors. I think I discouraged him for the moment, and perhaps you could do the same, at least for another day? Oh, and he does not know what any of this is about, and it is probably better that he stays ignorant. You understand, I'm sure." He gestured for Elena to pass the telephone over. "You dial nine first, and then your number."

The Virgin fetched his diary from his briefcase, and dialled Tom Forbes's direct line. Tom must have been waiting. "Jesus, Greg. What the fuck have you been doing? I've had this guy Hobson telephoning me five times a day all week. What's going on?"

"Well, he's here beside me. He doesn't want me to say anything in detail, but it's nothing to do with us, with MacAllans, I mean. He wants to visit with me tomorrow at eleven thirty - could we do that?"

"Let me check. OK. There's nothing that can't be delayed a little. Eleven thirty. But you tell him from me that if he doesn't come up with something pretty convincing, I'm going to have to go to Ron. I should have done that right at the beginning, and it's already been three days. He'll have my balls when he finds out, and quite right too. How are you, anyway?"

"Fine, fine. And you?"

"I'd be feeling a good deal better if you'd stayed in Tabriz, believe me. Anyway, what are we going to talk about tomorrow? We'll have to give you something to show Harris."

"Christ, I don't know. Do you have anything new coming up?"

"No. Not for you primitives in Tabriz, anyway. It's all North Sea up here, and if it's not expensive and off-shore, we don't want to talk about it."

"How about a transfer? You could always transfer me out of Tabriz, and we could talk about that."

"Possible. How long have you been there? It must be long enough by now. Right. Yes. We'll do that. I'll think of something smart. OK. I'm off home. Right. See you tomorrow."

"See you, Tom," said The Virgin, feeling that Tom was already half way out of the door on the way to his Hampstead retreat. He put the telephone down gently.

Hobson was looking at him with surprise on his face. "Is that how you talk to each other in the oil industry? I am surprised. It wouldn't do for us, I'm sure. We're much more old fashioned. How strange.

"Very well. Now, there are a couple of things we just have to get sorted out. Firstly, you are now in the realm of the Security Services, and we do things in our own way. And part of our way of thinking is that you are to be treated with the greatest suspicion until we have good reason to think otherwise." Again, he nodded at The Virgin to encourage his assent. "The first thing we shall do is a short polygraph test. You may also know the polygraph as the lie-detector. We have a technician waiting just outside. I would like to get the results to my office before the meetings tomorrow.

"Another part of the way we operate is that you will be kept under close surveillance until we are sure about you. Hence no romantic dinner with Miss Anthony." He looked round at Elena who coloured and whispered "Hobson!" in protest.

"Never mind. As she says, it may be possible on another occasion. This evening, the three of us and the technician, whose name is Mostyn, will dine comfortably on room service. You may then sleep as innocently as a babe while one of us watches over you, turn by turn through the night to see that the bogey-man does not come for you. You see, we do take some things very seriously.

"But firstly, let us call Mostyn in and get to work."

"Hobson, can we call for some coffee?" asked Elena.

"Why not, indeed? How do you like your coffee, Mr Cartwright?"

The Virgin was beginning to find Hobson irritating. The little man in the grey suit was rather too cocksure, rather too pompous.

"I'll have an Irish one, I think."

"Oh, no. Not before the polygraph. It would upset things, I'm sure. Would cappuccino do as a substitute? Good. I must call Mostyn in from the corridor and find out what he would like. And Elena is black, no sugar, I know. Could you please call room service, Miss Anthony?" Perhaps Hobson was getting to Elena too, because she ordered cappuccino as a protest vote.

Mostyn was a young man with untidy blonde hair. He too wore a tie and grey suit but managed to make the uniform look like a workman's clothes. He came forward shyly to shake hands, and then went to retrieve a deep aluminium suitcase from the wardrobe. He set it on the floor near the window and opened the lid. The lower half of the case contained an instrument panel. On the right hand side was a chart recorder with a glass window covering its roll of lined paper. In the centre of the panel was what appeared to be a cassette tape player, with various extra switches and potentiometer knobs below. The left hand side of the case was a deep slot for storing cables. 'Instructions for Use' were pasted inside the lid. Incised deeply into the panel surface was the legend 'Security Equipment Ltd, Sunbury, Surrey UK'.

"Have you ever seen one of these, Mr Cartwright?" Mostyn was not just any untidy young man. His accent was from one of the very best schools, which made him a well-educated, untidy young man. As he spoke he started to retrieve the cables from their storage and lay them out on the bed. "Well, they're quite simple really. All it does is to take readings of your pulse and blood pressure, and a couple of other things, while I ask you some questions that Hobson has prepared."

He seemed to have lost something and was emptying the storage compartment completely. "This is not really my job, you know, so you must forgive me if I seem all fingers and thumbs. I got roped into going to a course at the manufacturers, and now I can't get away from it. Every time something comes up, they seem to call for me. Never mind.

"Now; let me explain how we go about things. First of all, I have to attach the sensors to you. All the time you're wearing them, I must ask you to relax and sit very still. Oh look – you're feeling cold. Hobson, why doesn't he put some clothes on?"

"Why not indeed? Mr Cartwright, please get dressed. Something casual will do. And leave the door open. Miss Anthony will sit out of sight."

The Virgin returned to his room. Out of curiosity he looked for his room key on the bedside table. It was missing. The security chain on the door had also been put in place. He turned and found Hobson had followed him into the room.

"Excuse me. It's just until we are sure of you, that's all. Don't mind me." The Virgin changed quickly into jeans and shirt.

Back in Hobson's room, the coffee had arrived and they took a break before settling The Virgin back in his chair. As he had promised, Mostyn was all fingers and thumbs. He had three sensors. A rubber suction cup that fitted inside The Virgin's shirt just over his heart. This had to be stuck on with a dollop of silicon jelly. There was a sort of double sheath for the two middle fingers of his right hand as it lay on the table. And finally there was a blood pressure cuff over his upper arm. Mostyn tested the battery and the chart recorder, and settled himself in the chair opposite with a sheet of notes in his hand.

"Mr Cartwright, if we are to get this job done quickly and effectively, we shall need your complete co-operation. You must avoid confusing the machine, so sit very still and relax. I'll ask questions and you must reply with yes or no - only yes or no. Anything else is confusing. And above all, you must relax so that we can get good clear readings. Can you do that? I'll start off by asking some simple questions just to establish some background levels, and then I'll go on to the ones Hobson has given me. Oh, and we have to stop now and again to let the pressure out of your arm-band -

otherwise the readings get erratic." He placed a microphone on the table between them and tapped it, watching for a response from the polygraph. A small red light on the panel blinked.

The Virgin found that he felt nervous. He had been wired up like a laboratory animal and he was about to be tested for what? Was he really suspected as some kind of terrorist agent? A spy for the Tabrizis? He felt the same sense of alienation from reality that he had felt when Dov Nagel was staying in his house. Now there was a thought; could Dov have anything to do with this? He thought for a moment and decided that he could not. He was in the business of destroying chemical weapons, not ordering them.

Mostyn was ready to start. He picked up a push-button on a cable that led to the suit-case, and pressed a switch on the polygraph. The chart recorder started to turn and four uncertain ink traces appeared on the paper. He leant towards the microphone. "Cartwright interview, tape number one, time nineteen twenty-three hours, seventh of December." He looked up at The Virgin and grinned. "Remember please; yes or no only. Your name is Gregory Cartwright?"

"Yes."

"Your parents live at Tollands Farm, Morwenstow?"

"Yes."

"You work for MacAllans International?"

"Yes."

"Your date of birth is 27th of October 1958?"

"Yes."

"You are married?"

"No."

"You were married?"

"Yes."

"You are single?"

"Yes."

"You were born in Farnham?"

"Yes."

"You were born in London?"

"No."

"Your ex-wife's name was Joan?"

"No."

"Your ex-wife's name was Maria?"

"Yes."

Mostyn was examining the chart recorder. "Good. That's enough background I think. I'll just loosen your arm band for a moment. You can talk normally now, but stay relaxed."

The Virgin moved in his seat, more for something to do than anything else, but there seemed to be nothing to say. He felt a little like a contestant on one of the more gruelling television quiz games, but if this was how it was going to be, he felt he would manage. Mostyn allowed him a few moments, and then pumped up the arm band again. He started on a new leaf of questions.

"I know Mohammed Gamal Azziz?"

"No."

"I know Samir Ajouda?"

"No."

"I know Mohammed Sakran?"

"No."

"I know Ali Mehmet Majubi?"

"No."

The list was long, may be thirty different names, all Arabic. The only one that raised any response was Major Jamal Breki; he asked if that was the Major Jamal he knew and was sharply told to stick to either yes or no. They paused again to loosen the arm-band, and went on to more general questions.

"I am working for Tabrizi Intelligence?"

"No."

"I am working for Israeli Intelligence?"

"No."

"I have supplied the Tabrizi Government with chemicals before the current order?"

"No."

"I support the Tabrizi People's Revolution?"

"No."

"I have received money from the Tabrizi Government?"

"No."

"I support the Israeli people in their struggle for survival?"

"No."

"I support the Palestinian people in their struggle for survival?"

"No."

"I support Palestinian independence?"

"Yes."

"I knew of the death of Dr Hamed Ashrawi?"

"No. Yes. Who was he?"

"Let's stop a minute there, Mostyn," said Hobson, holding up his hand. "Mr Cartwright, it would be most helpful if you could give us just yes or no. We don't have many more questions to go. All of these questions are most important and you have just confused the machine by your last answer."

"How can I give you an intelligent answer if I don't know who he is? I know a Palestinian doctor involved with chemical weapons was assassinated last month. I was told that, anyway. But I don't know his name or any details."

"Ah, yes. I see your problem. Don't worry, we will return to that later, without the machine."

The Virgin stretched and Mostyn held a whispered conversation with Hobson. Then he pumped the arm-band up again. "My job with MacAllans is a front for intelligence activities?"

"No."

"I have a problem with debts?"

"No."

"I am being blackmailed?"

"No."

"The Tabrizi Government is forcing me to work for them?"

"No."

The Tabrizi Government has compromising information about me?"

"No."

"I have been in Tabrizi Government custody?"

"Yes."

"At the time I faxed Karelia I knew what tetra-ethylene disulphide was?"

"No."

"The Tabrizi Government are paying me personally to supply tetra-ethylene disulphide?"

"No."

"I expect to receive money for supplying tetra-ethylene disulphide?"

"No."

Suddenly, Mostyn had reached the end of his questions and he started to untangle The Virgin from the sensors. Elena passed a tissue to wipe the slimy jelly from his chest. Hobson was standing over the suit-case and peering at the chart. "Hey - wait a minute, Hobson," protested Mostyn. "Let me annotate it first and then you can have it. Or we'll get the time sequence all wrong. Let's get Mr Cartwright out of the way first."

Hobson stood back. "Miss Anthony, why don't you take Mr Cartwright next door and watch the television for a while? Mostyn and I will translate this, and then we can have dinner. And perhaps Mr Cartwright can talk while we eat. In fact, let's order now so that we'll be ready to eat once we have translated this tape."

"Hobson, do you think Greg - Mr Cartwright and I should order from his room? Then he will have the right sort of hotel bill in his brief-case when he goes home?" Elena seemed to be prompting Hobson.

"Oh yes. Very good idea - thank you, Miss Anthony. Mr Cartwright; what Miss Anthony is leading up to is that, when you return to Tabriz, certain people might wish to check on exactly how you spent your time in London. Now I don't believe you were followed here, but one can never be sure. In that case, we'd better not try to conceal your smuggling of Miss Anthony into your room for an evening of illicit pleasure. In fact it makes an ideal cover story for whatever happens during your stay. To that end you should collect receipts, tickets, all those sorts of things that confirm what you are supposed to have been doing. Are you with me? So off you go next door and order dinner for two. With champagne, if you can afford it. Is that the sort of thing you do on these occasions?"

"Er - I don't know. I mean, I never..."

"Come on, Greg, let's go and order. He's only trying to embarrass us." Elena led him next door.

"Do keep the door open, children," came Hobson's voice from behind them. "I'd like to know just what you're getting up to."

"I bet he does," muttered Elena. "Dirty old man. And he'd like to be doing it himself even more!"

"Doing what, Elena?" The Virgin asked, innocently. He had begun to come back to life as the shock wore off.

"Oh, don't you start! I hate it when they send me off on these jobs and then it's all nudge-nudge, wink-wink. Just because I'm a woman."

The Virgin laughed. "Relax. You were very professional. And nice with it. Who is that little creep anyway?"

"He's my Section Head. He's really enjoying pushing you around because he normally doesn't get the chance to do any real work. He just stays in the office and sends us out on jobs. But he can't do anything to you. It's the people you'll meet tomorrow who will decide what happens."

"Am I really in trouble? I mean, I didn't know what was going on. I was just doing my normal job of selling stuff." The Virgin felt she was human enough that he could confide in her.

"Oh, that's just Hobson laying it on thick. Don't worry. I suppose they could make trouble with your job and so on, but why would they bother? They've stopped the shipment, not that it was ever going to happen. Did the Tabrizis really order two thousand litres of mustard gas just like that? We didn't believe it in the office. In fact, I still don't."

The Virgin thought back to the idiocies of normal daily life in the Tabrizi Peoples' Republic. "Yes. It's quite possible. Sometimes you work with them and they seem quite normal, and then they'll be off doing something really stupid."

"It must drive you mad. I hope I never have to go there. I was born in Alexandria, you know. My mother's Greek and Daddy was in Marine Insurance. So I know what living in an Arab country's like. I don't like them very much."

"Oh, they're OK most of the time. The Tabrizis are, anyway. Get them by themselves and they're very pleasant. Always friendly and ready to help out. Not so good when they're in a group, or if some-one's given them a uniform."

"I still don't see how they could do anything so stupid. I mean, they must realise, surely..."

The Virgin was having trouble getting his mind around the idea as well. Major Jamal was an educated man. He must have some idea of how things worked in Britain. If he had been one of the younger generation with their minimal education and foreign experience limited to Hollywood videos, it would have been more believable. Perhaps he had fallen in to the trap of believing that the openness of Western societies implied a lack of vigilance. The Virgin hoped so, because if Major Jamal knew what he was doing, then he must have expected The Virgin's order to flash warning signals. He would expect The Virgin to be grabbed as soon as he reached England and brought into close contact with the Security Services. The implications of that would be to worrying to think through.

Dinner was a pleasant affair. The Virgin treated Elena to a bottle of Veuve Cliquot, and they shared it between them. Hobson refused to drink any because he said it was for 'the two love-birds', and Mostyn was too embarrassed to take more than a small glass. They both stuck to a bottle of house red. The Virgin did not mind; he was less in awe of Hobson now and less worried about his future. The meal was nearly over when the little man threw him another shock.

"Cartwright, now you've enjoyed this excellent repast and the glittering company," he nodded over his glass to Elena, "I am sure you will not mind answering a few more questions. Who is Danka?" The Virgin took a little time to realise what he was asking.

"Er - she's just a friend. A Polish nurse in Sabah."

"Just a friend? She is not, excuse me Miss Anthony, your lover?"

"Oh no. Just a friend. But how do you know about her?" The Virgin did not like the implications of these questions. Some-one in Sabah must have been supplying information. He had only been with Danka on a few occasions recently. He tried to remember when they had last been together in public, and who might have seen them. Any mention of Danka tended to start him worrying since that night on the beach. Should he tell the whole story? Was Hobson the man to tell?

Hobson ignored the question and returned to the attack. "What do you know about the death of Dr Hamed Ashrawi?"

The Virgin decided to back the feeling he had about Hobson's significance. "If he's who I think he is - was, I don't think I should really be discussing him with you." A phrase from spy novels jumped into his mind. "I don't think you really need to know."

The Virgin half expected Hobson to throw a tantrum and demand his co-operation but instead he reacted like Pavlov's dog to 'need to know'. "Yes. Well. Maybe you are right. Perhaps it's better left until tomorrow. But I was specifically told to ask about Danka."

"Well, you've asked about her. And the answer is nothing. She's just a friend, nothing else." Hobson lost interest and started to clear his plate away.

The Virgin turned in early. It had been a very long and very tiring day. As he dropped off Hobson was sitting watching the muted television in the darkness. He awoke once in the small hours and Hobson's place at the television had been taken by Elena. She was dressed in a soft grey track suit. He raised himself on one elbow but she pointed firmly at him, sending him back to bed. He slept heavily.

The Virgin woke early out of habit. It was already seven o'clock in Sabah and he should have breakfasted and driven to the office by now. In London it was still five o'clock in the morning and Hobson sat in front of the television, tired and unshaven. He was reading a paper-back. The Virgin grunted 'good morning' and made for the bath. Baths were a problem in Sabah. The cheap small-bore water piping of Tabrizi villas soon became clogged up with corrosion and scale from the brackish water, and running a bath was a slow job. A long comfortable bath is one of the luxuries of civilisation and it rated close to bacon for breakfast on the list of things The Virgin missed most. Following the hint that he had to meet important people that morning, he dressed his best.

Hobson gestured through the adjoining door and spoke quietly. "We'll let them sleep another hour at least. I've arranged transport for seven forty-five. They're opening the office especially early for you. I've just called for coffee. We'll have breakfast later." They sat together in silence, reading and waiting for room service.

Hobson waited until the last moment before having a last jab at The Virgin. "To be on the safe side," he announced, "By which I mean, to discourage any wild ideas on your part, I think you'd better give me your passport and airline ticket."

The Virgin thought for a moment about being bloody minded but it did not seem to be worth the effort. He opened his brief case and dug them out.

"And your wallet, I think. Your credit cards are here, yes? And your cheque book?" The Virgin went back to the brief case. "Do you have any traveller's cheques there? Eurocheques? No more cards? Good. Now, when the transport gets here, I would like you to stick very closely to us. Once we get you into the transport, we can all relax. Please don't frighten us. Perhaps Miss Anthony can take your arm, and Mostyn and I will follow.

"It's not purely for our peace of mind, you know. I am worried that certain unfriendly people may be watching you. That's why we changed your hotel, you understand. I dare say it fooled them, but we can't be sure. Our people are having a good look around at the moment to see who might be watching - you can't be too careful.

And when the transport is ready, I would like you and Miss Anthony to leave the hotel and get straight into it. Is that suitable?"

When the telephone call came they all packed into the small lift and dropped to the lobby. As the doors hissed open Elena slipped her arm through his and steered him towards the hotel entrance. A London cab with darkened windows was waiting with its door open and she pushed him straight in. The Virgin looked around for Hobson and Mostyn but Elena had shut the door firmly. She went to the microphone on the partition glass and said, "OK. Lock up." There was a loud click from both door locks. Hobson and Mostyn must have stayed inside the hotel.

Elena sat back and giggled. "Good. Now we're safe. The others will follow along later." She took his hand. "Did you sleep well? You were muttering about something but I couldn't catch just what. Who's Evelina?"

The Virgin felt himself colouring. "She's just a friend."

"Another girl-friend? How many do you have?"

"Well, I don't really. Not proper girl-friends."

"I see. You prefer improper ones. You bachelors are all the same. I was just going to ask them if we could go out this evening, but I might have to be improper too."

"I'd like that."

"I dare say you would, but I haven't said I'm volunteering yet. Seriously, I expect they'll let us out for a while if everything goes well. Do you mind?"

"Is this business or pleasure?"

"Both, really. I mean, I'm meant to baby-sit you anyway, but there's no reason why I shouldn't enjoy it. It'll be a pleasure doing business with you."

"Where are you taking me now?"

"To my office. You've got to meet some people. I expect you'll have a busy day. I'm going back to my flat to change, but they'll tell me when we're meant to meet up again. When do you go back?"

"I'm meant to travel tomorrow to Crete and overnight there. Are you coming with me?"

"That would be nice, wouldn't it? No. It would be too obvious. I'm meant to be just a girl you picked up on the plane. I expect some-one will travel with you though."

"It's just I must do some shopping. I positively have to. You know, small things, Christmas presents, stuff you can't get in Sabah."

Elena looked interested. "You have to?"

"Oh yes. There's a lot you can't get there, and you have to take every chance you can. I want to get some shirts and some CD's - a few other things."

"It wouldn't look normal if you went back without them?" It was a strange question to ask. "Fine. If it's important, I'll make sure you have time to go shopping. Can I come too?"

They were driving through the prosperous streets north of Oxford Street, busy with rush hour traffic. The pavements were crowded too and when the cab drew up the driver had to wait for the way to clear before he dived in to the burrow-like entrance of a basement parking area. The cab stopped but Elena waited until the metal roll-door closed behind them and the door locks clicked free. She led him to a small door in the dark concrete wall. Inside was a brightly lit, bare room, a section of corridor closed off by a heavy fire-door. She stopped and rooted in her bag. There was a small trap in the wall beside them where she delivered a pass. The Virgin noticed a security camera peering at them from above the door.

"Good morning, Miss Anthony," announced a heavily distorted Tannoy voice. "Would you mind asking your guest to stand clear of you?"

Elena looked back at The Virgin. "They just want a clear picture in the camera." She stood back against the wall. The Virgin raised his elbows and opened his jacket.

"That's fine," said the Tannoy. "Please leave the guest's brief-case at the desk outside. Does he have any identification?"

"No, he doesn't," said The Virgin. "You've taken it all already."

A clunk came from the door and Elena pushed through. Her pass was waiting at the reception desk beyond, and they left The Virgin's brief-case. There was a badge for The Virgin. It was a grey plastic slab like a radiographer would wear. The Virgin wondered if it contained some kind of tracking device. They went up in a tiny lift. On the fourth floor a man in a grey suit waited for him. "Ciao!" Elena said as she pushed him out. "See you this afternoon." The lift door closed behind him.

The Virgin was standing in a dark, carpeted corridor. Old fashioned brown doors in cream painted walls; fire-extinguishers and illuminated emergency exit signs. Dark oatmeal carpet well worn in the centre. The man in front of him was holding out his hand.

"Cartwright. Welcome. My name is Stanford." He was a thin man, about forty The Virgin guessed, with a hawk-like nose. His accent sounded vaguely Home Counties. Brown hair combed back. He was beginning to lose it, and a touch of salt and pepper had crept into the edges. "Come to my office. Like a coffee?"

His office was a narrow slot leading from the corridor to a tall sash window. His desk ran the length of the room and there was just enough space for a chair on either side of it. The only other furniture was a safe, and a personal computer on a shelf at the window. The desk was bare and the paper trays were empty.

"Sit down, sit down. How do you have your coffee? I'll bring it - there's hardly anyone in at this time." While he was away, The Virgin sat looking at the office. It had no character. No calendar, no photographs, no personal touches. Nothing to betray the likes and dislikes of its owner. The window looked down onto a neat Victorian street, its large houses all converted into offices. There was a small Italian restaurant across the street, but no shops. The parking meters were all occupied. Stanford returned, pushing the door open with his foot as he steered in the two coffee cups.

"So; enjoying being back in London?"

"I've been meeting some pretty strange people," said The Virgin.

"Yes. I can believe that. How did you take to Hobson? Ah, well, most people have that reaction. Never mind. He's not so bad and his report has been quite useful. I've just seen it. What's it like, working in Tabriz?"

"It's not too grim. The newspapers always exaggerate. I've never had any serious trouble, thank God."

"Hamdullah, you should say. But you said you've been in Government custody."

The Virgin was taken aback. I said that, he thought? Oh yes. I said it to the lie-detector. "Yes. That's right. I was held overnight once at a police post. It happens to everyone."

"Why were they holding you?"

"Just the usual. I was driving a company pick-up and they wanted to borrow it, so they held me until our manager came and told them he didn't have another one to spare. It happens all the time."

Stanford was looking at him in disbelief. "Go over that again for me, would you?"

"It was out in the desert, on one of the blacktop roads. The police never have any vehicles of their own out there. The new pick-ups all stay in town and the guys at the outlying posts are just dumped there and left alone. So if they want to go and visit their friends, they have to borrow a vehicle. They like to take our pick-ups because they're in good shape and are not going to leave them stranded in the desert. So if your documents are not in order, they just take your vehicle and you have to get a lift home from anyone passing. I knew the documents were good so I wasn't going to leave, and they locked me up."

"Good Lord! And that's normal?"

"It's normal in Tabriz. Everyone's been held up at some time or other. We carry a wad of documents around with each vehicle but they're always trying to find an excuse to take the pick-ups away."

"Hm. I hope that idea doesn't catch on here. Where were we? Yes. Danka. Tell me about Danka." He sat back and steepled his hands in front of him.

Christ! Danka again. What was it about that woman that they found so fascinating? How did they know about her anyway? The Virgin was getting rattled and decided to take the offensive, if only to buy time. "Look - I don't know what you want from me. I haven't done anything wrong, at least, I wouldn't have if I'd known what that bloody chemical was. I'd like to help you out, but I'm getting pushed around and asked all sorts of stupid questions without knowing why. I got screwed around on the chemical. OK, I admit it, but you've stopped the order now, so what's the problem? What's going on?"

Stanford thought for a moment. "Right. You're asking me what I'm doing. Well, you must see it my way. If you are who you say you are, no more than that, no hidden secrets, then we can sit and exchange information. Some information anyway. Of course, if you're not who you say you are, then I shouldn't even be offering you coffee. Not here anyway. That's the difficulty, you see."

He thought a little more. "I'm just going over your lie detector test again. Of course, Hobson's always a bit of a Devil's advocate; it makes him feel in the centre of things. I believe I am going to have to trust you a little, but give me a couple of answers first. What were you doing on the night of the third of November? Just a brief description."

"Oof. Beginning of November. I don't think I went to the desert then. I don't know; my diary's in my brief case downstairs."

"I think you'll remember. It was a Saturday."

The Virgin thought back. Saturday - that meant he certainly went to the Hash; it must have been that particular day. The one when Dov came marching into his life. "Er - I suppose I can talk about that sort of thing here?"

"Well if you can't, there's nowhere safe. Hm - I suppose that's true nowadays anyway. No, you're safe enough. We're swept at least weekly for bugs. Go ahead."

"Well, I was on the beach in the evening, for a swim. With Danka, as it happened. And we saw a bunch of soldiers come running down to the beach and taking off in inflatable boats. One got left behind and we took him home for the night. We sent him on his way next day. That's all. I haven't heard from him since, and I don't want to. I must have been crazy."

"Did he tell you why they were there?"

"He said they had just assassinated some Palestinian doctor who was working on chemical weapons."

"Do you make a habit of picking up stray assassins?"

They both laughed. "No. I'm trying to give it up."

"You would be well advised to. You see the difficulty. First we receive a routine information exchange concerning a friendly Englishman helping a foreign operative out of a particularly nasty hole. After a gung-ho raid to stop chemical weapons manufacture. Then we get another message, from a totally different source, saying the same friendly Englishman has just ordered enough mustard gas to poison a large town. Your credibility rating is not high.

"However, I am trying to piece together an explanation for the two events that makes sense, and I can't do it. It's completely bizarre. Which brings us back to the explanation that you have offered, unlikely though it is. I still don't believe it, but there's nothing else to believe."

Stanford stopped talking and concentrated on his coffee for a few moments before starting to muse again. "The thing is, you see, that if we just shut you down, it would be a huge waste. I mean we could slap your wrist and send you home, and the problem would end there. You could even tell Major Jamal what had happened to you; it wouldn't make any difference. The old rogue would probably swap stories with you.

"On the other hand, this might just give us a lead into some of the nastiness that goes on behind the scenes in Tabriz. These reports about international terrorists operating out of the desert are not entirely moonshine, you know. There are some very dangerous characters lurking in the sand dunes, and the thought of them having mustard gas at their disposal sends shivers up the Government's spine. In the right place, say a plane or an underground station - it doesn't bear thinking about.

"I would like to do something. Throw a spanner into the works. But to do that, I need you to tell me everything; everything you can remember and probably a few things you can't. At least that would get me started on the right foot and I'd have a chance of convincing my bosses." He sat forward and looked straight into The Virgin's eye. "What do you say? You show me yours, and I'll show you mine, a bit of it anyway. We really do need your help."

As Hobson had said, he really had no choice to make. Stanford was presumably on the side of the angels, and The Virgin had no particular loyalty to Major Jamal. Stanford produced several sheets of unlined paper and started to take him through the course of events in detail. He started with the Hash - he seemed to have met them somewhere else in the world and so did not raise an eyebrow - and went on to the way The Virgin lived in Sabah. He was particularly interested in the incident with the burnt soldiers being turned away from the hospital. "Probably mustard gas or something similar. Vesicants, that's what they're called. Blistering agents. You could easily confuse vapour or steam burns with mustard gas." He was less interested in Dov Nagel. He had probably heard the full story on that already. Major Jamal's part in the picture he wanted in great detail, even trying to reproduce the conversation word by word.

Questioning took a long time, especially as Stanford was taking notes in long hand. It was after ten when he looked at his watch, cursed and grabbed the phone. "Tom? Stanford here. Can you get us to Whitehall quickly? Good - we're on our way." He dropped the phone in its cradle. "Cartwright, we have to run. I'll just tell the manager, and we'll be off."

They seemed to be using the same taxi, and it made slow work weaving through the crowded one-way system. "Er - are you going to tell me where we're going?"

Stanford smiled. "We're off to the heart of the British Government. At least, that's how they like to see it. This is where it all happens, the people who turn the wheels. No, it's quite fun really. I don't come down here much normally, but the Private Secretary wants to see you. He takes these ideas into his head sometimes. He doesn't have any real contact with what we do - thank God - but every now and then he likes to feel he's in the swim. He's heard about you, though. Your fax did the rounds before it got to us. Don't worry. He'll probably do most of the talking himself."

"All this - all this running around and ordering the wrong chemicals - is that going to affect MacAllans? I mean, what are they going to think of me? If they think I'm a problem, they'll just tip me over the side, believe me."

"Oh, I expect we can do something about that. What nationality is MacAllans anyway? American, I suppose."

"Well, they're registered in the Bahamas but that's just for tax purposes. They're all-American at the top. Our regional manager is American."

"Mr Steenken? Yes, well, don't worry. I don't think you'll have any problems there."

The cab pulled onto Parliament Square and round into Whitehall. Just before the Cenotaph, it turned left into a side street. Classic Purbeck limestone buildings stood on either side. "Have you ever been here? You'll enjoy it. This is the old Colonial Office. We're going to the India Rooms. It's almost the way it must have been in the days when there we had an empire. I always expect to meet Curzon coming round the corner."

Security was more relaxed here. A policeman watched them mount the steps and push through the revolving wooden door. Inside, The Virgin's brief-case was inspected by a janitor who waved them through to a spiral staircase. It did not look grand at all. Even though it was stone-built with a marble balustrade, it seemed to be the back stairs. The lighting was poor and the stone walls grimy. At the first floor level an old-fashioned brown Bakelite light switch was crudely mounted at shoulder level. Stencilled in black paint beside it were the words 'Remember the black-out'. Untouched since the war.

They stepped out into a wide corridor. Rich red carpet hissed beneath them. Dignified portraits of Georgian and Victorian giants looked down at their passage. Stanford ushered him into a conference room and left him alone. It was incredible. The Virgin sat at the huge mahogany table and looked around at the paintings. Generals, admirals, old colonial administrators. There was a translucent view over the Straits of Penang in front of him, with small native craft and large Indiamen. The Majesty of Empire still permeated the building.

The tall double door opened and in came Stanford leading an old, heavily built man in a dark suit. The man was silver-haired and majestic, as if constructed to live in these very rooms, but he moved with an old man's concentration. "Cartwright, this is the Private Secretary. This is Cartwright, Sir."

The Private Secretary took his place at the head of the table and gestured The Virgin to sit beside him. "So you're stationed in Tabriz, Cartwright. Like it there?" He was examining The Virgin with blank watery eyes.

"Oh, it's not too bad, Sir. We get along." He could not remember when he had last called anyone 'Sir', but it just popped out naturally.

"Very good. Very good. Look, I'm afraid I can't sit and chat with you today. I'm busy and Stanford tells me you're only in town today. Never mind. Next time you can tell me a bit about what goes on out there. You could probably tell me a damn sight more than I get out of Stanford and his chums." He screwed himself around to look at Stanford who was still standing. "Meant to be running the department and they tell me bugger-all most of the time. Only drag me in when there's been some damn-fool cock-up.

"Anyway, don't have time today, so it will have to wait. Cartwright, I'm very pleased at what Stanford has been saying about you. Nice to know some of the old spirit still exists out there, and people don't only go overseas for the money. I'm happy to welcome you onto the team. I'm sure you're just the sort of chap we need nowadays."

Breathing heavily, he hauled himself to his feet and thrust a large paw out to The Virgin. "Well, good luck, young fellow. Do your best, and come and see me when you get back to London next. Always pleased to see you." He turned and searched for the door. Stanford guided him out.

The Virgin was standing like a bumpkin in a magic show when Stanford returned. He opened his mouth to ask, but Stanford held a finger to his lips. "Later. Let's get moving first." Moments later they were walking out into the open air and looking for their tame cab. It came rolling up to meet them.

"Come on, Stanford. What's going on?"

"Good, isn't he? No, really. I've got a lot of respect for him. There's a very sharp mind under all that, and you should see him chair meetings. He can really get things done when it suits him. And as for not knowing what's going on... I've known him come out with things that only the angels could have overheard."

It was not enough for The Virgin. "Yes, yes. But I don't mean that. What's all this about me joining the team, and being 'the right sort of chap'? I felt like he was sending me out to the North-West Frontier."

"He does that awfully well, doesn't he?" His voice took on the Private Secretary's gruffness "'Very well, Henderson. That's the job, and I'm sure you're the best man for it. Off you go and do your bit.' 'Thank you, Sir. I'll give it a try. Goodbye. Or is it au revoir?' 'No, Henderson, it's goodbye.'" The mimicry was wicked and had The Virgin laughing in spite of himself.

Hobson took him to the MacAllans office. As they walked in, the receptionist looked up with surprise on her face. "Mr Cartwright! Mr Steenken was just asking for you, and I didn't know you were in town. You'd better go in to him straight away - he seemed to be awfully keen to see you." The Virgin left Hobson in reception and walked past the modern, glass-fronted hutches that passed as offices here. Inside men in shirt-sleeves and loosened ties were staring at monitors and typing continuously. There was little noise.

Ron had an office near the end of the corridor and it was a longer hutch than the rest, with a chrome and glass conference table at one end. He sat stretched out on a reclining chair behind a futuristic assembly of shelves that housed his writing desk, his telephones, fax and computers. He jumped up when he saw The Virgin and walked round to shake his hand.

"Hey, stranger! What are you doing in town? How are you, good? Come on in. I'll just shut the door." Ron was an ugly American. Short stumpy legs supported an extravagant belly. His creased face showed every sign of hard living and the quid of tobacco behind his bottom lip made him look like a dumb good ol' boy. Within MacAllans everyone knew the appearance belied the fact. Ron concealed a sharp business mind beneath a Father Christmas image. He was not even from the southern States. He was from Boston, from a good family and with the education of a Brahmin. He had no more right to wear pointed cowboy boots than The Virgin. Not that that stopped him. He was wearing some repulsive mauve ostrich-skin boots today.

He closed the door to the corridor, and the one to his secretary's office, and slid back behind his desk. "So; I had the United States ambassador to London call me today." He waited for a comment and The Virgin made approving noises. The call had obviously made an impression.

"Boy, I don't know what you're doing and I don't want to know. I just want to tell you I'm real proud of you. It ain't every day that we get a chance to serve our countries like that, and I believe you're a lucky man. You have any problems, anyways I can help out, you just give me a holler."

The Virgin found his new role as an ace of espionage becoming an embarrassment. God alone knew what Ron was imagining, or how the ambassador had puffed things up, but it made The Virgin very uncomfortable.

"Well, it just sort of happened. I didn't do anything..."

"That's not the way I heard it. He said you were a gallant gentleman and he would take his hat off to you. That's just the words he used. Take his hat off to you. So you just carry right on and keep helping them out. I'll do everything I can to help you."

"Did you happen to hear anything from Tom Forbes? It's just they put the hard word on him to call me over to London, and he didn't know what to do. I'm afraid I'm going to get dragged into a lot of questions, that's all."

Ron reached for the phone. "Tom? Yes, fine, fine. And you? OK, listen up. I've got Greg Cartwright with me here. Yes, from Tabriz. Now I want you to know that what he's doing has my full approval, right? Yes - yes. I know. I know all about that. So just do whatever he asks and help him all you can - OK? Good. Good, thank you, I'm sending him down."

He grinned at The Virgin. "Now old Tom thinks he's got his pecker caught in his zip. Just run along and sort him out, will you? What are you doing for lunch?"

What was he doing for lunch? He thought for a moment and decided he would turn Ron down and take his chances that Elena would be free. "Well, actually, I'm being briefed all this afternoon and I fly back tomorrow."

Ron looked at him with something touching affection. "Boy, I wish I had your luck. I'd have done just the same. You ever want anything handcarrying in to Tabriz, or anything like that, you just call, right?" The Virgin shook his hand and left before he got too sentimental.

Tom Forbes was no trouble at all. He did not even want to see Hobson. He rushed The Virgin through a list of new products coming onto the market and gave him a heavy position paper on the developing markets in Eastern Europe. "Tell Harris we spoke about Russia and that I told you to keep quiet about it all. If he has a problem he can call me. Anything else you need?"

The Virgin decided to push his luck. "Well, I'll need to travel in and out a bit more now. Do you have any courses going?"

"Courses? Where do you want to go? What sort of courses?"

"Oh, anything on the technical/marketing side. And it doesn't really matter where, as long as they're outside Tabriz. The States would be real handy. In a couple of months time. Would that be possible?"

Tom was flicking through his diary. "There's a sand control school in Houston. February 12th. You any good at sand control?"

"I've done some in Balikpapan, but that was a long time ago. That would be handy. We've got a chance of some sand control work coming up for TAMCO."

"OK. And if you need more later in the year, give me a call. I suppose I'd better come and see your Mr Hobson."

"He's not mine. He's an obnoxious little prick, but I guess you could shake his hand. I've got to run anyway."

Hobson took him back to the office in a regular taxi. They had no sooner got there than they were sent out for a pub lunch. It seemed that he was now viewed as less of a risk. Stanford was ready for him when they returned.

"You've got to meet our Projects Manager. Edgar Crossman. He's got some questions for you."

Crossman's office was a builder's afterthought. It was reached by making a dog-leg at the end of the main corridor and dropping down two steps. It had a five-sided plan, and a fine view up the street. Crossman was a tall languid man. "Cartwright. I'm Crossman. Do sit down. Tea? How do you take it?" While they waited for his secretary to bring the tea, The Virgin watched him chatting with Stanford. He had feeling of not belonging. It was not only that the two men shared the same profession and knew each other well. They seemed to be members of a club, of a social caste that was not his own. He wondered if they were both ex-military and he was visiting the officers' mess. Or did it go deeper than that, to the deep roots of the county class?

The tea was left by a motherly lady who passed round the cups, and left with the teaspoons and sugar-bowl. Crossman sat forward at his desk and cleared his throat.

"I'd like to make one thing quite clear from the beginning, Cartwright. Despite the impression the Private Secretary may have gained from my silver-tongued colleague here, we are only asking for a little co-operation from you. We would not like to think of you acting as, say, a representative. Or our man in Tabriz. Nothing like that. Is that how you understood it?

"Good. Right. So this is the situation as I see it. The Tabrizis have asked us to supply them with some mustard gas. We have intercepted their request and have decided to play along with it in order to penetrate their chemical weapons programme. Yes, Stanford?"

"That's right."

The Virgin was horrified. "You're going to give them mustard gas? But that's - that's..."

"That would be unthinkable," finished Crossman smoothly. "What we shall send will be very smelly, and rather explosive. Does that answer your question?"

How nice, thought The Virgin, 'rather explosive'. But this would be loaded onto a ship chartered by MacAllans. "Hey, how explosive? This is going to be on our boat, don't forget. It's got to be safe or we're not going to be able to handle it."

"Yes. Yes, of course. Perhaps I gave the wrong impression. The material itself will be quite safe. And the container in which it travels. We will merely modify the container to provide a little surprise. A controllable surprise. But you're anticipating my next question. How will it travel?"

"We normally ship out of Rotterdam. We charter a five thousand tonne vessel and fill it full of cement and chemicals and send it out. We usually have a few containers as well, either below decks or deck cargo. How big is the tank?"

Crossman did not get diverted. "So you would like us to send the material over to Rotterdam? I don't think that's possible. I dread to think what would happen to us if anyone suggested sending it on a passenger ferry. Can you divert the ship to pick it up? That would be the best answer."

"I suppose so - but it will make things expensive. Where would you want to load it? Poole?"

Crossman looked at his colleague. "Does Poole have a harbour? Isn't it one of those dreadful towns that you learn about in school? The ones where the harbour silts up and everything ends up miles inland?" Stanford did not know, and neither did The Virgin.

"Never mind; it will be somewhere around there. Southampton, Bournemouth, I think Weymouth is all pleasure boats nowadays."

"How heavy is the tank?" asked The Virgin. "Are we going to need special cranes?"

"Ah. Yes. Now I'm in an area about which I know next to nothing. I was thinking of increasing the order size to five thousand litres, if you think your customers would accept it. Apparently that's the size of the tank they would have to use anyway, so they may as well have it full. Let me see; that would be six and a half tonnes of chemical. How much does a tank weigh? When do you need special cranes?"

"What sort of tank are you talking about?"

Crossman opened a drawer and pulled out a loose file. He sat back and read it privately. "It says here it is a five thousand litres, double-insulated tank, with an integral scrubbing system. Transport frame as for standard twenty foot shipping container. Does that make sense?"

"I don't know about the scrubbing system, but the standard container makes life easier. It'll be eight tonnes all up, I guess. Maybe more if it's a double tank. Say ten tonnes tops. That should be easy enough to handle. So what do you want from me?"

"Oh, your bit is easy. We need you to sell it to Major Jamal, and arrange for delivery. That's all."

The Virgin laughed. "That's the easy bit? I can see you've never been in sales. The selling's the difficult bit. The rest of it's easy. If I've got to sell it, how much are you going to charge me?"

"Karelia says the substitute chemical will cost £1.45 per litre."

"£1.45; that's around $2.10 per litre. I suppose you're talking FAS a southern port. Five thousand litres, $10,500. OK. And how much for the container? It's all one-way trips into Tabriz so we'd have to buy the container."

"They say the basic container cost is only £850 if we take a second-hand one. And then there's the modifications, of course."

"You're not going to make us pay for the modifications! Are you trying to make a profit out of this? Come on! It's going to cost us a bunch of money to come into Southampton and pick it up. Look; $10,500 for the product, say $1300 for the container, I'd better say $10,000 for the pick up and shipping, that's $12,000 plus... $22,000 altogether. We'll have to sell that for around $80,000."

The other men looked shocked. "How much is $80,000?" asked Stanford.

"Around £55,000."

Crossman whistled. "I had no idea. Are they going to buy that? Why's it so expensive?"

"Tabriz is a very expensive place to do business. We have to pay all sorts of taxes and rip-offs just to be there. And it's all paid in dinars at the official funny-money exchange rate."

Crossman thought for a while. "I suppose we could ask Karelia to reduce their price a little. And perhaps I could give you the container free. Would that help? And you could ask your manager to help, what was his name, the American?"

The Virgin laughed. "You can forget that. Ron might be very patriotic and stand up for the flag and all that, but he's not going to let it stand between him and a dollar. You do what you can, and I'll do my best. If the Tabrizis let it fall through, it means they're not really interested anyway. They've got the money, especially for military purposes."

They were clearly troubled. They did not want to see their project collapse before its birth just because of a lack of funding, but then again, they did not have much of a budget of their own. "I just hope Karelia can help us," muttered Crossman. "Now, what else do we have to discuss?"

"I have something," said The Virgin. "It's just occurred to me. How do we know they're not just blowing smoke up our backsides? I mean, they might string us along and then leak it to the Sunday Times."

"Ah, we thought about that," said Stanford. "There's no problem. Firstly, they're not ordering mustard gas. It's going to be referred to as Karelia SV 6 which is the catalogue reference of the real chemical but not a definition. So if there's a leak, they ordered a fairly harmless solvent, nothing more. It's all quite deniable. The press makes a fuss, the Minister orders an investigation, no problem is found, everyone's happy."

"Except for Major Jamal."

"Oh, yes. I see what you mean. Major Jamal would be a little upset. He'd probably be after your blood. Well, there's two ways to look at that. Firstly, no-one in their right minds is going to open the container and take a sniff. If they do, they'll choke anyway because there will be a good dose of tear gas in it. Secondly, the evidence is going to be destroyed by fire before they can use it anyway. Does that set your mind at rest?"

"Is there any way Major Jamal's going to suspect I've met you?"

Crossman dived in. "I don't want to hear this. I don't need to know. Stanford will take you away and sort all those things out between you. I just have to organise the shipment. What else do you need?"

The Virgin thought for a moment. "Nothing, I think. So Karelia will be faxing me with all the details?"

"That's right. You can sort it all out with them. We'll see everything you fax them."

"You'd better watch the telexes too; sometimes the telephones don't work at all."

He noted that in his file. "Right. That just about finishes my bit. It's been nice meeting you. We'll see you when you get back." He stood up and shook hands. "You're Stanford's baby from now on. Good luck."

Stanford had a list of things to cover, but The Virgin had his own priorities. "I've got to go shopping. I've got a pile of stuff to buy and I'm leaving tomorrow."

"Don't worry so much, Cartwright. It's the Christmas season so the shops will stay open late. And we're expecting Miss Anthony any time now. She's got your wallet and passport, and she'll take you shopping, and to dinner, and stay in the hotel with you."

His last words fell into silence as The Virgin's stomach turned a somersault. Stanford continued, "Of course, Mostyn will be there with her, so I suppose you can play three-handed bridge if you can't sleep.

"Right. Business. Major Jamal is not likely to know you were here. But we know him fairly well - we trained him, you know, in military intelligence - and I'm almost certain he'll check on what you've been up to. After he left us, the revolution came along and the Russians stepped in. They are really responsible for the way the Tabrizi security services have developed. I'm sure they'll have trained him in advanced paranoia, so let's assume he'll check on you."

"Jesus!" whistled The Virgin.

"Oh, don't worry too much. We talked this through and the way we see it, in no circumstances can he confront you. Let's assume he really is serious about this order; in that case he won't want you to know it's anything other than a harmless solvent. And if he's not serious he's trying to catch us out, not you. So he still wants your co-operation. Either way, he can't really interrogate you or you'd smell a rat and drop the whole deal.

"I expect he'll try and check you out by talking to you, try and find out how you spent your time, who you met. So what we are intending to do is make up an interesting couple of nights with Miss Anthony. You know, theatres, candle-lit dinners, all that sort of thing."

"Sounds nice. I wish it had happened."

Stanford smiled to himself. "Don't we all? Never mind; we're giving you an illusory girl-friend, so you'll just have to imagine what happened. She'll have all the details and will go over them with you this evening. She might even manage the candle-lit dinner if you ask her nicely.

"Do pay attention to her. She's going to be your contact with us. She'll give you her home telephone number and you can communicate using word code if you have to. But it shouldn't be necessary. We'll get all we need from Karelia. Just treat it like a normal shipment and you won't hear any more about it."

"Normal shipment! I just hope the bloody thing's safe."

"Oh, some things we can manage pretty well, even in these post-Communist days. You won't even notice. All you'll have to do is pick up your money, and you seem to have got that sorted out in advance. Let me just check if Miss Anthony's here."

He came back with Elena in tow. She was wearing a chunky sweater and jeans, and smiling happily. "Ready to go? Let's hit Oxford Street."

"I don't know what else Stanford has to cover."

Stanford thought for a moment. "Nothing else, I think."

"Is that all? I mean, what happens if something goes wrong, if I have to get in touch with you?"

"Miss Anthony has all you'll need about that. It's really not necessary because we'll be following you closely through Karelia, but you never know." He held out his hand. "Good luck. We'll have lunch next time you're in town."

"Goodbye. Or is it au revoir?"

The Virgin flew to Crete with butterflies in his stomach. Elena had been good company. She had rushed him up and down Oxford Street, accumulating nearly everything on his shopping list in a shorter time than any woman The Virgin had known. She was a creature of both taste and decision. Choosing the right warm shirts was just a matter of letting her look through the racks and handing over his credit card. She seemed to know her way around the CD megastore as well and he bought half of his discs unheard on her recommendation.

Back at the hotel he took a quick shower and she led him down to the coffee shop for his briefing. It had been disappointing. He expected a lecture on secret inks and silent killers, but she kept it much simpler. He was to call her at least once a fortnight, just to pass the time. If anything came up, he would just have to figure out a way to pass the message by word-code, as she called it. She was going to send him a package to arrive about the same time as the chemical or a little later. If he spoke on the telephone to her about a parcel, he was talking about the chemical; if it was a package, it would be the present she had sent. Apart from that, just two code words; if he mentioned blue cheese he was asking for a meeting; 'wheelbarrow' was the signal to panic.

She passed over documentary proofs of a non-existent affair between them. Theatre stubs for Cats; two pairs of used bus tickets; an opened packet of condoms. The condoms were called 'Sultan' and featured an enticing slave girl on the front of the gold packet. He sighed when he saw them and told her he would keep them for next time. The last item, a stuffed envelope, she produced a little reluctantly. She told him to keep it unopened until he was on the plane. She wrote her telephone numbers on the inside of a hotel match folder and handed them over. "This one's Executive Travel where I work - normal office hours - and the other's my flat. Call anytime; I always let the answer phone run before I pick up."

"And that's it? Nothing else?"

"What did you expect? Your job is to arrange for the shipment to get into Tabriz, and be our ear to the wall so we know what's happening. Don't even think about anything more. It could be very damaging to the mission, and to your health if anything goes wrong."

"What could go wrong?"

Elena played with her coffee spoon. "Nothing. In theory nothing could go wrong that would involve you. But you can imagine how it is in real life. Anything could go wrong. Anything you can imagine and then at least as much again that you can't. What you've got to do is forget about it all. All the people in our office, all the things you've discussed, all the things that might happen and probably won't. Just forget about it all and get on with your normal life."

"Do I forget about you too?"

She was human enough to laugh. "Well, maybe not about me. You've got to call me anyway. That'll be nice; I can just imagine how it is in Tabriz when it's January here. If we're lucky, we might have to meet in Crete later on for business. Would you like that?"

"Are you going to bring Hobson?"

"Don't be silly! No. If they send me on jobs like that I'm normally alone, so we'll have fun. When is spring in Crete?"

"I don't know. Late March I should guess. Do you travel much?"

"Oh yes. They're always sending me off to pick up little bits of information or to meet people. Nothing quite like this, though. This could be quite exciting." Before The Virgin could ask what 'exciting' meant for him, she was standing up and waving for the bill.

She took him to a Hungarian restaurant that night. Goulash and Bull's Blood, with little old men playing gypsy violins at their table. Elena's eyes were flashing in the candle-light, it was ridiculously romantic, and they enjoyed every minute. Mostyn was waiting for them back at the hotel. He sat watching television in the next room, and The Virgin's hopes of a romantic night rose. He had been cuddling Elena in the lift and was feeling very good. She left him to talk with Mostyn and then came back leaving the connecting door ajar. The Virgin took her into his arms and squeezed her.

"I'm sorry, Greg. I can't do it with him in there," she whispered. She held a long finger over his protesting lips. "I'd do it if it was for work, but... I'm sorry. Next time, I promise." With a long and passionate kiss, she left him. The imprint of her firm body remained pressed against him and now, flying away high over France, he could imagine it yet. He wriggled his brief-case out from under the seat in front, and looked for the envelope she had given him in the coffee shop. A pair of tiny black lace panties fell out. There was a card, a childish thing with two furry mice sharing an orchard swing. Inside she had written 'Hurry up and bring them back to me - Love, Elena'. Below her signature was a big lip-stick kiss.

Next day, Heraklion Airport felt deadly. This was the inward traveller's first contact with Tabrizis in mass and it always made The Virgin's heart sink at the feeling of being back home again. The oil-men with their doleful workmen's faces sat alone on the plastic chairs and drank steadily from cans of beer, the last real beer they would see for weeks or months. They were still travelling into Tabriz and could not even start ticking off the days on their calendars to when they would be back with their families. Tabrizi children ran everywhere while their parents sat surrounded by mountains of European shopping. The fat women with their head-scarves made a depressing contrast with the sexy Greek girls outside. At last the flight was called and the Tabrizis formed a scrum at the doorway. Oh well, thought The Virgin, Sabah here we come. A deadness settled on him and he made his way to the plane like a robot.

It was a windy evening in Sabah and the plane lurched down onto the run-way like a tired goose. The passengers wrapped their coats around them as they were herded into the broken-down airport bus with no windows. It was dirty and only half of the door next to The Virgin could be closed. It creaked its way to the low airport buildings. They waited in a bare terrazzo room for the two Immigration officials to start stamping passports. The foreigners lacked the enthusiasm to push and stood quietly in line while the locals fussed and called out, brown hands thrusting bunches of passports at the lethargic officials behind their glass plates. It was a slow business, even for the Tabrizis.

The Virgin's turn came eventually. Immigration was represented by a juvenile with an uncertain moustache. He was dressed in a scruffy combat jacket and jeans. Every passport that was put into his hands seemed to confuse him and he turned the pages slowly as if trying to buy time. When he came to The Virgin's picture he held it up and compared the image with the reality in silence. Without speaking he left his desk and disappeared through a door behind. Now it starts, thought The Virgin.

He came back quickly with his finger closed inside the passport. Rapidly he opened it and slapped a stamp and a signature over the re-entry visa. Still mute he pushed it back at The Virgin. Hamdullah, he thought, it's going to be easy. Through the open door to the apron he could see three men slowly pushing the baggage trolley towards the terminal. The tow truck must have broken down again. The passengers moved back onto the apron ready to pounce.

The line for Customs seemed to be moving quite quickly. Through the crowd The Virgin could see that the customs men were in place behind their low tables, but they were not interested in the baggage passing them. Aside from hauling in each Tabrizi and making him open all his carefully tied bundles, they were waving most foreigners through. Strange, he thought, that's something new.

Some of the oil-men were being pulled up but released after a passport check and a cursory bag search. The Virgin's turn came quickly. His passport caught some-one's eye again and was carried off for a second opinion. It came back in the hands of a well turned out officer. "You come inside. And your bags." The Virgin picked up his bags and followed him. The office inside was bare. A dilapidated desk filled one side, and cheap chrome chairs lined the wall. "Bags here," ordered the officer, pointing at the desk. The Virgin swung his hold-all up onto the desk and set his brief-case beside it. "Empty your pockets also." The Virgin was stunned. He had never had that happen, or heard of it with any of his friends. The officer was pointing at the desk and silently commanding. There was no choice. The Virgin's hands went slowly to his pockets. There was not much. Car keys, wallet, passport. "Also your watch." He unclipped his heavy diver's watch and laid it beside the rest. "Now you come with me."

The Virgin followed him down a dark corridor to what appeared to be the chief's office. It had carpet on the floor and a low table in front of the desk. There were two comfortable chairs for visitors and behind the desk an enormous modern manager's throne. The walls were empty except for the obligatory portrait of the Great Man looking over the shoulder of the manager. The Virgin sat and waited.

He must have waited alone there for half an hour. The room was completely silent and he was left to uncomfortable speculation about what was happening outside. Lurking behind him was the god of panic. He felt that at any invitation, any half open door, the god would burst through and overwhelm him. By instinct he refused to look at what he had been doing. He buried Hobson and Mostyn, Crossman and Stanford. Buried the Eminent Person from the India Rooms. Instead he thought of Tom Forbes and his plans for Eastern Europe. He tried to remember heading by heading the position paper he had flipped through carelessly on the flight over. He remembered Elena. He remembered taking her to the theatre, the address of the Hungarian restaurant with its little old violinists. Holding hands with her and walking down Oxford Street. Elena's black eyes as she raised her glass in the candle-light. Making love to her on their arrival at the hotel as soon as the porter left and the door closed. Elena's figure as she undressed; her lacy black panties, the ones in his brief-case, hiding very little. The shape of Elena draped naked over his hotel bed; making love half asleep two mornings later. Sharing the three-quarter sized bath tub, her perfect breasts hiding behind her knees. Plans for a holiday in the Greek islands when they would lie nude in the sun, like immortals.

Once he heard foot-steps outside, but they passed by. He returned to his remembering.

Suddenly the door swung open and the officer who had brought him there was standing in the door-way. He looked at The Virgin for a long moment without expression. "You have big problem. You have pornography in your bag."

"What?" The Virgin could not believe what he had heard.

"You have pornography in your bag. The chief officer is coming." He turned and left, the cryptic accusation still hanging in the air.

What were they thinking about, he asked himself, what has blown their tiny minds this time? It could not have been Elena's knickers, surely not. Even in Tabriz that could not be against the law. Was there something in the Guardian newspaper he had picked up at the airport, an advertisement with a naked lady perhaps? He could not remember one, and naked ladies were not the Guardian's style. What else did he have? Had they slipped something into his bag? Why bother? Were they just trying to frighten him? Again, why bother? Once in Tabriz they could do what they liked to him anyway. They were probably listening to him, or watching him right now. He looked around for a camera.

He sat back in his chair and started thinking of his toes. Slowly he moved his focus up to his shins, his knees and above. He was taking an inventory, tensing muscles individually, feeling them react. By the time he reached his ears, he was ready to start remembering again. In his mind he got onto the plane in Heraklion. The empty seat beside was filled by a pretty, no, a beautiful girl called Elena. They started to talk.

88

He was in the taxi into town, holding hands with Elena, when the door opened again. The same officer, but this time he was holding a magazine. The magazine he had bought in Heraklion and not read on the plane because he had Elena next to him. The one that had lain hidden and unopened in his briefcase throughout his trip. "This is yours, I think?"

Sick at his own stupidity, The Virgin nodded. "It is a big problem. The chief officer is coming."

The Virgin was alone again. They would watch him, he knew it. He played the part. He let the fear take a corner of his mind just to see what he would do. He got out of his chair and paced the room. He stood on tip-toe and tried to look out of the high window. He took a tissue from the ornate box on the table and wiped his brow. He sat down again in the other chair. Finally he tried the door. Outside was a uniformed man with a Kalashnikov looking straight at him.

"Er - I want to see the officer, please." The man waved him back inside with the Kalashnikov.

Back in the room he started to over-act. Or perhaps he was not acting, he was no longer sure. He paced. He stood on his chair to look out of the window, and paced again. The daylight had gone and he was losing sense of time. He did not know how long he had waited when the officer re-appeared. "What do you want?" he asked, woodenly.

"I want to see Major Jamal," said The Virgin in a voice that was barely his own. There was no sign of recognition in the man's face. "Major Jamal. He is in Military Security, a tall man, with a moustache. I need to talk with him. Or telephone. Can I telephone him?"

The man still showed no response but he answered, "Major Jamal, I will see." He turned and left.

Again he had no way of telling how long he had waited before the door opened. It seemed a short time, too short to have brought Major Jamal from his home but there he was, his large frame filling the doorway. With him was Captain Zella. They burst into the room bringing noise and light. The Virgin felt a wave of relief. "Mr Cartwright! How are you? Kefahlik! Did you have a good trip to London? How is your family?" Major Jamal was reaching out a rescuing hand and The Virgin shook it gratefully. He even felt benign towards Captain Zella as he shook hands. The Major took the throne behind the desk and Captain Zella sat opposite him.

"Major Jamal, I'm awfully sorry to have called you, but I've got a bit of trouble. It's just that when I was flying out to London I bought a magazine. One with girls in it. And I forgot to throw it away and it's still in my bag. So now Customs are upset and I needed some-one to speak for me and I thought of you, if you don't mind. I need your help."

Major Jamal seemed to think The Virgin was being far too hasty. "Did they give you tea? Or coffee? How do you like your coffee? I will call for some."

As he went to the door, Captain Zella spoke in a low voice. "It is a serious thing, what you have done. This is strictly illegal in Tabriz. To bring in pornography is a very serious thing."

"Er - yes. I know. I mean, I didn't want to do it. It was an accident."

"That is not important. What is important is that you have a very bad magazine. It is non-Islamic. Do you understand that it is a big problem?"

"Oh Jesus, yes! I wish I had never seen the damn thing. I haven't read it anyway. And I certainly wouldn't risk bringing it into Tabriz if I hadn't forgotten about it. But can you help me? Do you know what they will do?" Captain Zella was expressionless. He seemed to be much less of a saving angel than the Major. The Virgin refused to think of what might be going through his mind, how he would be thinking of the opportunity that The Virgin's slip-up had given him, how the lever could be used in the future.

Major Jamal came back leading a porter with a tray of coffee cups and Captain Zella slipped back into silence. The coffee was sweet and heavenly.

Major Jamal sipped delicately and started to question him. "How was London? Did you have your meeting with your manager?"

"Oh yes. He wanted to talk about Russia. It's getting very busy and they want to send me there. To Siberia. From the Sahara to Siberia."

"Really? When will they send you?"

"Oh, probably never. We're always making plans that don't turn into anything. But we've got to be ready, just in case. It won't be for at least a couple of months anyway."

"And did you get any news about our order of solvent?"

"I'm sorry. I was so busy I didn't even telephone the supplier. I'll have to get after that first thing on Monday."

"I see. So what else did you do in London?"

"Well, I met a friend and we spent some time together. You know, shopping, going out, that sort of thing. I was only in London one day really. I spent most of Friday in the office hanging around, so it didn't leave much time."

"I tried to call you at your hotel. I wanted you to bring me some shirts from Gieves and Hawkes, but you weren't there."

"Ah - yes. I didn't stay where I was going to stay. My friend didn't like that hotel so we went to the Holiday Inn instead."

"Oh. You stayed with your friend in a hotel?"

"Well, yes. It was a girl friend, you see, and she had stayed at the Rutland before and she was afraid they might recognise her."

"Ah. I see. That sort of friend. The one who sent you the card and souvenir of her affection in your brief-case?"

The Virgin felt himself colouring. "That's right. Look, Major Jamal, I'm awfully sorry about what happened. It was so stupid of me. Would it be possible for you to talk to some-one about it?" He was on the verge of offering to pay for his error but Major Jamal seemed too grand for that.

"Perhaps I can help. If everything is as you say, I will speak to the officer in charge now. Perhaps he will let you leave if you give me your parole. I know him; he is an old friend."

The request for parole dropped the whole affair another notch into unreality. How seriously was The Virgin meant to take the situation? A pledge on his honour as an English gentleman? It was absurd. He decided to play along.

"I would be very grateful if you could sort it out. Anything you need from me to help, just ask."

"Good. Come with me and we will fetch your bags."

His luggage was still on the desk outside. His hold-all lay open and had been clumsily re-stuffed. His wallet, keys and passport lay beside it. He followed the Major and Captain Zella out into the evening. He was free again; it had been that easy.

The Major was full of himself. "You will come home in our car. There is no need for friends to take taxis."

"But I have my car here."

"No problem. Then you can give me a lift instead. Captain Zella can drive our car." He gave Zella some quick instructions in Arabic and they left him, still silent and morose.

Major Jamal relaxed in the car. Sitting back with his legs stretched out, it was difficult to be suspicious of him. "Captain Zella is a very serious man," ventured The Virgin.

"Ah yes. He is serious. He is one of the new men who came up with the Revolution. There are many people like him now. All very serious, but not educated. His father was a poor man, you know. A baker. He had a small shop, one of the very small stalls you used to see before the Committees made them illegal. This man had his shop just outside the gates of the Muharraq army barracks, when the Great Man was stationed there. He used to like sweet cakes - he still does, that's why he is so fat - and he would spend his spare money with the baker. So, come the Revolution and suddenly the baker is a big man. That's how it was in Tabriz in those times. People from the streets were made into big men, and all the old families lost everything. All their money, their businesses, farms, everything." He was looking out into the darkness and remembering.

"Our family was stripped. The Committees took all we had. I made myself very small and shouted for the Revolution with the rest of them. What else could I do? If I couldn't live with the Great Man, I would lose my job and probably my head as well. So I sat on the Committees and helped him as well as I could. He knew me from before, of course. We served together. The Royal Tabriz Scouts, that's what our regiment used to be called. We were the old King's favourite troops. We had a small Camel Corps then, and a little Air Force. A few patrol boats for the Navy, that was all Tabriz needed. But we were the cream. We had English and Tabrizi officers, you know. All trained in Sandhurst. The Scouts would march past on the King's birthday and His Majesty would stand up straight and salute us - those were good times. A soldier was a proud man then. Afterwards, we all had to be politicians and play dirty games.

"Look at the soldiers now. Rubbish. Sons of street sweepers. Dirty, poor, ignorant rubbish. They don't want to be there and the Army doesn't want them either. All the good families pay a little money and their sons don't have to join the Army. They can go to University in Moscow or Czechoslovakia instead. Before I used to have proud men from the desert, and Sudanese who stood up straight and did just what they were ordered to do. If I had told them to lie down in front of this car, they would have done it. They would die for their King and be proud of it. Now, I can't even give the simplest order without dirty sons of Egyptian prostitutes coming to discuss it with me.

"The officers we have now are just politicians. Captain Zella! He should be minding his father's old shop. That would be more suitable for him. He would shit himself if he ever heard a gun fired in anger. And I have to drag him around because he is a revolutionary and they still don't believe I am. He watches me and reports back. All this time, and they still don't trust me.

"Maybe it will be better one day. Maybe. Perhaps the Great Man will retire before some-one helps him do it, and we can have a proper Army again. Too late for me. I'm getting old and this business of Security, it makes you old very quickly. Were you in the Army, Mr Cartwright?"

"Me? No, never. They'd finished conscription long before I was old enough and I went to University and then joined the oil business. Was Sabah very different before the Revolution?"

"Oh, Sabah was a good place then. People used to come here for their holidays. That is hard to believe, isn't it? It was a tourist resort. Italians, Greeks, English of course, rich Lebanese, they would all come here and enjoy the restaurants and the casino. We had rich men's boats in the harbour, and you could sit in the cafes on the pavement and drink wine with your pasta, and watch the girls go by. Ah, it was like the Riviera, believe me. We could go to those cafes also. The good families mixed with the foreigners, we lived just as they did. You would have enjoyed yourself. You wouldn't have to go all the way to London to find a girl-friend then.

"What was your friend's name?"

They were back to reality with a bump. "Er - Elena."

"What does she do, this Elena?"

"She works in a travel agency. She had a cheap ticket to Crete and we sat next to each other on the flight to London. Bloody idiot!" He swerved to avoid a taxi pick-up that had decided to stop in the middle of the road.

Major Jamal was watching him. "You didn't know her before?"

"Well, no."

"And she came to stay with you in the hotel?"

"Yes; but she's a nice girl. Not - um, you know what I mean - not doing it for money. I'd like to see her again. Perhaps we can go to Greece together."

"Ah-ha, Mr Cartwright! I believe you have fallen in love! And so quickly. She must be very exciting."

"Oh, she's certainly that. Very sort of glamorous and alive and - well, it was really good being with her."

"Perhaps you should bring her to Tabriz?"

"Wouldn't that be nice? But you know how it is. Single ladies can never get visas because they must be prostitutes."

"Don't worry about that. I am very pleased you thought of me when you had trouble today. Any time I can help you, you must ask me. I have many friends who will help you. If you want to bring your girl-friend to visit, I can get her a visa tomorrow."

They were getting into town at the worst time of day; the traffic was crazy and avoiding the other cars kept The Virgin fully occupied. "You drive very well, Mr Cartwright. You do not shout or complain like most foreigners."

"Ah, well. I guess I'm used to it by now. Getting excited doesn't help."

"You are right. One must be quiet and just keep on going. Can you take me to the People's Hotel? Captain Zella should be meeting me there. Tell me, do you think you will have an answer about our solvent tomorrow?"

"That's Sunday. I might have one waiting for me, but if they haven't sent anything I'll call them first thing on Monday. Don't worry. I'll let you know as soon as I have anything."

The Virgin pulled into the forecourt of the People's Hotel, a modern glass and marble palace built by the Koreans and run by Moroccans. A stiffly uniformed doorman ran to help Major Jamal. He struggled out of the car and turned with the door still open. "I am glad you had a good visit to London. I was worried that perhaps you would be delayed and so we would not be able to order our solvent quickly. It was good talking with you. Goodnight."

When he got home The Virgin found his luggage had been thoroughly searched. Nothing was packed the way it had been and every packet had been opened. But everything was there, even the offending magazine. He left his bag on the bedroom floor and boiled saucepans for a hot bath.

- 10 -

Seven o'clock next morning was a hard target to achieve. Still half asleep, The Virgin drove through the dark streets to the office. Driving and parking was easy at this time of day; everyone else had the sense to stay in bed until the sun got up. He made a coffee and started to call the desert. Life had improved sensibly since he had carried in an automatic dialling telephone. He could now punch in the number and let the machine do the work. Of course, the Tabrizi telephone system often defeated the electronics and the process stalled, but a touch of a button and it was clicking away again. He no longer had to sit with the hand-set wedged under one ear, spinning away at one of the old-fashioned dial phones.

As he waited, he started through the messages left by Abdul. Some-one in TAMCO had been trying to reach him. That would be Tayfun with some niggling problem on the RomDril-1 cement job. Tayfun could wait until he got to TAMCO later that morning.

There was a telex from Rotterdam announcing the scheduling of the next charter vessel. It should be loading 18th January. Wonderful. Any delay on that and the boat would reach Tabriz just in time for Ramadan. Things happened slowly in Tabriz at the best of times, but in Ramadan everything was twice as much trouble and took twice as long. Bless Rotterdam's little hearts. Their problem was that they did not want to load any earlier as that would mean making their preparations during the Christmas/New Year period.

His in-tray held a wad of supply orders wanting descriptions for Customs purposes. This was the critical part of The Virgin's job. Anything imported had to have a description in Arabic, and the wording of the description determined the duty payable. 'Water pump' would get off lightly at 10% duty but 'Water pump for truck engine' would get hit with 30% as a spare part. It could make a big difference. He put those aside for later in the day when he would have time to do them carefully.

There was a letter crudely typed in Arabic with a large green stamp over the signature. Abdul had written 'This is from the People's Agricultural Congress. They say they are the owners of our yard and we must pay rent to them from 1983. They want $100,000.' Oh shit! That meant another bunch of unwashed people would be pestering them for a month or two, waving a photocopy of some grandiose Congress decision and claiming that it gave them the right to blackmail whoever they wanted. It was a great strain to be polite to some of them when they crowded into his office, all smoking and trying to speak at once. It would come to nothing in the end. The Great Man's style of leadership left the local committees with a great deal of freedom to make rules and regulations, but once they started to interfere with the oil industry they would be brought up very sharply.

The lab tests for the RomDril-1 job were in. Nothing unusual there. He had better get to the rig that day and see how things were going. Still reading, his practised ear identified some useful sounds in the clicking from the telephone; it might have got an open line. He waited with his pen poised; the hollow buzz was broken by a ringing tone. Hamdullah! Another miracle of modern technology. He opened his telephone log and started to exchange news with Florian, the desert Operations Supervisor. Nothing much was happening, and everyone was waiting for RomDril-1 to reach casing point.

Duty done for the moment, it was time for another coffee while he continued reading the mail. No fax from Karelia yet. It was still too early. They might have got the go-ahead on Friday afternoon, so the earliest he could expect anything would be Monday. He wondered how Elena was getting on. It would be just before six in the morning there and he could not disturb her Sunday lie-in. Maybe later on. He switched on the computer and got down to work.

TAMCO was just starting its week. In Sabah they had their Monday morning feeling on Sundays. RomDril-1 would probably reach casing point sometime on Tuesday night and Tayfun was just putting the finishing touches to the cement programme. The trouble was losses. The hole was steadily losing around twenty percent of the drilling mud circulating. For every hundred barrels pumped down the drill-string and circulated back up to surface, only eighty actually arrived. It was not that the mud was heavy – the report said it weighed only 8.5 pounds per US gallon, just dirty water really. More probably the pressure generated by thousands of feet of liquid was making the mud leak off into some fractured limestone or very permeable sandstone. And if 8.5 pound mud was leaking off, it was a certainty that the two cement slurries planned for the casing would disappear. They weighed 13.6 pounds and 15.8 pounds per gallon. The hydrostatic pressure exerted by such heavy liquids was far higher.

Tayfun was in a corner. He would have to request really light cement, may be 10 pounds per gallon, with all the extra cost that entailed. The idea pained him and The Virgin enjoyed watching him squirm. In revenge Tayfun put up a stiffer fight than usual over the amount of excess cement that should be mixed. The Virgin settled for twenty percent over the hole volume as measured by caliper. Not enough really, but they could always make up the difference by a top job, pumping cement from surface down the outside of the casing to just top off the hole. He did not mind. It would cost TAMCO a second operation charge if they followed that route.

They counted out the timing together. Tuesday night the rig should reach casing point. Pull out of hole and run the drill bit to bottom again for a wiper trip, say Wednesday lunch-time. Then a quick surface logging run as this was an exploration hole, all finished by Wednesday midnight at the latest. Another wiper trip and they would be ready to run casing Thursday afternoon. The job would be in the small hours of Friday morning. Typically, the cement job would come at three in the morning, at the weekend, and it would surely be raining. He would have to rush off to RomDril-1 that afternoon and get a confirmed order for the light-weight cement. The desert would need to start blending and trucking immediately. And the desert lab would have to re-run the tests with the new cement weight, but that should not take too long.

He hurried back to the office just at twelve o'clock. No point calling the desert now, they took a two hour lunch break. Terry Jones on RomDril-1 would also be going for his rubber chicken lunch and then taking a siesta. The Virgin decided to give up for the moment and take a break at home. His microwave was beckoning and there would be plenty of time in the afternoon to get done what had to be done.

He did not make it back to the office until after four in the afternoon, but in his hand he had Terry's order for 4000 lovely cubic feet of light weight cement plus another 1300 of normal Class G. Life felt good at moments like this. It was like winning a race, or getting a pay rise. Like walking home in a student dawn after making love to the most beautiful girl at the party.

Florian in the desert was less excited. Some poor souls would be up all night blending the cement, and on top of that he would have to juggle his transportation around to deliver it on time. Whichever way you looked at it, he was going to need six trips. Two trips with the Class G at 650 sacks per load, and then if he could squeeze 1000 cubic feet of light weight cement into each bulk trailer he would need another four. He would get the Class G on the road straight away. Then it dawned on them that they did not have enough silo space on the rig. He could send up one more 1000 cubic foot silo but only if he could find a truck to carry it up. The Virgin promised to find him one tomorrow, and left a note on Abdul's desk telling him to fix it.

It was not until he was locking up the office that he realised he had forgotten to telephone Elena.

Florian managed to get two trucks on the road at six in the morning. Two contract road tractors hauling MacAllans bulkers. It would be faster than using the desert Kenworths with their great big balloon tyres and a top speed of only forty klicks. He had sent a bulk plant operator along to make sure the drivers did not stop at every restaurant on the way, so they should be on location by lunch time. The Virgin would have to go and receive them. Make sure the cement ended up in the right silos. No problem; he would be there anyway, checking that Terry had got RomDril all lined up.

Tayfun was waiting for him with a surprise. Bill Gordon wanted to have a meeting on the RomDril-1 job and had called Terry into the office for ten thirty. The Virgin liked that idea; Bill knew what he was talking about and was quite capable of putting his foot down if Tayfun tried pulling one of his stunts. He could even talk sense into Bassam Al Suleiman, the operations manager.

The Virgin tried to sit in the back-ground when the meeting got together. After all, he was only a contractor. All the others were TAMCO employees and far more exalted. Suleiman did not come voluntarily; he had to be led by Tayfun. Bill kicked off.

"Right. Everyone got a copy of the programme?" The Virgin raised a tentative hand. "No? Tayfun, do you have a copy for Greg?"

"I did not make a copy for him..."

"Oh, I think he ought to have one, don't you? He's the one who's got to get the job done and it would be nice if he knew what he was meant to do."

"I thought Terry would tell him."

"Sure will," broke in Terry, "But he'd just as well have one anyway. Save him stealing mine."

"Maybe I have another one in my file. I will give it to him afterwards."

"How about now?" Bill issued a veiled order. "Then he'll know what we're talking about." Accepting defeat, Tayfun left to fetch it and The Virgin settled to read carefully.

"So. From the top. The casing's all on site, yes? And being inspected? When will it be ready to run?"

"The casing hands reckon they'll be done this afternoon. It's in good shape. They've only rejected three joints so far."

"Good. And the hardware?"

That was The Virgin's department. The shoe with the one-way valve that went on the bottom of the casing to allow cement to be pumped out but to stop it flowing back when pumping stopped. And the bow-type centralisers that kept the casing centred in the hole. "They're all coming up with the cement this lunch time."

"That the last of the cement?"

"No. There will be another four loads after these."

"Jesus, Greg! You're leaving it a bit late, aren't you?"

Bill was right. Unless Florian rounded up another bulker today, they would be delivering cement right up to the last minute. "Well, it was the losses. We only got the order for the light cement yesterday afternoon. We'll be back-loading some pozzolan cement that we were going to use."

"And you will not charge for the transport of that cement, no?" Good old Tayfun. Never missed a chance to put the boot in.

"Oh no. You only pay for the cement you order. We sent the pozzolan up because we wanted to be ready. I'll let you have the transport for free." It was not much of a gesture. The pozzolan had been left over from the surface casing and The Virgin knew there was not a hope of making TAMCO pay transport.

"Never mind about that," said Bill. "Let's get on with the important bits. You're going to be able to get the cement there on time? Good. Mr Suleiman, is there anything you would like to add at this time?"

"Yes. The operation is too expensive." Oh Christ, thought The Virgin, Tabriz strikes again. Now he is going to ask for a discount. "I think that MacAllans should give us a discount."

Bill kept a straight face and looked at The Virgin. He pretended to consider the matter. "Well, I'm sorry, Mr Suleiman, but the operation is not expensive. It's just that it's so big. The casing is set at 1800 metres and that means a lot of cement."

"But it is so big that you must give us a discount."

The Virgin wondered what line Tayfun had been feeding him. "I don't know how we could make it cheaper. We could go back to ordinary cement I suppose."

Bill glared at him. "Not a chance. We'd lose the lot as soon as it hit bottom."

"Or perhaps less cement..."

"No way. This is an exploration well. It's got to be cemented back to surface."

The Virgin pretended to consider. "Well, I don't know what to suggest." He looked at Tayfun; the man really thought that MacAllans would give discounts away just because his boss asked for them. "I think you've given us a very large and difficult job to do and I don't see any other way of doing it." The room fell silent and eyes turned from The Virgin to Suleiman. The Virgin let the silence increase the pressure and Suleiman shifted uncomfortably in his chair. Eventually, Bill rescued him.

"How much does the job come to, Tayfun?"

"Ah. This is not for us to say. The cost must be worked out by MacAllans."

Just as The Virgin had thought. The demand for a discount was merely a reflex. No-one knew how much they were talking about, and still they knew it was too expensive.

"Greg?"

"Well, I haven't worked it out either, but off-hand I'd guess it's not as expensive as Mr Suleiman has been worrying about." He smiled at Suleiman and nodded encouragingly. "Four thousand sacks of light cement and tail in with one thousand three hundred sacks of Class G neat. Delivered to location you're only talking about $400,000 or so. Say another $100,000 would cover everything else so I'd guess around half a million dollars. That's not so much for a job like this, is it Mr Suleiman?" He nodded again at Suleiman. Suleiman could not help himself. He was nodding in agreement. As if half a million was loose change. It was all funny money to TAMCO, anyway. They never saw a dollar for the oil they produced, and the oil ministry footed the bill for every dollar they spent. God bless the Great Man and his devotion to socialist economics, thought The Virgin.

"Right," said Bill with that swept aside, "What about your casing tally, Terry? I want the pipe set with a sensible stick-up this time."

Terry's turn for embarrassment. On the last job he had selected the joints of casing so that when the pipe reached bottom there was still twenty feet of it sticking above the rig floor. That made connecting the cement head a nightmare. The MacAllans' man had flat refused to go up to insert the plugs and operate the valves because RomDril had no working harness and the air-winch was down. A rig hand had ridden the cat-line up in the end, with one leg stuck uncomfortably through a loop of chain. Terry kept quiet and made a note in his tally book.

Suleiman cleared his throat. "Now I must go, excuse me. Mr Tayfun will tell you everything that has been decided. Thank you." He sidled out of the room.

"Greg. Anything from your end?"

"Couple of things. There's only twenty barrels of wash in the programme. At normal circulation rates that'll be gone in only a minute and a half. I don't think that'll clean much mud."

"Tayfun? What's the mud like?"

"Oh, the mud is very good. The programme says Marsh funnel of less than forty seconds."

Terry snorted. "Guess the mud man forgot to read the programme. The shit he's got me pumping probably wouldn't go through the funnel. I've been telling him but he says he doesn't have low temperature thinner."

"Have him use some high temperature stuff then."

Tayfun was outraged. "High temperature thinner is very expensive! He must just use more water."

"I don't care what he uses. Terry, before we run casing, the last wiper trip, I want the Marsh funnel below forty and you'd better give us at least four hours of circulation before you pull out. Until the mud's coming back in good shape. Let me know if you're not getting what you want and I'll kick some-one's ass. What else, Greg?"

"Even with the mud in good shape, twenty barrels of wash is still not going to get the hole clean. That's a lot of hole you're trying to cement."

"OK. A hundred barrels of wash. You'll write it in, Tayfun?"

It was not Tayfun's day. "But we could use water..."

"Good idea. A hundred barrels of water. And then a hundred barrels of wash."

Tay fun swallowed. "But it will be expensive."

"Oh, come on, Tayfun," Bill said. "Wash doesn't cost much and I don't want to screw up a half million dollar cement job for a couple of thousand dollars worth of wash. What else, Greg?"

"You've got us doing the displacing."

"Shit! I signed that? Show me. Jesus Christ, you're right. What's going on?"

Everybody knew what was going on. In a normal operation, MacAllans would pump the cement into the casing and then the big rig pumps would take over, pumping mud behind the cement and forcing it down the pipe and out of the bottom. Pumping large volumes was just what they were set up to do. Trouble was, normal rigs had stroke counters on their pumps that let them measure accurately what they were pumping. RomDril-1 had stroke counters but they did not work.

"I've tried pushing them," said Terry, "But there's no way. They're never going to get their counters working. The only way we can get a measurement is to use the MacAllans truck. But I don't believe we should be displacing a 13-3/8 inch job with a pump truck. It's too slow."

"What about another pump truck?" asked Bill. "We ought to have a back-up on a job like this. If the unit goes down half-way through it's going to cost us a fortune. Can you get us a back-up, Greg?"

Why don't I have more days like this, The Virgin asked himself as he made for his office phone? The job had a momentum of its own and Suleiman was smart enough to keep out of the way. The Virgin revelled in the relief of doing things properly for a change. Sure it would be expensive. In the States you could probably drill a regular well for the cost of just this one cement job, but that was not MacAllans' fault. The costs were high here because Tabriz was a very expensive place to work. Taxes were ridiculous. The artificial exchange rate racked prices up every time you turned around. The old men at the yard gate - night watchmen who actually had a bed in their little shack and would no more dream of staying awake at night than a child - were being paid three thousand dollars a month in real money by the time you figured in their taxes, holidays and other excessive benefits. And that was just one example. The Customs department really believed that by soaking foreign companies they were making money for Tabriz. They just did not understand where the money was coming from.

It suited foreign contractors to have high costs. They made sure their percentage profit remained the same by adjusting their prices, and at the end of the year it was better to have a percentage of a big figure than a small one. The numbers got really silly when it came to big jobs, but who cared? Tabrizi oil was good quality and easy to produce, and the share of the profits that foreign contractors were getting was still only a fraction of the Government's take. But not by much.

Florian tore his hair out at the thought of having to get another pump unit and crew up to Sabah, but it had to be done. He would get the truck on the road first thing tomorrow and the crews would come up twenty-four hours later. He even let The Virgin keep the bulk plant operator who would accompany the cement delivery. There would be enough to keep him busy for the next day or two. The Virgin went off to take lunch with Terry and to meet the cement.

The two bulk trucks ground onto location mid-afternoon. Big Mercedes tractors with oil-field winches and purpose-built head-ache racks. Probably provided originally by some crazy Government scheme to encourage transport co-operatives, they were now privately operated. The drivers would be paying off some-one high up in the co-operative organisation and using the trucks to make themselves money. It all worked well enough as long as the trucks did not break down. Thank God that a Mercedes could take a lot of hard work.

The bulk plant operator they brought with them was a Filipino called Felix, a calm, hard-working man who had been with MacAllans in Tabriz for years and knew his job inside out. The Virgin put his coveralls on and between them they hauled the four inch hoses off the bulk trailers and fired up the trailer compressors. Blowing the cement off took an hour or so and The Virgin ended up dusty and greasy, and with the inevitable cement in his hair. As he stripped off his work clothes at the back of his car he felt good about the chance of being able to do a little practical engineering for a change.

He waited until Felix had chased the truck drivers out of the canteen - free meals were irresistible to Tabrizis - and he watched the two bulkers roll out of the gate. Tomorrow morning he would give their departure time to Florian in case they returned late. Felix took his travelling bag and went off to find the camp boss and get himself a bed for the next few days.

There was no fax from Karelia until Tuesday morning. The fax bell rang and the paper curled slowly off the machine. 95p a litre ex-works with a minimum order of 5000 litres. Container to be purchased with the chemical at an additional £850. As he pondered the shiny fax it occurred to him that somewhere in town Major Jamal was probably doing exactly the same. He called Harris. "What mark-up shall we put on this solvent for Security?"

Harris did not even pause for thought. "Whatever you can get out of them."

"Well it's letter of credit, so that makes it better. I'll try them with 100%"

"What! Christ Almighty! It's not Christmas yet. I'm not going anything less than 400% or it will screw up my margin. Are you talking before or after on-costs?" Harris's reaction was pretty much what The Virgin had expected.

"After, of course. And our on-costs are minimal because it's FOB Sabah in our own charter."

"Well that makes it a bit better I suppose. But I'm still not in the charity business. If they want it, they'll have to pay. Tell them we're not negotiating and I want a 50% field margin. You know what that means, don't you? $50 in every $100 has got to be clear profit, right?"

"Right, Harris. Do you want to see the letter before it goes?"

"No. I guess not. Just don't screw up or you're here for the next ten years."

So there it was. Five thousand litres at 95p a litre came to £4750. Plus £850 for the container was £5600. Say $7800, $8000. He would have to call Rotterdam to get the cost of diverting the boat to Southampton. That would probably cost more than the chemical. He caught himself wondering if they should ship some other items from UK at the same time, just to provide camouflage. He was beginning to stand on the wrong side of the fence, he told himself. This is a normal solvent, nothing more, and we're picking it up in

Southampton to save the safety hazard of trucking it across to Rotterdam.

It was time to dip his toe in the water so he called Major Jamal with an outrageous price. "That solvent you asked me for. We can do it but you have to take a minimum of 5000 litres and it's going to cost you $63,000."

There was only a moment of silence from the other end, then Major Jamal's unhurried voice came back. "Very good. And the delivery charges?"

"That includes delivery. Everything, container as well. FOB Sabah, payment by ILC."

"I see. $63,000 complete. Mr Cartwright, I will come to your office tomorrow and you can write me an official letter for the bank to issue the letter of credit. When shall I come?"

The Virgin was stunned. Major Jamal was not meant to go for this price. The Tabrizi did not exist who paid the first price asked. Bargaining was an essential part of purchasing whether shopping for a dozen eggs or a dozen oil-wells. "Nine o'clock would be good, I guess."

"Very good. I will see you then." The Virgin was left listening to the dialling tone in disbelief. Then he started to call Rotterdam to make sure he had not made a mistake over the shipping charges.

- 11 -

Major Jamal picked up the official quotation next morning. He was in a fine mood and took a cup of coffee before he left. The Virgin found himself warming to the big man with his animated grey moustache who sat overflowing from the upright office chair. Major Jamal had been out in the world enough to treat foreigners as equals, and that made him comfortable to sit with. Although his profession made him suspicious of everyone, he was smart enough to see that the threats to the Great Man's regime were much more likely to come from home-grown malcontents than from foreign engineering companies.

On RomDril-1 things had begun to happen. Another load of cement had come in on Tuesday, and the back-up pump unit had already left the desert. The rig should reach casing point during the night, or maybe at breakfast time. The lead cementing engineer would arrive during the day, and on his morning telephone sched The Virgin promised Florian he would be on the rig to meet him.

He passed the back-up pump unit as he drove to the rig. The big black and grey Super Kenworth was thundering along the highway at its painfully slow maximum speed, its General Motors Detroit turbo-charged 12V92 diesel roaring smoke. The huge balloon tyres made it appear even more slow and ponderous as it rolled deliberately in through the location gates and pulled up outside the company man's trailer.

"Hey, Greg!" shouted Terry from his doorway. "Tell him to move that heap of junk out of my window. I can't see a dammed thing" .

Joe Milut the Maltese driver climbed back up to the cab and fired the beast up again. The Virgin dived inside to get away from the noise. "How's it going?"

Terry looked pained and shouted over the truck engine. "Be a dammed sight better when he's moved off. Good. He's going. I don't know when you guys are going to give up those GM engines. Don't use them in North America no more. Say they don't meet the emission standards and they won't have the noise. Health and Safety won't allow it and a damned good thing too. Everyone's changing to Cats - even your guys."

The Virgin shrugged. "You know what Tabriz is like. Twenty years behind. They're probably shipping all the old engines out here."

"Man, you should change too. Those Cats are reckoned to do 35,000 hours before rebuild. Guaranteed, so they say."

"Makes a lot of sense in a place like this. They won't let you re-export old engines for re-build, they can't do it themselves, and hiring mechanics to work in the desert would break your heart. We must have a yard full of old GM's. Never mind. TAMCO can afford it."

"Ha! You say! They might think so now, but times are changing." This was Terry's favourite theme, the inevitable slow decline of the Tabrizi oil-fields and the cold winds of economic reality that would be starting to blow any day now.

The Virgin interrupted him before he could get into his stride. "Our guys here yet?"

"What? Yes, sure. Guess they're having lunch. You coming?"

To say the food on RomDril-1 was basic would be polite. Most of the service hands used stronger language. Nobody understood what the Romanians thought of it because none of them spoke English. The Virgin knew what would be on the table before he got to the mess trailer; boiled potato, canned peas and stringy chicken. The Tabrizi government subsidised chicken production, and frozen chickens were cheap and plentiful. People reckoned you could tell an oil-field hand from Tabriz because he had feathers under his arms instead of hair. The Virgin borrowed Terry's bottle of Tabasco in an attempt to draw some life from the dry white meat.

The cementing crew sat at the next table. Rene De Groot was lead engineer, a battered, white-haired veteran of a couple of thousand cement jobs. He had brought Bjorn the Norwegian trainee, and two more Filipinos, Edgar and Manny. All good guys. It was a relief that they had got a steady man like Rene. Any cement job could get a little tense. The man on the pump truck was the star of his own show with everybody watching his performance. Once water had been mixed with cement, it would start to set. A fact of life, and it was up to the cementing engineer to make sure it was in the right place when it did so. Losing your temper, shouting, throwing your hard hat at people would not help when things were going wrong. Rene inspired confidence and made everything seem easier. Right now he was ragging the Filipinos about how they managed their three month hitches in the desert without access to women. They were in a weak position because not so long ago two of the Filipino catering hands had been caught by a Tabrizi watchman while deeply engaged. Now everyone chose to pretend that they had only been reported because the watchman was jealous, and that there had been no more reports because some-one else was keeping the watchman happy.

After lunch The Virgin walked around the MacAllans gear with Rene. Things were looking good. The silos were all set up and tested. There was a cement bulker due anytime, and the last two loads were due in late that night. The main compressor had been fired up and was good, and they would have the trailer compressors as back-up. That would get the cement to the pump units, no matter what. Both units would be rigged to mix and pump down hole, but Rene was planning to use one for mixing and one for pumping. He should have no trouble going down hole at ten barrels a minute, provided the rig kept the mix-water coming. They walked over to the rig together. It was a good piece of gear - a National 130 from the States - but bore marks of RomDril neglect. For a start it was filthy, covered in grease and old mud. And it was battered. During every rig move you could expect some damage to be done rigging down and then up again. A western company would do its best to straighten out damage immediately but RomDril tended to just leave things. An experienced glance could pick out bent railings, damaged stairways, pipe-work loose of its mountings.

Even the location was filthy. No surface ditches had been dug and to reach the shakers they had to skip across pallets dropped into a pool of overflow mud. They stood for a while watching the steaming mud pour over the shakers. The drill-pipe was on bottom and they were circulating to condition mud. There were few cuttings being shaken out of the mud now but The Virgin and Rene were looking at the viscosity. It was pouring in smooth heavy curtains onto the shakers. They trekked back over the pallets to the mud-man's shack. It was empty. Leaving Rene to supervise rigging up the two-inch cementing line, The Virgin went over to speak to Terry about the mud.

"How's your mud, Terry?"

"Pretty good; why?"

"We've just been looking at it. It looks kind of heavy."

Terry reached for the clip-board with the daily report. "No, it's OK. 8.6 pounds a gallon and low viscosity."

"Want to put a beer on it?"

Terry looked at him long enough to read that he was serious. "Aw, shit! Come on, let's go look."

Together they stood in the steamy warmth of the shakers. "OK. You win. That sure ain't what was on the mud sheet this morning." He was letting it run through his fingers. "The weight I'd believe but... Jesus, you can't believe anything round here. Mud-man's not there, I suppose. God dammit! I tell you, it's a real bind being this close to town. Any chance they get and they've disappeared. OK. I'll get after him when I can find him. Hey, you guys know you're displacing?"

"What? You're joking! I thought we'd sorted that one out."

"Nope. RomDril must have been talking to some-one in town and the programme stays the way it is. You to displace."

"Jesus. I hope they can get us the mud fast enough. But you're still not going to get much more than ten or twelve barrels a minute down our line. It's only two inch, don't forget."

"Yeah. I know. But that's what the mudirs want, so that's what they'll get."

"You'll have RomDril hooked in, just in case?"

"Yeah. Sure. And I'll make sure they dip their tanks and are all ready to go. Just in case."

They climbed up from the shakers onto the rig floor. It was empty. The kelly was half-way down and the block and swivel swung above their heads. The kelly hose was pulsing with the beat of the mud-pumps and the whole structure beneath their feet vibrated in sympathy. The brake was chained down but there was no sign of the driller. Terry looked into the dog-house. Also empty. The Virgin could see he was pissed off from the set of his jaw. They met the driller as they stepped off the stairway onto the ground. He was a small man in soft rubber boots and a navy-blue coverall. There was no hard hat covering his thinning hair.

Terry attacked him. "Where the hell have you been? How many God-dammed times have I got to tell you to keep some-one on the floor all the God-dammed time?"

The Romanian did not bother to say anything. He just shrugged sheepishly and showed Terry the packet of cigarettes he had been fetching from his cabin. When there was no response, he offered them round. Terry turned abruptly away and stumped off across the dirt towards his cabin. "I don't know why I bother. Always the same.

I can't believe it. Not on the floor because he'd run out of cigarettes. Jesus! If he'd been caught smoking in Canada, his ass would have been out of the location gates in thirty seconds. Here running out of cigarettes is a reasonable excuse for leaving the floor. Jesus! It's like trying to teach a cat to do tricks. They're just smart enough to know that they don't want the hassle."

The next thing on the schedule, once the Revard's truck had turned up, would be to pull out and log the hole. That should not take too long; just one pass at this depth, say eight hours including rigging up and down. Then another wiper trip and run casing. That would definitely put the cement job on Friday. The Virgin's day off. Oh, well. He drove back to town carefully, looking along the road for the big blue Revard's truck.

Back at the office he decided to give Elena a call. It was a thrill to hear her distant voice. "Executive Travel, good afternoon. How can I help you?"

"I'd like to buy a ticket from Sabah in Tabriz to Crete. Do you have any special fares?"

"Greg! Where have you been? I've been waiting for you for ages!"

"Yes - well. I didn't know if you'd want me to call you at work."

"Of course I do. Or at home, it doesn't matter. How are you anyway? Did you get home safely?"

"Oh, I'm alright. I got stopped at the airport though. I'd left a stupid magazine in my brief-case and they wanted to put me in calaboosh for importing pornography."

"Jesus! What happened?"

"I had to ask them to telephone a friend who works in Security, and he helped sort things out. They were quite kind really, considering the magazine was a bit naughty."

"What are you doing with naughty magazines anyway?"

"Well I've got to have some kind of substitute for the real thing. Otherwise I'll forget what real ladies look like." He imagined a snort of disapproval from the other end.

"I'm sure I don't look like that."

"Like what?"

"Like your magazine. No-one looks like that."

"Well I remember when we were in London..." but she cut him off with a scandalised shriek. She was playing her part.

"Greg! You told me that the police listened to telephone calls!"

"Yes, but they can't listen to them all. Anyway they haven't seen what I've seen."

"If you don't stop it, I'll call the police at my end and tell them I've got a pervert on the line. Talk about something else. How's the weather there?"

"The weather? Now you're being dreadfully English. We haven't spoken for ages and you want to talk about the weather. Well, it's the Mediterranean, you know. Just about cold enough to wear a sweater during the day. The sun's out and all's well with the world. How is it there?"

"Oh, you know. Awful. Raining, windy. The tube's packed with people trying to get home with all their Christmas shopping. No-one's got enough money..."

"Oh yes, and it's hard to get from one pub to the next before closing time. It must be tough. I bet you have parties every night and a two-week break over Christmas and New Year, right?"

"Well, there are a few parties, but you know Christmas is on Saturday this year so we have to be in work on the Tuesday. What do you do? Do you have Christmas over there?"

"Sort of. Harris lets us go home as soon as we finished the work we have to do, so I expect I'll get myself an invitation for lunch somewhere. And that's about it. There's not too many people around. All the ones that can have gone home for Christmas."

"Poor you. What shall I send you for Christmas? Another naughty magazine?"

"For God's sake don't do that. They wouldn't believe me a second time. What about an exciting photo of you instead?"

"If you think I'm getting photographed in the nude so that you and your sex-crazed friends can drool over me..."

"We wouldn't drool, honestly. It's bad manners. We'd just sigh respectfully and wish you were here. Just for the quality of your intellect."

"Intellect my backside!" Elena snapped.

"That too, that too," said The Virgin happily. "I can just picture it in my mind's eye."

"You really are a pervert, aren't you?"

"Of course. Didn't you realise? But I'm a very nice pervert."

"Oh Greg, Greg. What am I going to do with you? No, I shan't ask you that because I can guess what you'll say, and anyone listening in will think I'm as bad as you. Oh, my boss is coming. You'll call me again before Christmas?"

The Virgin put the telephone down with a happy glow in his stomach. It was nice to have a dream-girl on the end of the telephone. Which gave him a sudden desire for female company. Evelina possibly, but she was too much like hard work. Perhaps he would just close up the office and go to Barani to visit Danka. Or maybe Wanda. There was not much to do in Sabah of an evening, so he may as well do it in company.

Barani was living up to the worst of its reputation. He steered car around the rubbish-strewn lagoons of foul water, trying to keep to the higher ground. Winter was here and every hollow was full. Still, at least it was too cold for the mosquitoes, he reflected as he stood at the windy foot of the Polish nurse's tower, waiting for an inmate with a key to come out or go in. At this time of the evening it did not take long. A woman popped out to shop in the local store, and The Virgin popped in.

The hall-way was dark and he felt his way cautiously up the three marble steps towards the lift. He peered towards the lift doors; if the lift was working the red floor indicator would be alight. Nothing broke the darkness. Oh, well. Eighth floor here we come, The Virgin thought as he fumbled for the stairway.

There were lights on most of the floors above. The bulbs were less likely to get stolen than the ones in the entrance and most of the girls had rigged up some sort of light outside their apartments. They wanted to check visitors through the peep-hole before they opened the door. He was breathing deeply by the time he was on Danka's doormat. A magazine picture of three puppies had been cut out and pasted to the door. Written above them were the names of the inmates with drawings of bells; Danka had two bells. He rang twice.

"Czesz, kochanie!" Danka's plump figure was wrapped in a thread-bare dressing gown, and her face was still pink from the shower. "It is so long before that you come here. Come in, sit down." The Virgin ignored her efforts to steer him to the bleak central room where the windows rattled in the wind, and headed instead for the kitchen. Wanda was inside cooking. Their ash-tray, a cleaned sardine tin, lay with coffee glasses on the table. The Virgin squeezed himself into the folding chair between the table and the refrigerator. The atmosphere was cosy, redolent of the soup Wanda was stirring. Danka put the kettle on and sat opposite him.

"So. You have news from my friend Dov?"

The Virgin's heart skipped. "Er, who?" He tried to glare at her but Wanda was looking straight at him. "Oh, him. No, nothing. But why would he write to me? I only met him once and I'm not sure if he even knows my name. What about you?"

Danka laughed and passed two cigarettes to Wanda. "The letters never come. I gave to him the number to hospital but really it is not possible."

At last Wanda was busy, bending down to the gas to light the cigarettes one after the other. The Virgin got his opportunity to glare and kick her gently under the table, but Danka was unrepentant. "Never mind. It is nothing. You did not come to Hash last time."

"No. I was in London."

"Boże! London. It is so easy for you. For us we must have visa from Captain Zella before they will give us ticket. And must have ticket before they will give travellers cheques. Next time that you go, I will come in your suitcase, OK?"

"Where is the Hash this week?"

"Holey Rock. Good. I am happy that you are here. Now you can take us to Hash, OK?"

"I guess so. I've got to come this way anyway. What time are they starting now?"

Danka consulted with Wanda in Polish. "It will be on five o'clock. Now you have soup with us. Flaki soup; you like?"

Wanda was offering him a brimming spoon to try. "Uważaj - bardzo gorąco!"

"She says is very hot," Danka translated. "You like?"

The soup was clear and peppery, good for cold windy days. Danka set her cigarette in the sardine tin and started putting bowls and spoons out. It was always the same when he visited Polish friends. You had not been with them for more than ten minutes before they were trying to feed you. And after the food the vodka would come out. Why not, he thought to himself. It beats sitting at home alone.

Major Jamal called him early next morning. He brought the letter of credit around immediately and stayed for a coffee. His queries about timing were cursory; the order did not seem to interest him at all. What did intrigue him was The Virgin's exotic girlfriend in London, and he quickly steered the conversation around to her.

"Are you going back to England for Christmas? No? Your girlfriend will miss you. Really, you must invite her to come to Tabriz. I am sure it will be interesting for her here."

"Well, maybe. Better in spring though. There's not much to do in winter, really. The days are too short and it's cold."

"True," he nodded. "I find it cold and I think you do also, but she is from England so even winter here will seem warm to her. Tell me again, what is her name?"

"Her name? Elena. Elena Anthony."

"Elena. Such a pretty name. And where does she work?"

"She's a travel agent, didn't I tell you? She can get cheap tickets to go anywhere."

"So. She must get a cheap ticket and come here. But I am sure you have other girl-friends, Filipino ones and Polish ones. There are many European ladies here. I thought you had a Polish friend."

That would be Danka. "Well, I have some friends, but no-one special. Not a real girl-friend."

Major Jamal smiled happily. "Ah, you are a young man. You play with all the girls and don't settle down. Very good. We are the same except that we marry our girl-friends. If our old wives are not happy, they can always leave.

"But tell me. How did you find our chemical?"

"I just sent faxes to the company you told me about. You remember, Karelia. Why do you ask?"

"Oh, it is nothing. I just wanted to know if you had found it with Karelia or tried other companies. And so you will order from them? Definitely?"

"You can make it a condition of the order if you like. But don't worry. We don't have time to run around getting competitive quotations. It has to be ready to ship at the beginning of the New Year."

"Good. It is better that you don't ask further because we do not want too many people knowing our business. Did you see Karelia in London?"

"No. I was too busy to worry about it."

"And your office in London? Did they help you?"

"About this? No. Not a chance. They're so involved in doing their own thing that you can't expect any help from them at all. I expect the order will be placed from Rotterdam and payment made from there."

Major Jamal seemed pleased by his off-handed responses, and The Virgin felt bold enough to ask a question that foreigners always steered clear of in their dealings with Tabrizis. "May I ask you something? I was wondering about the political situation here, the economic situation. Do you think it is going to stay the same?"

"As it is now?" Major Jamal gave it a moment's thought. "You must understand that this country is not like Europe. It is a different sort of democracy. We have our congresses, and every man can stand and say what he wishes. This is true democracy, as the Great Man wrote in his book. I think that America and the West don't understand this. They keep saying that the Great Man is another Stalin, but believe me, it's not true. Any man can get up in the congresses and speak about most things. Not all, of course.

"You know the Great Man always says he is not the leader. He says it on the television and the simple people believe what he says; he is only the servant of the people. What the congresses want, he says, they can do. Of course, the truth is that although they can say many things freely, no one will dare to say anything directly against him. Not a word, because he has the army behind him. And the police. And all the different security forces. They are all his people.

"You see, most of the officers are not like me, old men from before the Revolution. Most of them owe everything to him. He meets us; he sits and eats with us. These things are very important in Tabriz. He takes care of us, and we all know that everything we have, every dollar we receive, (Did you know that? He pays us dollars so we can travel outside) everything comes from his hand. So we are his people, and we work for him because we are working for ourselves.

"The ordinary people, they are different. They receive what they can take and they must be happy, because anything else is not permitted. Believe me; sometimes a man will make a lot of noise in front of his friends in the congresses. He forgets where he is and starts to speak as if this was America or England, and then one day, two days later, he disappears. Disappears completely. His family know what has happened, of course. But what can they do?

"So you ask me, will the situation change? As long as the Great Man is there, and as long as we can protect him from his enemies, nothing will change. But he does have enemies. Many enemies from different families. Especially from his own village and the country around there. One day he will be caught, I think, because no security net can be perfect. He will play with some-one's sister, or be rude to the wrong old man and one of the young men close to him will kill him. That is our way here. Young men will die for their families, and if they do not fear to die themselves, the life of a leader can finish in an instant."

"And then what?"

"Ah. Now you have asked a very difficult question. What will come in his place? I don't know. I can hope only that whoever comes next is a strong man, or everything will be lost. We must have a strong man who will control the army and the security forces, and then we will have peace. And it would be better if it was some-one close to the Great Man."

"Close to him? I would have thought people would want a change."

"Maybe. Maybe the people would want that. But let me tell you a story, young Gregory (May I call you Gregory?). There was once a wounded soldier lying on the battle-field. He was badly hurt and his wounds were open and bleeding. A friend came to him and saw that his wounds were covered with flies, so he wanted to chase them away. But the soldier would not let him. He said that the flies had already eaten as much as they wanted, and they were not troubling him much. If they were chased away, their places would be taken by fresh and hungry flies who would attack him fiercely. This is a good story for Tabriz, don't you think so?"

"Yes. I can see that. And it would certainly be better for us, for the foreign businesses. We all wish the Great Man a long and happy life. I'd hate to be around if there was another revolution."

"Oh, I don't think it would touch you. You could just hide in your house for a couple of days. But there is a lot of old blood to be paid for. There will be many old debts paid. You know, when the revolution came, people were shot. Some were shot in their houses, in front of their women and children. Some were even hung in the football stadium. Good people, from good families, strung up like criminals. For every one of them, there will be ten of the people who did these things hanging in the wind. Believe me; people do not forget wrong things like that, not in Tabriz. And everyone knows who will be hanging there." Major Jamal sat musing. He seemed to be looking forward to the day.

"How is Captain Zella? I haven't seen him for a little while."

"Captain Zella? He will be one of the first! No, Captain Zella is improving his Islamic and revolutionary education by visiting Amsterdam. He has even arranged that a foolish Greek company pays all his expenses there. And when he has finished playing with the white prostitutes, he will buy a Mercedes and return. I wish he would play with the girls in some African countries and then he would definitely catch a vile disease and bring it back to his family." Major Jamal was vehement in his hatred. "Have you heard of what he does in the hospital? He is in charge of the visas for the nurses, so if they want a visa and he is feeling sufficiently like a man, they must sleep with him first. He tells his brother officers about the things he does and who has been forced by him. And then some of the younger ones from bad families go and make trouble for the nurses at their homes. I have had to prevent all security officers from entering their buildings in Barani, or we would have visits from their consul every day. Has anyone you know had trouble with him?"

The Virgin was on the edge of telling him about Evelina's problem but an urge to appear uninformed held him back. "Well, I know the nurses all hate him. He seems to enjoy making them suffer. He's no gentleman..."

"Exactly. He's not a gentleman and never will be. One day he will do something too ugly and foolish, and his masters will have to transfer him. I hope for the sake of those ladies that it will be soon.

"Enough about Captain Zella. I must enjoy my freedom from him while I can. Now, you will call me as soon as you have any more news about our shipment? This order is very important to me."

"And me too. My manager is keen that everything should go well, and then maybe you will order more material through us."

"You never know." Major Jamal was rising. "How is the telephone? Working well?"

"It's fantastic! I can call my parents, and Elena. And business is so easy. It's just like being in America."

Major Jamal laughed. "Why not? Everything is possible in Tabriz, if you know the right people."

Friday dawned grey with the wind rattling the ghibli blinds. The Virgin crawled out of bed and looked at the sky. The wind was coming from the sea, bringing rain and English misery with it. And today was the cement job. What was it about cementing that always seemed to attract foul weather? First he had to decide what he would wear. MacAllans insisted on fire-proof Nomex coveralls. The artificial fabric might be safe to wear, but it felt unbearably hot and sticky in summer. Conversely, on a winter's day like this, wearing Nomex alone would feel like standing around in the nude. He had some thermal liners left over from an assignment in Germany but he was too embarrassed to wear them here. He settled on jeans and a thick sweater under his coveralls. And no matter what MacAllans said about proper uniforms on location, he would wrap himself in an old ski jacket. He might get wet but at least he would be warm.

The wind-blown streets were empty as he drove to the office to make his morning call. Florian was bitching about the amount of equipment tied up in Sabah. He wanted everything and everybody back tomorrow morning if not sooner. Apart from that, nothing was happening. About normal for a week-end when all the work-over rigs some-how managed to get themselves onto dull repetitive work with no decisions required. He would have to go to the rig to sit out the hours before the job.

As he left the empty car park he thought about going to church, to listen to Evelina and the other girls singing hymns in their Filipino country and western style. Sunday fell on Fridays in Sabah and he would be just in time for mass. Perhaps he could pray for a good cement job. It was not just his clothes that stopped him; it was hard to be enthusiastic about anything on a day like this.

As he jolted up the location road towards the rig he could see the travelling block moving up in the derrick. That meant they were still running casing, and when he pulled up outside Terry's shack he could see they had another thirty or forty joints on the racks. Terry was reading a novel.

"Hey, guy! You're here early. You piss the bed or something? Or your little Filipino nurse have early duty? Like a coffee?" Without waiting for a reply he reached for his miniature percolator and a paper cup.

"Just thought I'd stop by and make sure you're not giving our guys a hard time. How's it going?"

"Hey, it's good. The casing crew's good. Haven't cross-threaded a joint yet. They're keeping up a steady twelve joints an hour. We'll be done by lunchtime. Haven't seen your guys. They're out there on the mud-tanks somewhere, mixing up your God-damn expensive chemicals that we don't really need. Sugar, isn't it?"

"Yes. And milk if you have it."

"It's in the fridge. If you like canned milk. No, they seem to have everything about straight. That Rene, he's a good hand."

"Oh yes. He's been around a while. We still displacing?"

"That's what it says in the programme. And here's one foreigner who ain't going to change any programme. That's playing with fire, that is."

"Well, I hope they can get us the mud fast enough."

"Don't worry. Even RomDril can pump mud at ten barrels a minute. And we'll have the mud pumps hooked up just in case. You hear the news last night?"

"No. What's up? Price of oil tripled?"

"No such luck. No, it's those Yanks again. Sounding off about Tabriz. Old Clinton was carrying on in his state of the Union speech last night, making out how they've been supporting terrorism and all that. Probably buying toys for the Palestinians."

"So - what's new? Name me an Arab country that doesn't give money to the Palestinians. It's just conscience money to save them doing anything positive to help. Clinton's got an election coming next year and he's looking for some-one to push around. The Great Man's such an obvious target."

"Yeah." Terry seemed to be wondering whether he disliked the Tabrizis or the Americans the most. "And the Great Man doesn't help himself, either. The mud man told me he was on television last week saying how the Arabs should be getting together to push Israel into the sea."

"Why does he mess with that stuff? If Tabriz wants a quiet life all it has to do is to keep selling the oil and making babies. Start being rude to Israel and you'll have the States down on you in a big way. Look what they did to Libya."

"You're right there. I wonder if the Arabs could ever get it together."

"Not a chance," said The Virgin happily. "Old Lawrence of Arabia tried that at the end of the first war. They just had to hang together for a couple of months and they could have strangled Israel at birth. They couldn't do it; they hate each other too much. They had to run off and do their own Arabic things, and look at them now. What would they be if they didn't have oil?"

"Yeah. I'd sure like to see them trying to push Israel into the sea. They wouldn't even make it across their borders. Those Israelis don't take no shit from no-one."

The Virgin thought of the one Israeli soldier he had met. "Yes. They're a pretty tough bunch. The Egyptians didn't get very far with them even after they'd caught them with their pants down and got across the Canal. But I do wish the Great Man would leave it all alone. Doesn't he have problems enough without that?"

"Problems? The only problem he's got is how to spend the 750,000 barrels of oil he makes every day. Just think of it! That's around a half barrel a day for every Tabrizi. If they make fifteen dollars a barrel, that's seven and a half dollars a day each, just for waking up. And seven and a half dollars goes a long way here on the black market."

"Don't believe they get to see it! The Great Man has to get his cut first. And then there's the army and all his other toys. I wonder how much they actually make."

"That's easy enough," said Terry, reaching for his calculator. "750,000 barrels a day at $15 per barrel that's - let's see now - $11,250,000 a day. Wow; every day. Over a year that's 365 times - $4,106,250,000. Four billion dollars a year. You could run a pretty good country with that."

"It's not all profit, though. I wonder how much getting the oil to surface and onto the ships really costs them. I bet it's pushing $10 per barrel."

"Could be right. You've seen the way they piss money away down in the desert. It should be hitting the boats at a couple of dollars only, but I guess you're right. Not all of it goes to greedy bastards like MacAllans though. A lot of it stays in Tabriz as salaries."

"Yes, but how long does it stay in the country? They don't produce anything except tomatoes and dates, and even then the farm workers are Egyptian. All the workers in town, building houses and the like, they come from Egypt. Ninety-five percent of their money gets sent home. All their canned food, clothes, everything, it's all imported. They must be the world's most efficient consumers."

"Guess we shouldn't complain too much. If they ever decided to work for a living, they might take our jobs." Terry chuckled at the thought. "It might take them a year or two to learn how it goes, but that wouldn't stop them."

"You're right, though," said The Virgin. "Isn't it terrible? Whenever two foreigners start talking about Tabriz, they always end up complaining. And it's not so bad really. You can find a way to live here and be comfortable enough. Sure it's a bit strange, but I'll tell you what; there's no-where I could be saving the amount of money I do here. They pay us extra to be here because it's such a pain, and there's nothing to spend it on."

Outside the wind was getting stronger and even the half-hearted attempts to rain had left the hard red clay of the location slick and treacherous. The equipment was looking good, its grey and black livery shining in the rain. The cement would soon take the shine away. On the mud tanks Rene and his crew were manhandling drums of chemicals, pouring them into the dirty water and carefully turning it into the exact solution they would need to prepare the cement slurry. Casing was being rolled from the racks onto the catwalk, and hoisted up to the rig floor a joint at a time. Suspended up over the hole, one of the casing crew on the stabbing board half way up the derrick held it straight while his companion down below threaded it and made it up tight using the hydraulic power tongs. They should be finished in a couple of hours. Then all that remained would be to circulate the mud for an hour or two to clean up the hole, and the cement job could start.

It was late afternoon when the cement head was sent up to the floor. Terry had made good his promise of spacing out correctly, and the top of the casing protruded only a couple of feet above the slips. The massive grey cement head held the two large rubber tampons that would be pumped ahead and behind the cement, physically separating it from the mud in the casing. The rig crew had made themselves scarce and Terry was forced to operate the air-winch to bring it up to the floor. He inched the head over the casing and the MacAllans crew carefully made up the threads and hammered it tight.

Then the high pressure line from the pump trucks had to be brought up. The heavy-walled joints of pipe with their Chiksan swivels and hammer unions were laid across the floor to the cement head like a disjointed snake. As soon as pumping started it would be vibrating fiercely, and the Chiksans gave the flexibility that would stop it shaking itself to pieces. They put a tee in the line to allow the rig pumps to be connected into the system. If anything went wrong with the pump trucks, the rig could take over and displace whatever cement was in the casing before it was too late. The last thing to do was to thread a steel safety cable through eyes on the pipe. A failure under pressure could see the heavy joints of pipe whipping around like grass in the wind and the cable would at least restrict it.

MacAllans were very tough on safety, and every job had to start with a meeting. Rene called the crew over to the shelter of the cement silos and waited for Terry and the rig crew to join them. Darkness was gathering as Terry plodded towards them on the wet catwalk. Alone.

"I couldn't find the cook. He must be in his pit or something and no-one wants to go get him. So it wasn't worth bringing the driller because he wouldn't understand anything without the translator. Right. What's the plan?"

Rene was the man on this job, so he took the meeting. "First off, I've got to test the lines. 2500, 3000 psi for five minutes. That should be enough for a job like this. Then there's a hundred barrels of water and a hundred barrels of wash, and we can drop the plug. The bottom plug."

"You sure that's the bottom plug, Rene?" asked Terry, only half joking.

"You bet. Put them in myself. OK. Then we start mixing the lead cement. I've got it in this silo, in that one there, and over here. We'll be blowing it across during the job. Save us having to run the hopper around. Until we get to the tail anyway. That's in this tank and we'll move the hopper across for it."

"What are the quantities?" asked Terry, opening his tally book.

"I've got 883 barrels of lead at 10 pounds per gallon. Then 55 barrels of tail at 15.8 pounds per gallon. And 886 barrels of displacement."

"886 of displacement. Right. You using both trucks to displace?"

"Well, I'll try to go at 12 barrels a minute, so I'll probably need both to get it down the two inch line. Oh, about the weight. This 10 pound lead is real critical. I only have to be a point or two pounds per gallon up or down, and we'll run out of cement or water before we've mixed enough. So I'm not listening to any yo-yo with a regular mud balance telling me I'm wrong. I'm taking the weight off the densitometer panel. Greg'll check it with the pressurised mud balance so you'll have some kind of second opinion."

Terry smiled, knowing that control of slurry weight was what made for a good cement job. "Sounds fine. I don't expect the mud-man will be available to give you a hard time anyway. Just make sure you keep me some surface samples, that's all. What else?"

The Virgin took the floor. "About the timing. We've got 938 barrels to mix. Say we go at 8 barrels a minute, that's 120 minutes plus a bit for stopping and starting when we go onto the tail. And then dropping the top plug - say two and a half hours. The thickening time on the lead cement is only five hours twenty minutes so we've got two hours and fifty minutes to displace. Maximum, no allowances. We better plan on getting it away in two hours, so that's just about seven and a half barrels a minute. If we're not displacing at that rate, we'd better expect to have it setting up on us before we've finished displacing."

"OK, OK. I hear you. If the mud's not coming across at that rate or better, or if one of the trucks goes down or something, we'll switch over to the mud pumps. I'll have them all standing by. Promise. What else?"

Rene took over again. "Er - the usual. Fire extinguishers are all around - you can see them. The eye-wash station is the back of my pick-up over there. We'd better make sure we're all wearing our safety gear because Greg's here and he'll be writing an audit report, I'm sure. And that's about it. Greg, you going to get on the floor for the pressure test and dropping the plug? Can we trust you to do that?"

"If you've loaded it right, I'll drop it right."

"Good. So let's move." After a last look around, he climbed up onto the nearest truck. He flicked on the working lights and stood above them like an orchestral conductor. Leaning on the air starts he fired up both engines and the job officially began.

The Virgin took a valve bar and made his way along the catwalk and up to the rig floor. It was deserted. The big grey cement head stood glistening in the rain. He checked that the lower circulating valve was open and walked to the railing. Rene and Edgar stood on the truck, looking up at him. He joined his hands together and held his arms over his head making a big open circle, the signal that the valve was open and pumping could start. He saw Rene concentrate on his panel controls and the deck engine of the pump truck raised its exhaust flapper and belched smoke. The pipe beside him started to pulse as Rene pumped water into the hole.

After a few barrels, he stopped and held his arms crossed over his head. The Virgin went over to the cement head and slipping his valve bar into the control wheel, swung on the circulating valve to pull it closed. From the railing he sent a confirmatory crossed arms signal. Again the deck engine lifted its exhaust flap as Rene slowly pressured up against the closed valve. The Virgin retreated behind the drill-pipe standing in the derrick. If a union or a swivel was going to blow, this would be when it happened. The pumping stopped and Rene and Edgar were standing close together staring at the DAC display, looking for signs of a leak. Sheltered from the wind by the drill-pipe, The Virgin watched drizzle slanting through the derrick lights. There was a light clunk as Rene bled off pressure and the Chiksans relaxed. He was signalling for the valve to be opened again.

Pumping the fresh water and the wash took twenty minutes, so The Virgin took himself off to the dog house. Inside the driller sat smoking in front of an electric fire that glowed cherry-red. He waved The Virgin to a seat beside him and offered him a smoke. They sat together in silence until the vibration of the line stopped and told them that the wash had been pumped. The Virgin hurried to the railing. Rene was holding his nose and pulling an imaginary lavatory chain. It was time to drop the bottom plug. The Virgin stood on the casing slips and turned the wheel. As the 25 millimetre thick rod pulled back, he heard the retaining spade drop inside the head. The plug was now free to be pumped down into the well. He closed the circulating valve and routed the flow through the centre port above the plug.

Everything was nearly ready at the trucks. Rene had transferred onto the mixing truck; he would control the critical part of the job himself. Edgar would pump down-hole with the other unit. Felix was giving the equipment a last-minute spray with diesel. Cement dust would stick to it but it would not set hard the way it would with water. It made washing up so much easier. Bjorn the trainee had been given the easiest and dirtiest job, controlling the flow of dry cement into the mixing hopper. He was in full safety gear. Hard hat, goggles, dust-mask and ear defenders. It made him look like a refugee from Paschendaele. They all stood looking at Rene, under starter's orders and waiting for the off.

Rene, the respected actor alone on his raised stage, was making last minute adjustments to the DAC. Then almost casually he walked back to the mixing manifold and hauled open the master valve. At the control panel he fired up both engines and the hopper began to throb as the hidden jets roared with mix-water. He brought his arm down and Bjorn swung on the twelve-inch valve at the bottom of the silo. For an instant nothing happened then the dry cement crashed down, filling the hopper and avalanching over the sides. Dust was everywhere and Bjorn was struggling to get the valve closed again, to achieve some kind of balance between supply and demand. The mix-water gushing into the tub changed into liquid cement. Rene watched carefully, making sure of an even flow while he stabilised his weight. It took seconds. He was holding his thumb up to them while fine-tuning the weight with his other hand on the by-pass valve.

From behind the dust cloud Edgar fired up his unit to suck from the tub and pump down-hole. For an instant The Virgin's heart leapt; Edgar would not be able to see the tub through the dust. The thought had hardly come to him when the wind cleared the dust away. Rene had rigged it up that way, the wind blowing from the trucks across the hopper, keeping everything clear.

On the mixing truck Rene had no need of goggles or dust mask; he was above it all. He smiled at The Virgin and kissed his fingertips. Everything was going to be alright.

There was little for The Virgin to do during the job. Terry tried to take him off for a coffee, but his conscience would not let him go while the job was on. He felt like an old-fashioned officer. If the men were getting wet then, dammit, so would he. He ran a couple of weight checks with the pressurised mud balance. Spot on. He filled two tin cans from the kitchen with cement for Terry's surface samples and left them out of the rain under the catwalk. Apart from that, there was the service quality audit to be done. He wondered around the equipment making notes, counting fire-extinguishers and examining their service tags. They were all up to date. An old hand like Rene would not be caught out by details.

The warmth and comfort of his car beckoned but he fought against it and climbed up to join Rene. After the day's rain everywhere was muddy, and the way up to the operator's deck of the pump truck had to be negotiated with care. His route took him past the deck engine, screaming away at its optimum 2000 rpm. It was covered with tempting handholds but you did not have to be long around pump units to learn that they were all burning hot.

On deck, Rene was standing at the panel, his belly protruding over it, hands ready to throttle back at an instant. When he felt the deck grating move under The Virgin's weight he looked up and smiled. Conversation was impossible with both engines running so he returned to his panel. As time went on, pump unit control panels were becoming more and more complicated. This one looked like something from a small plane. There were monitoring dials and lights for the vital functions of both engines and their transmissions, temperatures, oil pressures, revs. And the auxiliary equipment, the hydraulic and air systems that kept things running together. The great pumps needed oil pressure readings; the make-up and pressurising centrifugals needed hydraulic pressures. The two sides of the panel were dominated by the throttle and shift control for each engine, and the two vital dials for each pump, rate and pressure.

On his left, mounted separately over the mixing manifold, hung the densitometer panel, displaying a radioactive density reading. It was steady on ten pounds a gallon, occasionally flicking up or down a point just to show it was alive. To the right of the panel on a heavy bracket was the DAC, the data acquisition computer. It was recording rates, pressures and fluid densities from both trucks. The total pumped showed 425 barrels and climbing. They were not yet half way through the mixing.

Behind Rene, Manny was working the twin displacement tanks. He was filling one ten-barrel tank while Rene was pumping from the other. Every couple of minutes, as a tank was drawn down to the zero marker, he would switch valves and start the new tank. At each change, he slid a washer from one side of a miniature croquet hoop to the other. It was a primitive but effective totaliser. He knew exactly how much mixwater had been pumped and if the DAC had gone down, they could still finish the job accurately.

The Virgin settled himself down on the DAC transport box, wedged into a corner between the deck engine and the displacement tanks. It was windy up here, but at least the engine gave some warmth. He settled his ear defenders more comfortably and lost himself in his thoughts.

He was brought to by the engines throttling down abruptly. It was time to switch to the tail cement. Felix, Bjorn and Joe Milut were wrestling to get the hopper off. They threw it to one side and man-handled the mixing bowl with the goose-neck and heavy hoses still attached around the silo legs until it was under the right silo. Bjorn wanted to put the hopper back on, but Rene was shouting and waving him away. Felix knew what he wanted and unwound the diesel spray hose from its cleats at the rear of the truck. Rene wanted the cement to drop through the hopper without sticking to the sides, so Felix sprayed the insides with diesel. Attention to detail.

They were standing again waiting for Rene. Pausing to send a quick signal to the DAC, he opened the mixing manifold and fired up the engines. Again he brought his arm down down and Bjorn swung on his valve handle. The Virgin watched as the densitometer readings climbed from water at 8.32 pounds per gallon up to 15 pounds. Then slowly up to 15.8 pounds per gallon, the norm for Class G cement. They were in business again. He tapped Rene on the shoulder and set off for the rig floor. It would soon be time to drop the top plug.

Joe Milut hurried up the cat-walk ahead of him. He would warn the rig to start delivering mud for displacement. Joe could talk to anyone, even Romanians. The floor was still deserted. Looking back beyond the end of the cat-walk, the MacAllans' equipment was a small island of activity. Blowing cement dust blurred the outlines and trapped the light around the trucks. The pipe across the floor pulsed with the beat of the pumps and everything on the rig rattled in sympathy. Even the stands of drill-pipe towering above him were swaying to the music. He waited at the railing for Rene's signal to drop the top plug. It came soon enough and he backed out the pin and switched valves again.

Edgar was not watching for his signal. He was hanging over his displacement tanks waiting for the mud to arrive. It surged into the tank, a silver fan in the lights. A few moments and they would be ready to go. The pipe started to vibrate as Edgar brought his pumps on line. Displacement had started. All they had to do was pump the top plug all the way down the casing before the cement started to set.

When The Virgin reached the units he could see there was a problem. Rene had switched trucks and was standing with Edgar. They were staring at the displacement tanks and timing the inflow. The Virgin clambered up to join him. The DAC showed they were pumping at 4.5 barrels a minute. He lifted one side of his ear defenders to let Rene shout in carefully articulated words, "Get more mud quickly, OK? Or the rig will have to displace."

"Keep pumping!" was all he could reply before running off to find Terry.

Terry had been watching from his window and met him half-way. "What's up?"

"You've guessed. They're only giving us four and a half barrels a minute."

"Oh fuck! What do you want?"

"Either get them moving or we'll have to go to Plan B."

"Shit - I hope it don't come to that. They don't have stroke counters or nothing. Hang around, I'll get the cook and the tool pusher."

The Virgin took a moment to steal a quick coffee from Terry's percolator. It tasted good. He was still sipping when Terry came back from the camp with the stocky figure of the tool-pusher and the cook still in his apron. The four of them hurried to the back of the rig, round the motors to the mud pressurising system. The tool pusher had a quick conference with two relaxed hands smoking at the door of the motor man's shack, and relayed the results to the cook.

The cook passed them on to Terry. "He say they not pump any more."

"Why the hell not? They're only doing four and a half barrels a minute."

The tool pusher was explaining something to the cook with gestures that meant nothing to Terry and apparently very little to the cook. "He say they must pump backwards to do this and so they not pump any more."

"Pump backwards? What the fuck's he talking about? Backwards? Have him show me!"

They clambered over pallets and old sacks towards the mud system pressurising pumps. The tool pusher pointed out the line leading forwards to the pump unit and showed where it was flanged into the yellow manifold. It came from a tee on an eight inch line.

The Virgin and Terry stared at it for a moment. Something looked wrong and it was Terry that picked it up first.

"Holy shit! That's on the suction side!"

The tool pusher was showing the valve between the eight inch line and the neighbouring tank. It was closed. Then with his hand he showed the route the mud was taking. It was being sucked out of the next tank by one big centrifugal and delivered to a shared manifold. The off-take from the manifold was closed so the mud carried on to the neighbouring centrifugal. This one was switched off because the mud was being forced back through it to the suction side and so out to the delivery line.

"Jesus. Pumped backwards. I don't believe it." He wound his hand vigorously around, asking the tool pusher to increase the flow. The tool pusher raised a stubby finger and waved it like an inverted pendulum.

The cook translated unnecessarily. "He say, not possible."

"Fuck it! OK. Tell him the rig has to displace. Now. Quickly. Twelve barrels a minute."

The tool pusher looked baffled. "He say, how much fast?"

"Twelve barrels a minute." Terry held up fingers for twelve. "OK. Does he understand?"

"Oh yes. He understand good." The tool pusher seemed to have caught some of the urgency and positively bustled up to the rig floor. He roused the driller out of the dog-house and started to blow the electric horn to summon the rig-hands from their hideaways. The Virgin and Terry climbed slowly after him. When they got to the floor, the driller was trying to spin the valve on his mud manifold, to open the line to the well. It was stuck. Then a large roustabout appeared with a sledge hammer and started to pound on the valve wheel. The cast iron wheel splintered under the punishment.

"Oh, Jesus, I can't watch," moaned Terry, and they moved to the furthest corner of the floor. Two Westerners and the cook presiding over the beginnings of a disaster. Some floor hands had appeared and, arguing amongst themselves, they set about opening the valve with a pipe-wrench. It took two of them swinging on the pipe-wrench to get it started. The Virgin stepped out to open the MacAllans' valve allowing them to pump into the well and then joined the crowd at the driller's panel. The toolpusher had taken over and was slowly winding up one of the mud-pumps. The Virgin ran to the railing and waved to Rene to stop pumping as the rig pumps took over. He checked his watch. The whole performance had taken over twenty-five minutes.

Rene puffed up the stairs and they met in the dog-house to look at the situation.

"How much did you get away?" asked Terry.

"Ninety-seven barrels."

"OK. What's the timing, Greg?"

The Virgin was working on his pocket calculator and writing results on the edge of an old Romanian newspaper. "886 barrels to displace. Less 97 comes out at 789 barrels left. We started mixing three hours and eight minutes ago, that's 188 minutes. Thickening time on the lead cement was five hours fifty, that's 350 minutes, so we've got 162 minutes left. How much has he pumped so far?"

"Christ - he won't know. He's only been pumping five minutes and you'll never pick that up by dipping tanks. Say 50 barrels; should be on the safe side."

"OK. We've got 739 barrels to pump at 12 barrels a minute - 63 minutes. Heaps of time. If he slows down a bit after 55 minutes, no worries."

Terry led the cook outside to explain the plan to the driller. The driller had no watch so he left his own on the top of the panel. The floor was empty again; even the tool-pusher had disappeared. The cook would have left as well but Terry sat him in a corner of the dog-house with a newspaper and told him he would have to stay until the plug bumped. They sat staring dopily at the electric fire.

The cement was falling inside the casing under its own weight, displacing the lighter mud that was outside the casing. It was like the school physics experiment, pouring mercury into one side of a U-tube filled with water. It would keep falling until the level of liquid cement was about the same inside and outside the casing. Then the mud-pump would start doing some real work as it lifted the column of heavy cement on the outside of the casing by pumping lighter mud down the inside. The pump pressure gauge on the driller's panel would start to climb slowly as the mud forced down the level of cement inside the casing, and lifted the level of the cement outside.

Everyone was waiting for the top plug to bump. It would arrive at the bottom of the casing and seal against the float collar. The mud-pump would be unable to force any more mud into the casing, and the pressure would increase sharply. Then they would bleed off the pump pressure and check that the float equipment was working - the check valves in the casing shoe and collar that prevent the liquid cement surging back into the casing. End of job, and everyone could go for a coffee.

For the moment, they had nothing to do but wait. It should be another quarter of an hour or so before the driller's pressure gauge started its slow climb. Rene left to check on the boys cleaning up the cement units. From where The Virgin sat, he could look out across the floor, past the cement head to the stands of drill-pipe racked vertically in the derrick. Silver rain caught by the derrick lights swept past the blackness of the pipe.

He must have been dozing when the driller came in. He was pointing his finger up and saying something to the cook. "He say, the pump is going up. He say you come and look."

"OK," said Terry, swinging his feet down from the bench. "I guess it should be - Christ!"

There was a metallic clap of thunder from outside and the floor leapt as if from a giant hammer blow. An unseen force seemed to catch the driller between the shoulder blades as he stood in the doorway and slammed him across the room into the opposite wall. Then everything happened too fast. There was mud everywhere, bursting through the doorway, jetting in every direction. They were covered instantly. As he tried to shelter from the tide, The Virgin found himself looking at the fire. It flashed blue and the lights went out. The walls of the metal room were drumming and shuddering fiercely. Outside they could hear the sounds of a freight train collision. His mind caught the fatal ringing sound of falling drill-pipe. Oh God, the derrick's going over, was the first thing that came to him. I must stay in the dog-house. The ringing of falling drill-pipe was continuing but the dog-house floor was not tilting. A heavy vibration was shaking the walls and the overwhelming noise deafened him, but they were not falling.

The deluge of mud continued. Squinting through his fingers, he could make out the grey of the doorway through the spray. Some-one was on the floor, flat on his stomach, trying to wriggle out. He could make out the shape of the driller huddled at the foot of the wall where he had fallen. The figure on the floor was Terry, fighting his way out below a solid column of mud that was battering its way in and exploding on the opposite wall. He disappeared and an instant later the mud stopped, and with it the noise. It was completely quiet outside. He could hear the wind blow.

It took him a few moments to understand what he saw on the rig floor. Most of the drill-pipe was still standing in the derrick where it should be. Swaying from the shock and sometimes ringing together, but safe. Only two stands had jumped from the fingers of the monkey board a hundred feet above the floor and they were leaning drunkenly against the other side of the derrick. The cement head had gone. The casing stuck up from the rotary, naked. It was full of mud that was slopping from side to side and occasionally bubbling up with trapped air. The float equipment's holding, was the thought that sprang into The Virgin's mind, the mud's not flowing back.

Terry was standing at the driller's panel, covered in thin mud and his hair awry. "Well, I guess we bumped the plug," he said.

The Virgin sat alone in Terry's shack, drinking a coffee and feeling warm in borrowed shirt and jeans. He had conflicting feelings inside him. Glad to be alive and safe, and with a good job in the ground, he was still furious at the gross incompetence that had nearly blown him away.

Terry and Rene came in. "So - what's the news?" The Virgin asked.

"Pretty good, I'd say," said Rene. "TAMCO have just bought one 13-3/8" cement head, three straight joints of treating pipe and two Chiksan swivels."

"How's the driller?"

Terry shrugged. "Idiots like that are always alright. He's walking around. His back's OK but he's got two beautiful black eyes where he hit the wall. The cook shat himself, so he's too embarrassed to talk with anyone. You know, that goddamn driller was bumping the plug and he didn't even shut the pump down? 5700 psi we got to before she blew. I thought he was trying to tell us the pressure was starting to build. God knows what rate they were displacing at, but it sure wasn't twelve barrels a minute."

"Yeah. I was watching," Rene was smiling. "The cement head took off like a rocket on a string. It bounced off the drill-pipe and whipped round on the safety cable. It's made a great crater in the vee-dore. If it hadn't been tied down, it was heading straight for us. Just like a rocket. I've got it all on the DAC. Edgar's making an extra copy for Terry right now."

"How about the job?" asked The Virgin. "We got it all away?"

Terry laughed. "We sure as hell bumped the plug. That wasn't no flash set. No, we'll know for sure when we run in to drill out, but I bet you it's good. Tool-pusher doesn't know how much we pumped, of course. I should have been standing over them while they strapped the tanks, I suppose. Goddamn RomDril. They're cheap, but cheap is dangerous in this business."

It was only nine o'clock when he drove off location. He would visit Barani. He felt the need for some home comfort. He would beg some food and real Polish flash in a hot, steamy kitchen. Almost like the real world.

- 13 -

He had little important work waiting when he reached the office next day. The cement job had finished, and it would be at least four weeks before the rig was ready for the next one. Rene was on the rig doing all the clearing up and getting the tickets signed, so The Virgin should have been getting on with selling something new. Except that it was Saturday when TAMCO did not work, and even Harris in Almadi was inclined to get in late and leave early at lunch time. The main business of the day would be the Hash that afternoon.

The girls were waiting for him at the foot of their tower. They scrambled into the car and immediately lit their cigarettes. That was the trade-off. Love me, love my cigarettes. And nurses were the ones who spent their days watching victims dying from lung cancer and heart disease. Never mind, he thought, it's no use fighting some-one else's addictions. Years of living in Third World countries had taken the spirit out of his fight for clean air. Picking a minor gap between the on-coming cars, he squeezed into the bedlam that was Sabah's evening rush hour.

This week the Hash was running at Holey Rock, a stretch of open, stony ground named for the large limestone slab with a hole in it that had been turned up on edge near the road. It was twenty minutes away, quite far enough on a winter's day. The Virgin jockeyed his way through the traffic and headed out of town on the airport road.

Danka had some news. "I know where burnt soldiers come from."

"What?"

"You remember. Those soldiers that come to hospital the day Captain Zella tries to rape Evelina. The ones that make too much trouble. They come from camp behind tannery."

That made The Virgin's new persona sit up and listen. The tannery was another piece of socialist idiocy. A purpose built factory designed in the West and staffed by a tight group of Poles, turning Tabrizi hides into passable leather. Right next to the plant another Government factory employed Egyptian women to make the leather jackets that were so popular with the Security forces. The product was fine; the difficulty lay in what could be done with it. Priced in official dinars it was far too expensive for export or selling to local shops. And after every young policeman had received his glamorous black leather jacket, the only market left was the friends of friends who got their jackets for nothing through the back door.

The Virgin knew there was an Army base behind the tannery; that was why the tannery gate security was so strict and so few outsiders visited. He had been there only once - some-one's name-day party - and found the Poles were a more or less happy bunch considering their confinement. They were housed in ramshackle cabins in the corner of the tannery grounds. A tiny East European enclave where they were discreetly permitted to indulge in their two passions - distilling large quantities of high quality flash, and then drinking it.

"So what were the soldiers doing to get burnt like that?"

"This I do not know. There are some new Russians there; they have come only one month before. You will ask them"

"Russians? In the Army camp? I thought they'd all been thrown out years ago."

"These are private Russians. Not official ones. There are two of them, one professor and one more. Is not normal, but they come to Polish people to be friends and to talk to normal people. You know, Polish people hate Russians, but here everyone is very friends. Stupid, no?"

"No. Not at all. I can imagine they must be going nuts if they only have themselves and Tabrizis to talk to. You have to be an Arab to fit into the society here. But I'm surprised the Army lets them visit the tannery. I thought everyone would be locked up tight, especially foreigners."

"To start it was not possible; they were locked up completely. And then the two men say they like to go home again, and so now they can visit. They have made a special gate in the wall. Anytime they like to visit tannery the door is opened for them, and when they go back they ring the bell and the Army lets them go in again. But they cannot leave tannery. That is not possible."

"How do you know all this?"

"I go to a party and stay at night with my friend there. I did not want to speak with Russians, but they are OK. They say they want to come to church with us. You are surprised? Russians going to Catholic church? I am not surprised. Now Communist Party is finished, everyone is Christian. Only they don't know nothing about Mass and church in Russia. So going to Catholic church is no problem. They know nothing about that also."

The picture Danka painted sounded frightening. The Virgin wondered if she would ever make the connections. First the burnt soldiers, then the murdered Palestinian scientist, and now two private Russians working in the place the burnt soldiers had come from. He steered her away from the subject.

"So you stayed there with your friend, all night after the party. How naughty! What will the priest say?"

"Boże, Virgin. You are jealous!" She reached over and patted his thigh. "Never mind. I will come and make you happy too. Very soon, I promise."

God forbid, thought The Virgin, God forbid.

The Hash had gathered at Holey Rock, jumping up and down to keep warm in the sea wind, and ready for the off. Noddy tootled the Hash Horn and away they went, skipping heavily around the limestone rocks and trying not to slip on the red clay between them. The girls made no effort to run. They were content with a short walk, then back to the cars for a cigarette.

They waited nearly an hour before the real Hashers returned, red-faced and boisterous. It was no weather for standing around chatting and soon they were off in convoy to the De Jonge's camp for the Bash. De Jonge was some kind of Dutch construction outfit, steel fabrication, making jetties, bridges, pipe-work, anything in steel. Their camp was mostly Thai, which made for good cooking, but management was in the hands of a few hardened expats, Dutch and English. The Hash crowded into the bar, half a trailer set up for darts and drinking. De Jonge had got their Thai carpenter to make up a real bar out of used packing case timber, and he had done quite a homely job. He had added a shingled temple roof complete with gold-painted Buddhist curleques. The effect was bizarre, but pleasing. The room soon filled with muddy footed Hashers, all waiting impatiently for the beer to be poured into the insulated urn. It tasted awful, as usual. Nobody brought their best beer to the Hash.

"Hey, Virgin! You in for Christmas?" It was Noddy, clip-board in hand.

"Certainly am. They don't let me out unless I really kick and scream."

"Just as well. We're going to be a bit thin on the ground. Nearly all the Canadians have wangled Christmas at home. New Year as well, most of them. What are you doing for Christmas Day?"

"Hadn't thought really. I might go down to the desert for Christmas lunch. But you know what we're like, strictly no booze. They have a football match and then a dry lunch. It's a bit boring. What are you doing?"

"I'm going round to Forfar Ironworks. Want to come?"

That was a Scots company. A good bunch, but hard drinkers. They would not do much for Christmas except party, which for them meant standing at the bar until standing became too much effort and some-one dragged them out horizontally. "No. I think I'll give them a miss. They're bad enough weekdays, but I keep away at week-ends and holidays. I don't know how they keep it up. They'll all be seriously tired and emotional by lunchtime."

"You know what your trouble is, Virgin? You don't have any Celtic blood in you. You're just an English wimp." The Virgin's weak head was famous in the Hash.

"You're right there. Not a drop. Of blood or alcohol. No, I might just go and visit the Filipinos. I expect they'll have something going and it's much less damaging to your health." Noddy shook his head and went in search of other victims.

The Virgin scanned the room, looking for Eytie Joe. He found him in a corner with a plump Serbian girl on his knee. Joe had a good reputation with the local ladies and they chased after him whenever he was free. For the moment, the Serbian girl was in luck. She was enjoying her exalted position and chatting animatedly in blended Slav with a couple of Polish girls. The Virgin squeezed into a seat beside Joe and tried to draw his attention away from his latest toy.

"She'll keep you warm on a cold night, won't she?"

"Of course," said Joe happily. He gave her hips a squeeze that she acknowledged with a wiggle of her ample bottom. "I like them this way. She is the same shape as me."

This was an exaggeration. She would have to put on a good deal of fat before she could match Joe's girth.

"Joe, did you know there's Russians around again?"

"Really? Where?"

"Danka said she'd met a couple up at the tannery. They're working on the Army base up there. You know the one I mean - it can't be so far from your place as the crow flies."

"Of course I know where is the tannery. Every time the wind is coming from there I'm reminded, believe me. And when it comes from the other way, the noise from your drilling rig is impossible."

"It's not mine or it'd be making even more noise. Anyway, it's the tannery I'm talking about. The army camp behind it. Danka says there's a couple of Russians working there."

"I tell you, I am not surprised. Before the Government has bought so much equipment from Russia. All the Army radios and electronics. Planes as well. Everything. All original from Russia. So I suppose that Russians are the best to maintain it. But I think the Russian Government had finished with Tabriz."

"True. But these are private Russians. Working for themselves, I guess. Neo-capitalists. One of them is a professor. I wonder how much they're being paid."

"I am sure that it is not much. You can get Russian engineers for nothing now, but I hear they are not much good."

"Oh, I wouldn't say that. They're just products of their system. MacAllans are getting a bunch of good people out in Siberia. We have doctors and teachers out there just driving trucks. Some of them want to work their way out of the mess they're in. Once they've learnt English and how to be a bit responsible for their own work, they're not stupid. I'm surprised that some of them found their way here though."

"It's money, Virgin. Money can make you do anything, especially if you don't have any. But I am surprised too. I wonder if we'll see a lot more of them. The Government would like that. Their nurses must be even cheaper than Polish ones."

"Come on, Joe. Don't tell me you want to try Russian girls as well."

"To tell you the truth, no. I have tried before and they were, well, not so good. They were really fat, believe me, and they did not like to wash too much. No, I am happy with what I have." He gave his girl another squeeze. "For the moment anyway."

"Joe, you ought to settle down with one of these girls. At your age you should stop playing around."

"Why? I tell you, I have been married three times. All good women, but they turned out impossible. Now I always say, it is time I stopped marrying my cooks. They can come, and as long as they make me happy, they can stay. And when they go, there is always another one."

"Hash Cash wants your money!" shouted a voice in their ears. It Hilary's Husband (know in real life as Dave Clinton), Hash Cash, collecting five dinars a head from all the men to cover beer, paint, food, anything else that the Hash needed to keep functioning. Joe and The Virgin reached for their wallets.

"Jesus, Dave, you must have enough to retire to South America by now," said The Virgin handing over the five dinars.

Hilary's Husband took his job seriously. "I'm going to order some special tee-shirts for the eight hundredth run. I'll soon have enough money."

"How much have you got?"

Before he could reply shouts of "Charge your glasses, charge your glasses!" were raised around the room. The ceremonies were about to start and the men crowded around the beer urn to fill their plastic cups.

It took a deft hand to control the Hash, and Noddy had the touch. In just a few minutes he had everyone standing around him in an expectant half-circle. The Master of Music had lined up his choir to one side, and this week's Hares were standing sheepishly in the centre. Noddy climbed up onto a chair. He raised a straight arm in a Nazi salute and shouted at the top of his voice, "Welcome to De Jonges! Sieg heil!" Everyone knew that Dutch men loved to be mistaken for Germans. "Sieg heil!" roared the Hash in reply.

"So what did we think of that weak-kneed excuse for a trail?"

"Rubbish!" "Fit for pansies!" "I never saw any paint!" "Waste of effort!"

"I thought so. And I would have been happy to give the Hares a glass of this excellent amber nectar. Instead they can retire to a corner and think of a song to sing us in a minute. Master of Music, serenade them off stage! After three!"

"Three!" shouted the Master of Music and everyone started to sing.

Here's to the Hasher, he's a blue.
He's a bastard through and through.
He's a bastard, so they say.
And he'll never get to Heaven in a long, long way.
Drink it Down, Down, Down,

Down, Down, Down, Down,

The ritual was under way. Hashers were called out into the centre and forced to drink a cup of beer for offences such as providing beer or food for the Bash, short-cutting the run, getting a hair-cut, fondling their partners before the run, anything that took Noddy's fancy. The choir sang out the Hash song at the top of their voices. The victims stood with their cups in hand until the song reached the words 'Down, Down, Down,' and then gulped their beer down if they could, or up-ended their glass over their heads if they could not.

The Virgin had long ago stopped marvelling at the strangeness of it all. He had hashed in several countries over the years, and they all had the same childish spirit. Perhaps it was necessary for up-tight northerners to let their hair down once a week and behave like a bunch of school-boys. He had noticed that the more confined the location and the further removed from home, the more frantic became the partying. Tabriz was a culture and country apart, and the Hash here was even stranger than normal.

The ceremony ended with Rubberdy being nominated as 'Hash Shit' for the week, because he had forgotten to bring the twenty litres of beer he had promised. He drank his down-down wearing a toilet seat about his neck, and he would have to wear it for next week's run as well. "On-on!" shouted Noddy and business closed for the week.

They started to queue for the best food in Sabah - Thai cooking from De Jonge's camp. The exquisite fiery flavours even made the beer taste good. The Virgin squeezed half-way onto Danka's chair and started on his food. Danka had already finished and was smoking.

"Virgin, this food is too pikantny. Too hot. I cannot eat."

"Poor girl. This is ambrosia - food of the Gods. I could eat like this every day. Perhaps I'll go and live in Thailand when I grow up."

"I am sure is very bad for your intestine. This chilli is toxic for humans."

"It's very good for you. Lots of vitamins and it helps with your slimming."

"It helps because I cannot eat, that's why. What do you do for Christmas?"

"I don't know. Maybe I'll go to church to the English Mass and then back with the Filipinos."

"Good. I will come also. First is the Polish Mass, but I have duty and cannot go. So you take me from the hospital, I change quickly and we go to the English Mass. It will be different. And then we go to the Filipinos. And then to tannery and visit my friends. They will having a big party."

The Virgin thought about that. It was not that he objected to being organised; it was just that turning up at the Filipino flats trailing Danka would put Evelina in a bad mood. Never mind. The tannery would be more fun than the Filipino party anyway. He would drop in on Evelina during the week by way of making amends.

He found himself next to Rubberdy in the queue for second helpings. "Hash Shit again, Rubberdy?"

"Yes. I think Noddy has it reserved for me. I ought to carve my name on that toilet seat. He had a couple of other offences lined up even if I hadn't forgotten the beer."

"Oh yeah? What have you been up to? Playing with little boys or something?"

"No. He somehow heard I'd been down on the beach with my cart." Rubberdy was famous in Sabah for his plan to walk down to the desert oil-fields across the desert. He had started to build himself a small two-wheeled cart rather like a miniature pony trap to carry his water and supplies. As it developed, he took it to the beach for proving trials.

"How's it going? You got it right yet?"

"I'm getting there. I put fifty litres of water in it this time and it still seemed to move reasonably easily. There's something you could help me with, though. I've just been pulling it along by the shafts but I think that's going to be too tiring for a long trip. I started some blisters just going five klicks along the beach and back. I'm thinking about some kind of harness belt that I could wear. At least that would leave my hands free. Your guys in the desert have some kind of safety climbing belt I could steal? You know, one of the wide canvas things that workmen use up scaffolding or telegraph poles."

"You're really serious about this, aren't you?"

"Certainly am. You've got to do something in a place like this or people will stop believing in eccentric Englishmen."

"But that must be four hundred klicks across the desert!"

"Sure. Most of it's a hard surface though. I'm hoping for forty klicks a day there. And there's some sabkha not far away, twenty klicks from here, and more a hundred and seventy klicks later. That's a big one, about forty-five klicks wide where I'll cross it. They should both go pretty fast. You know, you could probably drive a regular car most of the way, if it wasn't for the rocky bits and the sabkha. It's just the last fifty klicks that are a bit soft and you'd need four wheel drive. Once I get there, I can always dump the cart and make a dash for it."

"Rubberdy, you've been out in the sun too long. You're nuts."

Rubberdy grinned. "Certainly am. But how about the safety belt - can you help there?"

"Why not? You work for TAMCO, so I'll requisition one and put it down to client entertainment expenses. Though I guess it's going to be more entertaining for everyone else than for you."

"Thanks, Virgin. I'll let you put a company sticker on my cart, if you like."

"So we'll recognise it when some-one finds it in the middle of the desert two hundred years from now? I'll think about it. Anyway, I've got to go down to the desert next week. I'll see if I can pick the belt up then."

With everyone well fed and half-full of strong beer, the party started to swing. The stereo system was wound up and a disco compilation put on. The Polish girls started to drag their men onto their feet to dance. The trailer floor bounced under the load of leaping hashers so that even the wallflowers felt the beat. The Virgin looked at his watch. Coming up to ten o'clock. Just about pumpkin time for some-one who had to be up at six o'clock next morning for a long day's work. Not that Danka saw it that way. She would happily dance all night and go to work like a zombie next day.

"Virgin, you are too serious. You must stay and dance! Come on. I will keep you here." In the end, only Wanda rode back into town with him. She had duty next day and would have to be up even earlier than The Virgin to catch the hospital transport.

As they jolted back along the mud track towards the main road she took the chance to confirm some gossip. "Virgin, you like Danka?"

"Er - yes. She's OK, I suppose."

"I mean, she is your girl-friend?"

"Girl-friend? No. Definitely not."

"Ah. She is saying that she stays in your house."

"Well, yes. But only once and she didn't sleep in my bed."

"Really? She sleep by herself?"

"Er, not exactly, no. But you'll have to ask her about that."

Wanda stored away the information and started to probe further. "So. You have girl-friend, Virgin?"

A good question. He knew that whatever he said would be common knowledge by the end of tomorrow. Perhaps now was the time to admit to Elena. "Well, I do have a friend in London."

"Really? Virgin, all Filipino nurses will be jealous!"

"All of them? I don't have any special girl friend there, let alone all of them."

"Yes. All of them. They very like you. I am surprised you don't come with some of them to Hash."

That was the problem of course. Some of them. A group of Filipino nurses might agree to come, but only in a group and only with some Filipino men to escort them. Splitting the girls up was next to impossible. He was pondering the old problem as he drove through the night when a strange thing occurred to him. He suddenly realised that he no longer cared. Girls just did not seem to be that important any more.

The road to the desert was familiar as well as tedious. For the first eighty klicks south of Sabah it followed the coast. Where the beaches and sand dunes turned west along the bottom of the Gulf of Almadi it came to a giant roundabout. Most of the traffic took the main highway west along the North African coast. Oil-field traffic carried on south into the desert on the Cape Town Road. The Great Man had built the highway to carry the light of his Green Revolution down into Africa. In a famous speech he had foreseen the day when Tabrizi revolutionaries would solve the problems of black Africa and reach Cape Town itself. The Virgin supposed it was Arabic words from that speech that were inlaid into the concrete monolith in the centre of the roundabout.

Leaving the empty coastal highway behind, the road reached into a desert that was even emptier. The vast divided highway struck forcefully across a gently rolling landscape. Low heather-like scrub rapidly petered out and soon there was nothing but bare sandy emptiness. Nothing and no one lived here. Sometimes there were camels, usually dead beside the road, but apart from them there was no interruption before the village of Blida far, far to the south.

A fact of the desert is that nothing changes and nothing decays. Throw a bottle from a truck window and you can send your grandchildren out to pick it up in fifty years time. Along the roadside lay the debris of all the years since it had been constructed. Old truck tyres were the most prominent; tins and bottles the most common. Beside them twisted wrecks of cars that had lost arguments with trucks or simply driven off the road. And sometimes the trucks themselves, chassis contorted into impossible shapes when their heavy momentum came to a slamming halt. A few years in the desert and the steel had a dull black gloss from the sandblasting ghiblis. Over many years it would be completely worn away. Perhaps fifty years for the thin body panelling and hundreds for the load-bearing beams and running gear.

The Virgin's destination was Lima-7, the MacAllans' main desert base. South on the Cape Town Road two hundred and thirty-seven klicks, skirting the western end of the Al Ha'il Depression, to a double stacked oil-drum painted gray and black. This lonely monument marked the point the MacAllans' track left the highway and struck out fifty-six klicks across the desert. The road got longer each time The Virgin travelled it but he did not let it frustrate him. At least driving the empty road was easy and the only danger that of falling asleep. He just put his mind in neutral and let the car count the klicks.

The Virgin did a lot of his thinking on these long drives. Sales projects, budgets, analyses, all became clearer after a trip to the desert. Now work had been driven from his mind by other events. He did not know exactly why, but he knew the Russians were an important part of what was going on. They must be replacing the murdered Palestinian doctor, so the chances were that at some stage they would be confronted with his container of solvent. You had to assume they would want to take samples, to test its contents. But then, you would have to assume that someone would be taking samples anyway. What exactly were Standford's plans at that point? If the container caught fire on arrival, that would be fine. No one would ever be sure what had gone up in the flames. Things would not look so good if samples were taken before the accident. Then everyone would know that Tabriz had been cheated and the finger would point straight at The Virgin. He was sure Major Jamal would not just accept a bland statement of ignorance from him, and Captain Zella would relish pulling out his fingernails. He flexed his hands on the steering wheel. While he still could.

He always enjoyed reaching the double drum and turning onto the gravel of the open desert. It felt good to drive freely where ever you liked, eating up the klicks and rolling up and down the low hills. In December the desert was clear and sunny, but with a cold wind. The drive into Lima-7 was easy; a carefully marked road with black oil drums standing like tree stumps at half-klick intervals. All the same, he set his mileometer to zero as he bounced off the road. Take all the precautions every time and you would probably never need them. The drill required that you knew the compass bearing and distance of your destination. If you had driven more than 110% of the distance to your target and not found it, it meant you were totally lost. Then you had to stop and wait for someone to find you.

The desert here was smooth and undulating. Soft sand in some of the hollows but as long as you did not stop, an ordinary car could cope with it. A maze of vehicle tracks of all ages wound in all directions. No hope of salvation by following them if you got lost.

You could end up anywhere, so MacAllans people were meant to stick closely to the oil drums and not take short cuts. It always seemed a shame to The Virgin to cruise in so much dramatic wilderness and yet to cling to the ugly traces of man. He drove well to the side of the drum line, keeping them just in sight on the horizon. Even here there were signs of previous travellers. No matter where you stopped you would not have to walk more than a few hundred metres to find a scrap of blown paper or an old sardine tin. All the rubbish thrown away since the Tabrizi oil-fields had started work still lay on the desert surface somewhere.

The Virgin counted the kilometres. Twenty-seven klicks out and he came to a way crossing, where one trend of vehicle tracks crossed another. In daylight there was no danger of taking off along the wrong line of drums, but you had to watch out for deep wheel ruts crossing your path. When the sun was strong over-head they cast no shadow and he might run across them at high speed. That was a good way to roll the car. At about thirty-five klicks from the Cape Town Road he might see the smoke coming from the refinery flare, but on a windy day like this he had to wait until he saw Lima-7 itself. That happened when he came over a slight scarp at forty-three klicks.

Lima-7 was suddenly there in front of him. A distant island of trees on the desert horizon. The orange of the refinery flare flickered up behind them and the plume of black smoke was rushed away by the wind. He felt hungry but he was too late for lunch. He would be hungry all afternoon in the safety meeting he was attending. Perhaps that would keep him awake. The yard gateway had its barrier open, the gaffir enjoying an afternoon nap in his cabin. Even the hustle of the international oil-field could not keep him from his siesta.

The Virgin parked in line under the eucalypts and switched off the engine. The afternoon washed sleepy quiet around him. The only sound was the continuous drip of irrigation water at the foot of each tree. He went into the low wooden building to look for Florian.

Late that evening he was tucked up in bed recovering from a long and tedious safety meeting followed by too much dinner. The desert air always made him dog-tired and he was having trouble keeping his eyes open to read. A knock at the cabin door woke him. Standing on the sand outside was Florian in a track suit. A ragged Tabrizi soldier with an AK-47 stood behind him.

"You picked the wrong day to come down, Greg. These guys want your car."

"You're joking!"

"No. They want three pick-ups and your car. You'd better give me the keys."

"No way! They can't do that! Besides, my sunglasses are in it."

"Come on then. But you'll have to give it to them. The silly bastards will shoot you if you don't."

The Virgin threw on his clothes and stepped outside. There was a bitter wind blowing. Just my luck, he thought, coming when the Army has run out of pick-ups. Standing outside the office lounged several more soldiers, all armed, dressed in a promiscuous assortment of military and casual clothes. Most wore sandals, and loose turbans outnumbered berets. The gang leader was dressed no differently but stood at the front of his men.

The Virgin hurried into the office and found Florian trying to sort out keys and documents for the three pick-ups the soldiers had selected.

"Give me the phone. I'm going to call a friend." He dialled Major Jamal's number. It was a relief to hear his deep voice answer. The Virgin controlled himself long enough to go through the greeting ritual before laying out his troubles.

"Well, Greg, I must tell you that they can do that, you know. No-one will sell us military equipment anymore and companies like yours must help Tabriz. But I am surprised they are looking for three pick-ups and a car all from one company. What does the receipt say?"

"Receipt?" He looked over at Florian who was shaking his head. "They didn't show us a receipt."

"No receipt? Ah, now I can help you. They are taking the cars from you but giving the receipt to one of their friends to collect the compensation. How could you get paid if they do not give you a receipt? Call the officer to the phone and I will see what I can do."

The Virgin went outside and called for the gang boss in pidgin Arabic. "Mudir. Mudir - telephone." The man followed reluctantly, laying his pistol on the desk as he sat in Florian's chair. His expression went from confusion to horror as he held the phone to his ear. Major Jamal was doing the talking and the officer only managed occasional words. Still listening, he reached into his jacket and brought out an envelope. It held the receipt and copies, complete with signatures and multiple stamps. His hand trembled as he filled in one of the main lines. He pushed it over to Greg and handed him the telephone.

"All is well, Greg. I have spoken to the lieutenant and he has given you the receipt. It is for one pick-up only, just as I thought. The other two and your car were just a little private business. But you must give him a reasonable pick-up."

"I was going to ask you about that. They've picked out three of our newest units."

"Oh, you don't have to give them those. But it must be in working condition."

"How about something two or three years old? We could manage that without upsetting anyone too much."

"Only three years old? Greg, the Army will be delighted with something so young, and I know MacAllans always keeps its vehicles in good condition. Just take the licence plates off and give the lieutenant only a photocopy of the log book. You must give the original log book and the plates to Security in Blida with a photocopy of the receipt."

The officer had left Florian's chair and was standing respectfully with his hands together. "Major Jamal, thank you so much! You cannot imagine how much help you've been to us."

"Don't worry Greg. Call me any time. If I can be so much help just with a few words on the telephone, I will do it whenever you need, believe me. Now just give me back to the lieutenant for a moment and I will make sure none of his friends bother you for a while also. Goodnight."

The Virgin enjoyed the cup of coffee he had with Florian afterwards. He had met the enemy and won three new pick-ups and a car. Anything was possible in Tabriz, if you knew the right people. Florian was stunned. In all his long years in the desert, he had never seen the Army beaten off like that. The Virgin was a hero for the moment.

The Virgin had little enough to do next day. Planning the 9-5/8" cement job on RomDril-1, visiting the lab and discussing likely cement recipes, having a tuna and onion sandwich with the Filipino store-man in an effort to prise some spare photocopy paper loose from the store. He decided not to wait for lunch. He would rather get on the road and be back home in Sabah before night fell. After fuelling the car and filling in the travel board, he swung out of the gate and raced off across the desert. Another still and clear day. Each time he reached a hillcrest he could see forever in the cold winter air.

It was on the way back that he firmed up his decision to ask for a meeting. He would run past the office as soon as he got back and call Elena. Would she come herself, or would she fix up a trip out of Tabriz?

Christmas in Sabah was a covert affair. The church had been strong before the Revolution but as foreigners were pushed out, so the mosque achieved dominance. The cathedral had been taken over and loudspeakers now called the faithful to prayer from the old bell-tower. Not that Christians had been suppressed, for Islam is generally tolerant of other faiths. Christianity now existed discretely in the back streets. The central Roman Catholic church for Sabah was the old convent chapel. Concealed behind high walls in the maze of the old town, a flame flickered. The Tabrizis tolerated it, and for the most part ignored its presence.

The Virgin picked up Danka from Barani after work on Christmas Eve and ferried her into town. The evening streets were busy with shoppers and through the bustle came Filipinos dressed in their Sunday best. Along with them was a smattering of Africans, Arabs and Indians and a few Europeans, mostly single men far from home at Christmas time. But the goodwill was there. As they picked their way through the cars patiently inching their way down streets designed for donkeys, The Virgin and Danka were greeted by most of the people they met. She was famous from the hospital, and most of the Filipino girls knew The Virgin. Being part of Christmas made them feel good, and it felt even better in the church, packed together and standing at the back while the timeless ritual went on around them.

The congregation dissolved rapidly once Mass was over and The Virgin joined the stream heading back to the hospital. Here one of the roofed verandahs had been decorated with ribbons and computer print-outs and the party was ready to go. Children dressed in doll's clothes ran screaming in and out of the adults' legs, tolerated and caressed. Music came from a straining ghetto blaster. The nurses were bringing large plates of food from their bed-sits and passing around plastic cups of watered-down cola. There was some disgusting flash available if you went and chatted to the small group of men in the corner, but most of the party was building up its spirit on cola alone.

Danka did not get any affection from Evelina but she was welcomed by the rest of the nurses, all of them junior to her. Evelina got The Virgin into a corner and started to grill him. He had expected that she would be fishing for gossip about Danka, but now she had other things on her mind.

"Why has Captain Zella been asking about you? What have you been doing with him?"

The Virgin did not need to fake surprise. "Zella? What's he up to?"

"Caridad went to him for a visa stamp and he made her sit down and answer questions about you. What have you been saying to him?"

"Jesus! What does that bastard want? He came to my office once, with somebody else, and wanted to give me a hard time. What did Caridad tell him?"

Evelina shrugged. "What could she say? Just that she knew you, and that you come visiting sometimes. He kept asking if you had a special friend here and she said no. He wanted to know about you and me."

"Damn him. I bet I know what he's thinking. He'll be reckoning that I'm after him for what he did to you, and he'll try and get rid of me first. Has he spoken to you since then?"

"Do you think I'd say anything to him?" said Evelina fiercely. "I'll stay here forever before I ask him for a visa. I'll just wait until he's on leave, or I'll get the Director to ask for me. But don't talk to him, will you? He'll only make more trouble. For both of us. He was asking about you and Danka too."

"I guess that's good. Better to keep him confused."

She looked at him quizzically. "He's not the only one who's confused."

"Good. I shall have to take more ladies for parties now and again. Make him really blow his fuse."

"Greg, you're crazy. You should get a nice girl-friend, a Polish girl who will give you what you want."

"Oh yes? And what's that? And what can Polish girls do that Filipinos can't?"

Evelina looked at the floor. "You know! Polish girls are different. They'll do anything."

"Evelina, you have a totally exaggerated view of what I do in my spare time. And of who I want to do it with. When are you coming to visit me again?"

"Don't start again! Have a party and we'll all come, but I'm not coming by myself. People will talk."

"They talk anyway. You ought to let your hair down and give them something to talk about." She smiled and left him standing.

They did not stay long at the party. Danka wanted to get to the tannery before everyone got too drunk, and while there was still some good Polish food left. When they drove up, the ornate gate complex looked dark and dusty. The steel gates were shut and chained. No one came from the gatehouse; the gaffirs did not want to come out of their warm hut and open the gate. With resignation, The Virgin climbed out of the car and took his driving licence from his pocket. The gatehouse had a small window for communication but it had been closed with cardboard against the draught. He went around to the door. Inside three old men sat in a bare and dirty room. Heat came from an electric fire element laid across two concrete blocks.

The Virgin offered his driving licence. "Salaam Alleikum" he said with as much enthusiasm as he could manage. Without bothering to reply, one of the men took his licence and waved him in. He went out and looked at the gate. The chain at the centre was not locked. He swung open the gate and drove in. For a moment he toyed with the idea of leaving the gate open, but the old men had his driving licence and they were quite capable of refusing to return it if he upset them. He climbed out of the car and closed the gate.

The Polish contingent lived in two lines of tacky wooden sheds, probably the accommodation used by the workers who built the tannery in the first place. They were clean and functional, but very basic. The party was in the mess hall and had already warmed up. At a long table along one side all the tannery workers and several nurses were sitting on benches. They nibbled Polish snacks and passed bottles of flash along the table. Cigarette smoke was heavy on the air. The Virgin was swept up and sat in front of a plate of pickled fish and potato salad. Seconds later a large flash appeared. "Na zdrowie! Na zdrowie!" shouted his neighbours holding up their glasses. Convention demanded that he sink the first glass in one gulp but The Virgin had long since given up trying to compete. He shouted and smiled with the rest but drank no more than a swallow. There was enough flash in the glass to lay him out for the night, and he had only just arrived.

Some time later Danka appeared at his elbow with a tousled young man in tow. He had a bemused smile on his face and looked like a stocky elf. "Virgin, come and meet Janusz. He is electrician and makes best flash in tannery. He does not speak English; also he is very out of order because he started party at lunch time." Janusz held out a rough paw and smiled some more. Danka manoeuvred him onto the bench beside The Virgin and went back for his glass.

She squeezed herself between two men on the bench opposite. "Janusz says if you want work for your house or office, he is happy to come."

"Thank you very much. Is he good?" It was an interesting offer; competent electricians were as rare as pork sausages in Sabah.

"Excellent. He can fix refrigerator and air con. Also water pump. He fix my washing machine." She explained to Janusz what was going on. Still smiling, he gave her a long reply. "Now he is talking about family in Poland. Excuse me."

The Virgin sat quietly and let his mind drift above the Polish conversations around him. His neighbours were good people; hard-working men here to earn some real money for their families. Most of them probably sent home three or four hundred dollars a month. It was a sad situation but with conditions at home changing rapidly, it was the only avenue open to most of them. You had to admire them.

The door at the back of the hall opened and two men slipped in. The older one was short and stocky. He had a full beard and his hairline had receded so far that his frizzy grey hair was standing up around his face and pate like an exotic monkey. His face was red and smiling. His companion was a tall young man with a stoop, quiet and dour. As soon as the crowd noticed them a shout went up. "Victor, Victor! Wesołych świąt!" The old man was in amongst them, shaking hands and shouting. Someone put a large flash in his hand and he sank it without effort. A real Slav.

"Virgin, this is Russians I tell you about. They work for Army." She jumped up and thrust her way through the crowd to drag Victor over. "Virgin, this is Professor Victor Ivanovitch Kuryagin. Virgin is an English man."

"Ah, Mr Virgin! Now I will practice my English again. How are you?" His handshake was as full of energy as the rest of him. "Do you work with this people?"

"No - I'm an oil-field engineer. And you?"

"We work for the Army here, but I will not talk about this. Not for Christmas. Now we must drink! You have whisky?"

"Hah! Some chance! No - just flash like everyone else. But this is the best flash in Tabriz. Janusz made it."

"My friend Janusz. He is very good technician. Before my laboratory has good equipment. Then the Arabs work here and now everything is finish. Believe me; completely finish. Janusz come and fix everything for me. I give him meat from the Army - very best beef from Bulgaria. He come and give me his expertise. He is more useful than professor, I think. Here, you must drink for Janusz. Na zdrawie!"

Mechanically, Janusz raised his glass with the Professor. The Virgin was forced into taking another swallow. "Mr Virgin, you will meet Boris. He is cousin of my wife. We work together." Boris reached across the table to shake hands, but said nothing.

"Now I will dance," announced the Professor, taking Danka's hand and leading her to the floor.

Boris took his place on the bench. Leaning forward, he said in a low voice, "My name is Boris." His English accent was American.

"Hi, Boris. Are you enjoying Tabriz?"

He considered for a moment. "No. It is not good here, but I am here for money."

"Aren't we all? No one is here because they like it. What's it like working for the Army?"

"It is not very bad. There are many officers who have been in Russia and understand how to work in laboratory. They try and help us, but the young Tabrizis are not good. They do not understand."

"What are you doing for them?"

"This I cannot tell you. I do not understand exactly why we are here. Now I am helping Victor repair the laboratory. I am not for this work. I do not like to be welder and carpenter and electrician. I am medical technician. My training is for working with blood. In Russia if the equipment is not working we have special technicians who will repair. Here Victor must do the work. He has nothing. Not even books for equipment."

The Virgin laughed. "It all sounds very familiar. How did you come to be here?"

"It was very easy. Victor wanted laboratory technician so he call my mother and she sent me. I think she not know how it is here. It is like prison. We cannot go outside. Now it is possible to come here, but is not enough. Polish people only smoke and drink and talk. There is no culture here, no sport. Do you have culture in Sabah?"

"Culture? You mean concerts and ballet?" He had to laugh at the idea. "Not a chance. I don't know about the Tabrizis; maybe they play music in their houses. But they certainly don't go out to concerts. It's not part of their tradition. All the men seem to do is visit each other's houses in the evening and drink tea. Their women don't go anywhere. Sometimes they take their families out for a picnic at the weekend. Or to the beach in summer.

"You'll like it better in summer. I'm sure they'll let you go to the beach with the Polish people if you keep asking them quietly. The beach is really nice here. Much better than anything at home."

Boris thought about that for a while. "They say we can go to the church with the Polish people. Is that good?"

"Ah, well. That depends on what you feel. Are you a Christian?"

"My mother was a quiet Christian, and now she goes to church. She likes it. I went with her once. It was very historical. Is it the same here?"

"Pretty much, I guess. Though it's Roman Catholic here so it will be a bit different. The Polish people are very religious. I suppose it was almost a political statement for them. To go to church under communism was like attacking the Government. Now they must be wondering what they've been encouraging. The Church can be very conservative."

"I understand this also. The Church is reactionary. Maybe I will not go."

"It's not so easy to write the Church off like that. Parts of it are reactionary for sure. Then in other parts, say in Latin America, it's much more progressive. This Pope isn't helping much, and he was brought up under communism. And anyway, the Church isn't all there is to Christianity. There are lots of Christians whose churches are completely different."

"Then I think I will go for the experience. How is it for sport in Sabah? There are clubs for sports?"

"There might be, but only for Tabrizis. Foreigners aren't allowed to have clubs of their own, and it's difficult to mix with the locals. It only leads to trouble in the end."

"What sort of trouble?"

155

"Well, first they invite you to their houses for tea, and then they want to come to yours for alcohol. After the first time you've invited them they feel free to come anytime, and if you've offered them alcohol once, they'll be back every day until you throw them out, and then you've lost a friend.

"Then there's Security. If Tabrizis keep going to a foreigner's house, eventually Security get interested and the next thing you know you're being raided. They're not allowed to do it in theory, but they just force their way in and take all your flash. And they keep doing it every week or so until they realise that you're not keeping alcohol any more. Then it's not worth their coming round, so they leave you alone. But it's a real pain while it lasts. The best thing to do is to keep away from the locals after work. It's safer."

"Then they are like the KGB. My uncle was working here for a school. He was from the KGB and he was teaching the Tabrizi officers. The KGB was very strong. It is still strong, but now the best officers are in business together with some bad people. Is it the same here?"

"The Security people? God knows. I've never had anything to do with them and I don't want to start now. Do you see them?"

"I don't know. Here it is difficult to know who is from the Army and who is from Security. They do not dress correctly. They do not like to wear uniform."

There was a crash beside The Virgin as Janusz fell off the bench. He lay on his back, still cradling an empty glass. He was sleeping with his curly blonde hair spread on the floor. He looked child-like. His friends crowded round laughing, and carried him bodily from the room. No one showed surprise or concern, and the party went on without a break. Boris showed signs of wanting to talk again so The Virgin made for the dance floor. He hijacked Danka and let her lead him through some of the stand-up dances that Poles love.

Midnight found him standing outside in the cold, shaking his head and trying to decide whether to drive home or not. Inside the party was still roaring. Danka showed no sign of wanting to stop dancing, and The Virgin had absorbed as much flash as he could hold without falling over. His stomach heaved as the fresh air reached him, and he crashed into the bushes looking for support. Leaning over a branch he threw up gratefully. Definitely, he would not drive home tonight.

The morning light woke him in the back of his car, wrapped in a sandy blanket he kept for picnics on the beach. He felt cold and wretched. He went looking for a washroom and a coffee. Cold water woke him up but did not improve his fragile condition. He looked into the mess hall; it was empty and squalid. If he wanted a coffee he would have to drive home. He had to do that anyway. If he was going to the office, he needed to shave and get a shower. After all, it was Christmas Day and he could not let Abdul down by arriving at the office looking uncivilised.

It was not until the day after Boxing Day that he received any indication that his plea for a meeting had been heard. A fax from Karelia curled off the machine. Mr Thorpe, Sales Manager Africa, would appreciate an appointment. He would be in Sabah from the 3rd of January and could Mr Cartwright recommend a hotel? Please reply by fax as he will be out of the office.

Things had begun to move. The Virgin left a note on Abdul's desk to make a hotel reservation and faxed a welcoming reply.

- 16 -

In the cold of the year, The Virgin had started to feel paranoid. He took to locking his inner office door at night, leaving a key with Abdul just to show that there was nothing personal in it. As he walked the town in the evening he found himself looking for faces. Driving the streets, he was checking plates on the cars behind. He rationed his visits to Danka and made a point of taking Wanda on shopping trips as well. That should confuse Captain Zella.

Most of all, he visited Evelina. If Captain Zella was asking questions, Evelina would be the first to know. She was welcoming but distant, and The Virgin often found himself happier with some of the other nurses around. He would sit in their crowded bed-sits, drinking coffee and listening to the cassette player. They seemed to like having him around. Always friendly and smiling, when they did not call him 'Mr Greg' they would call him 'Uncle'. Still, he was an outsider and there was something about them that he could not quite penetrate. As he sat musing with the Tagalog chatter going around and over him, he wished they were all out of Tabriz and back in the Philippines. He would sit quite happily with them under the palm trees and watch the sun set over the South China Sea. When the time came for him to leave the warmth of their apartments, they wished him goodbye in the same friendly calm with which they had welcomed him.

The New Year began with a disaster. The gaffir in the office building was waiting for him when he arrived. He led him upstairs to his office where the door was open. Someone had used a heavy lever to force an entry. Inside, his office door had suffered the same treatment. The sight made The Virgin's hangover worse. Nothing seemed to have been disturbed. The office safe was still behind the door and the papers scattered on his desk were no more disorganised than normal. He called Eyetie Joe for a carpenter to repair the mess, and toyed with his work until Abdul came. Leaving the gaffir sitting officiously on a chair at the door, they walked together downtown to make a police report.

The police investigation department was in an old stuccoed Greek building. It must have been impressive in its day. A solid four storey edifice with a u-shaped plan, so that the colonial police could parade in the courtyard. Today the stucco was flaking off and rainwater dripped from blocked downspouts. The courtyard held dead cars whose owners were helping the police with their enquiries. A heap of builder's debris in one corner made it look as if some maintenance had been attempted, but the weeds growing through it showed that nothing had moved recently.

Abdul led him to a small doorway halfway down one side of the building. It led through bare offices to a large room with a desk, two small chairs and an iron bedstead. A faded poster of the Great Man hung behind the desk. The Virgin sat and waited while Abdul went looking for someone to report to. He came back with a smartly uniformed young officer who shook hands and went to sit behind the desk. He said something in a low voice to Abdul.

"He says he is sorry this has happened. It is the Egyptians or Palestinians who come here to work." The policeman continued and Abdul translated. "Now we must make a report and they will investigate, but first I must buy some carbon paper so they can make the report."

The Virgin and the policeman sat looking at each other until Abdul came back with a box of carbon paper under his arm. The policeman accepted it gratefully and pulled a school exercise book from his desk. Working carefully he removed two double pages from the centre and sandwiched a sheet of carbon between them. He started to write and ask Abdul questions. The Virgin sat and drifted.

It took about half an hour for the policeman to write the details of the crime and the people reporting it. He wrote precisely, making a tidy letter in Arabic. Then he passed it over to The Virgin. "You must sign here," said Abdul. "It's OK. It just says we found the office had been broken open but nothing was taken." The Virgin signed.

The policeman stood up and shook hands with them both. "He says he is sorry and now they will investigate."

"Ask him when he will be coming to look at the office."

Abdul had a short conversation with the policeman. "He is asking if it is necessary to come to the office."

The Virgin opened his mouth to insist, then gave up. Why bother? It would not make any difference. "No - tell him to do just what he normally would."

Once they were outside on the street, he could say what he thought. "Jesus, Abdul! Why did we bother coming here in the first place? They're not going to do anything."

"We must make the report," Abdul insisted, "Otherwise people will think that we did it."

"Did what? Nothing's been touched. And how did anyone break open the door without the gaffir knowing?"

"Perhaps the gaffir does know, but he does not want to make trouble."

"But that's his job! He's meant to make trouble if anyone comes into the building at night."

"Maybe the people who did this were his friends. Or perhaps the police. Then he could not stop them."

"The police? What do they want in our office?"

"Money, maybe. Or alcohol. They must know that we do not keep gold in our office."

It all had a twisted logic behind it. If you assumed that property rights for foreigners were just a Western conceit, then why should you expect a night watchman to protect you? Of course the gaffir knew what had happened. Just as The Virgin had to make a police report, so the gaffir had to let any friends or policemen do whatever they liked with the offices under his care. It was all part of the system.

When they got back to the office Eyetie Joe's carpenter, a taciturn Slav of some description, was already splicing a new section into the door jamb. The Virgin made him a coffee and sat at his desk. He thought of telephoning Major Jamal, but what could he do about it all? Instead he called Elena at home. She was out - away for the holiday he guessed. He recorded a message on her machine and left for TAMCO. The 9-5/8" casing job on RomDril-1 was getting nearer and he needed to push Tayfun into getting some planning done.

When he went home for lunch he found his villa had been broken into. Nancy was there, cleaning as usual. She had come in about ten o'clock and found the garden door ajar and the front door forced open. Nothing had been touched. Even the bottle of flash in the refrigerator was still there and the Tabrizi burglar who would have left that had not yet been born. He ate a thoughtful lunch.

He did call Major Jamal in the afternoon. One break-in could be dismissed; two on the same day would upset an honest man. The Major was sympathetic and played his part. There was nothing he could do, of course, but he did offer a trustworthy Sudanese gaffir for the villa and strongly recommended that The Virgin should take him. The Virgin spent the afternoon searching the office for bugs. It was a difficult thing to do while maintaining the normal office sounds and he found nothing. Not that he had any idea what a bug would look like.

Mr Thorpe from Karelia arrived two mornings later. He called The Virgin from the People's Hotel sounding a little dazed, and The Virgin went straight round to meet him in the coffee shop. The glass and marble lobby was full of life. Foreigners and influential Tabrizis met quietly below the enigmatic and badly translated green signs extolling the Revolution. The Virgin was scanning the coffee shop for a fair-skinned Englishman when his heart skipped. Mostyn sat there looking at him. Jesus Christ, he thought, they've sent Mostyn. Of all people. Why didn't they warn me?

"Er, excuse me, are you Mr Thorpe?" They shook hands as strangers. The Virgin's brain was turning somersaults. Someone must be watching. For sure the Tabrizis knew he was meeting someone from Karelia. The question was, were they listening as well as watching? Was Mostyn smart enough to keep his mouth shut?

"Shall we order coffee? The cappuccino tastes like mud here, but that's what I'm having. And you? Now tell me, how do you like Tabriz? Have you been to Almadi yet?"

Mostyn looked lost. "It's - er - different. They really don't try to help, do they? I got lost at the airport because I couldn't read any of the signs. And they took all my spare money and changed it into dinars."

"All of it? Changed it officially? Jesus, I hope you've got an understanding boss back in England. How much did they change?"

"All my cash, which was £240 and two one hundred dollar traveller's cheques. You don't get many dinars, do you? And the taxi down here was really expensive."

"Welcome to Tabriz. You'd need to be Paul Getty to spend money at the official rate. And you won't be able to change it back if you have any left when you go. Never mind, there's not much to spend it on anyway. What are you doing here?"

"Well, I'm not sure really. My boss wants to look at the market here. After all, there must be a lot of money around and everyone needs laboratories. I was hoping you could help me."

"Jesus! He's really thrown you in at the deep end. I don't know how you'll go here. We don't get any salesmen cold calling at all. It's not worth it. Any foreign company is going to buy what it needs outside, and I don't know what Government departments do. They never seem to have any money to buy things, or maintain them. I suppose you could try the Ministry of Health. They must buy their laboratory supplies somewhere. We'll try and get you a couple of introductions. They didn't give you any names at all?" The Virgin found the incompetence of his cover story hard to swallow.

They walked to the office. It was not too far, and at least they could talk. Then The Virgin's new paranoia got the better of him and he refused to open his mouth near Thorpe's briefcase. In his office he passed a note 'assume everything is bugged' which limited them to talking about the weather and the incoming shipment. He would have to get Thorpe somewhere safe, but where? In the meantime he called Eyetie Joe again, looking for somewhere to send Thorpe where he might sell some laboratory supplies. It pleased him when even Joe was stuck for an answer, but eventually he came up with a name from the Ministry of Agriculture.

"Sure," he said, "They will not buy nothing here. Your friend must go to Almadi, but at least he can find out where in Almadi he should be going. He must say that he is coming from me, and in Sabah they will help him. If my friend is there, of course. You know, they don't work too much in Agriculture." The Virgin thanked him and got Abdul to volunteer to act as a guide.

As Thorpe was led away, he called after him. "Do you jog?"

"Jog? Yes, sometimes. Why?"

"Good. You can come running on the Hash on Saturday. Got your trainers with you? Abdul, would you mind taking Mr Thorpe to buy a sports suit and some running shoes?" Thorpe was looking confused. "It's worth it, believe me. Most of the foreigners go, and someone might have ideas about who else you can visit. Just buy something cheap. There's not much choice here and none of it's very good, so I hope you're not particular. I'll pick you up from the hotel at four o'clock." Poor Thorpe. He would be spending tomorrow and most of Saturday alone in his hotel room. The Virgin hoped he had brought a good book.

Danka was off-duty and The Virgin picked her up on the way to the hotel. Thorpe was waiting in the lobby dressed in a shiny tracksuit and multi-coloured trainers, the best that Egypt could provide. He left Thorpe to talk to Danka while he negotiated his way through the traffic. He was watching for company. It did not take long to pick them out. A dented green Mercedes with three men in it, keeping always two or three cars behind. The Virgin ignored it and drove on. The Hash was not far away this week. As they passed out of the edge of town the Mercedes became even more obvious. The Virgin wondered if they would try to follow the Hash on foot, but the Mercedes swept past as he slowed down to stop.

This week the run was at The Pinnacle, a rocky outcrop near the town limits. The Virgin parked in the rubble and rubbish dumped beside the blacktop and waited in the car until the others arrived. They came in a rush. Soon everyone was milling around exchanging news and greetings, waiting for the off. Noddy came up with the Hash Horn in hand. "New blood, Virgin? One of yours?"

"Hi, Noddy. This is - what's your first name again?"

"Geoffrey - Geoffrey Thorpe," said Mostyn, offering his hand to Noddy.

"Pleased to meet you Geoffrey. First time out? Or have you hashed anywhere else?"

"I'm not sure. I don't think so."

Noddy laughed in delight. "I like that! Doesn't know if he's hashed before. Believe me, you'd remember if you had. Call me Noddy."

"Noddy?"

"Yes - Hash name. Everybody's got to have a Hash name. If you're a good boy, we'll give you one too."

Hash Horn was winding his bugle and the mass of people straggled up to the top of the outcrop - the traditional start of runs from this venue. On top the paint of many old trails was dotted on the rocks. Noddy climbed onto a boulder and shouted at them. "Good evening, Hashers all. Welcome to yet another exciting Pinnacle run. There's so much damn paint around we'll have to find another location soon. The Hares this evening have used a colour they persist in calling puce. I think that's because they don't want to admit its real name is lavender, and only poofs would lay a trail in lavender. Soooo; Sabah Hash House Harriers, running on lavender, ON-ON!"

They jogged carefully through the rocks to a dirt track that led away from the blacktop and into the deserted buildings of the old chicken project. One of the small blessings of the Revolution was the amount of derelict State land around town. Sabah's equivalent of parkland. The dots of lavender paint led out through the buildings to the fields beyond. The Virgin took the chance to slow Thorpe down and get some talking done. They walked as other Hashers ran past them.

"You're very nervous about bugging, aren't you? Do you think they're on to you?"

"No, I don't think so," said The Virgin, "But they're certainly interested in you. They broke into my office and house as soon as they heard you were coming. There must be some bugs somewhere, but I couldn't find them."

"Hmm. Better leave them alone if you do. I guess that means my hotel room is bugged as well. That's no surprise. Anything else?"

"They followed us here tonight."

"Yes? In the tatty green Mercedes?"

"That's not tatty! Well, not by local standards anyway. I guess they're waiting on the road. No, don't go that way. It's a false trail for sure, because there's an Army camp over there - nowhere to run. They'll be back in a minute. Head this way and we'll be well placed wherever the trail goes next.

"Right, while we've still got time, listen to this. I asked for a meeting because there are a couple of things that Stanford ought to know and I had no other way of contacting him. First the soldiers I told Stanford about, the ones that turned up at the hospital with terrible burns. They definitely came from the camp behind the tannery. Danka told me that, and she's sure. She's got contacts with the Polish people in the tannery.

"Second; they've got a couple of Russians working there now. The only foreigners in the place. They're working in some kind of laboratory, I think. The boss man is called Victor Ivanovitch Kuryagin. He's about fifty, black and grey hair and beard, bald on top. Gold framed glasses. About five foot eight and fatter than me. Calls himself professor. He's got an assistant, a nephew or something, not much use, just brought him along for the ride. Called Boris and he says he used to work in a blood bank as a technician. Boris can't be much over thirty. Dark hair, heavy build, near six feet

I'd guess. Very good English. Seems a bit of a lightweight when it comes to work, though. The professor is definitely in charge. They're doing a lot of repair work in the laboratory and Boris is complaining because he doesn't know anything about that sort of thing. The professor is using a Pole from the tannery called Janusz to help with the repairs. That's what I wanted to tell Stanford."

Thorpe thought about it. "Do you think it means anything?"

"I'm bloody sure it means something, I just don't know what. Stanford will have to figure it out himself."

"You may have something, from the sound of it. OK, let me repeat it." He was good; almost word perfect.

As they walked on behind the pack, Thorpe started to question him. He seemed to be more interested in Boris than Victor. "What I'm thinking," he explained, "Is that maybe Boris is a minder, just keeping an eye on the professor. A couple of years ago he would have been KGB for sure. Now, I don't know. Perhaps they are just two ordinary men looking for some hard currency. Anything's possible in the new Russia. Any chance of meeting them?"

"It would look a bit strange, wouldn't it? You're not meant to know anything about the plant, after all."

"You're right, I suppose. I'd only get my wrist slapped when I get home for thinking for myself. Do they ever leave the plant?"

"Well, they're allowed to visit the Poles next door and that was all until recently. Now they say they're going to church on Sunday evening with the Poles as well."

"On Sunday? You told us Sunday comes on Friday here. I particularly remember that."

"That's right. Delights of Tabriz. So the morning mass is on Friday and everyone's off work. But the Poles have their service on Sunday evening, and that's when the Russians are going. Anyway, I don't think they've seen the light or anything like it. They just want to get out of the plant for a while.

"I'll tell you what's bothering me though. I guess these guys are going to be the ones receiving the shipment. I don't know how long it's going to be before the professor figures out he hasn't got what he expected, and then you can imagine whose door they'll be knocking on. That's another good reason for this meeting. So what are you planning?"

"Planning? God knows! I certainly don't. They just sent me to bring some moral support. You know, tea and sympathy. Why are they running over that way?"

The Virgin was stunned. "But you've got to do something! Listen, I'm scared of these guys. If they receive that tank of solvent, I'm finished. I mean, chopped up in little pieces and fed to the cats. So whatever you do has to happen very fast, OK? And it has to be guaranteed."

"Don't worry. I'm sure Stanford's got it all thought out. Look, they're getting away from us - shall we run for a bit?"

The Virgin jogged alone for a while. He was shocked at Thorpe's nonchalance. It's OK for him, he thought, he'll be safely tucked up in his London bed while Victor is testing samples of the solvent. The solvent would come off the boat during the day - no one worked nights in the docks. He was sure that Major Jamal would not have to wait for Customs clearance; he would have a truck standing by beside the boat. That meant the container would be in the Army camp the same day the vessel docked, and you would have to assume that Victor would drain off a sample as soon as he could. That gave a maximum time window of half a day to trigger the explosion. Any earlier and it would not damage the plant. Any later and The Virgin might already be on his way to an appointment with Major Jamal's manicurist.

He looked around for Thorpe. He looked fit and had worked his way through the pack and was running down a likely false trail with some of the fast runners. The Virgin took a guess at where the real trail must be and took off to one side. It was his lucky day; a lavender paint spot appeared at the base of an old fence post. Another, two metres further on, was hidden behind a small stone. In spite of his troubles, his blood was up. "ON-ON! ON-ON!" he cried and following the paint spots he plunged into the scrub beside the path. Behind him the rest of the Sabah Hash took up the cry. For a rare few minutes The Virgin led the pack.

By the time Thorpe came up behind him, The Virgin felt he had run enough for the moment. He slowed to a walk and reined Thorpe in as well. The rest of the pack jostled past them, seeking for the next check. "Look, we have to get this sorted out now because it's about the only place we can talk. You have to tell Stanford that I want to know one hundred percent that the container is going to be triggered as soon as it gets to the plant, or I want out. We had more time when the Tabrizis were going to receive it themselves. It would take them a little time to sort out what they've got. But now..."

Thorpe looked at him. "Well, I'm not really sure what you're talking about. I mean you're talking about things that I obviously haven't been told about. Things I don't need to know. So I can't answer you. All I can do is tell Stanford you're worried."

"Tell him about the Russians too. It's important!" but Thorpe had already run on.

The green Mercedes trailed them to the villa where the party was held. Noddy decided to call Thorpe 'Jeremy' after the British politician with the unusual sexual tastes.

Once Thorpe had gone, The Virgin was plagued by the sensation that he had been launched on a terrifying roller-coaster ride from which there was no escape, and quite possibly no happy ending either. Life went on. He kept calling Elena once or twice a week. The 9-5/8" cement job for RomDril-1 was getting nearer and Florian had started to send up cement and chemicals already. Tayfun in TAMCO seemed more interested in his forthcoming Athens field-break than planning the job. He was happy to cut and paste an old cementing programme, changing the casing setting depth and cement quantities.

Abdul had received advance copies of the shipping documents for the charter vessel. The documents for the solvent had come separately because that would have to be picked up in England. The Virgin called Major Jamal and passed them over. The next thing to be received by Abdul would be the original invoices and bill of lading. And the anti-Israel declaration that stated that every part of the vessel and its cargo was absolutely untainted by contact with the International Zionist Conspiracy. Last of all to come, if the Tabrizi Embassy in The Hague could be persuaded to co-operate in time, would be the legalised certificates of origin. An unlegalised certificate was absolutely unacceptable. The certificate had to be delivered to the Embassy where, at the price of a large fee and a delay of a week or two, a clerk would put a rubber stamp on the back of a document which he could not understand. That made the shipment safe for Tabriz.

The Virgin was waiting. Waiting for the cement job. Waiting for the documents to arrive. Waiting for the ship to arrive. Waiting for the start of Ramadan, now only days away.

He had mixed feelings about Ramadan. It was true that it made life very much more difficult. Devout Muslims always refrained from smoking, alcohol and of course fornication, but in Ramadan they also refrained from eating and drinking from sunrise to sunset. Instead they meditated on their sins over the past year and strove to improve themselves. It was a time for quiet fasting and self-mortification.

The reality differed from the ideal even more than a Western Christmas does. In Tabriz, Ramadan meant that every Tabrizi worked six days a week from nine o'clock until two o'clock. They slept in the afternoon until dusk when they would sit at the family table, cutlery in hand, until they heard the muezzin's call. Then they would tuck into a large meal. These evening breakfasts were grand affairs; a minimum of three different kinds of meat were required, plus a selection of side dishes and sweetmeats. After breakfast and a period of relaxation to aid digestion, it was time to go shopping. During Ramadan the streets were deserted at the time of the evening breakfast and then burst into life with the shops open from eight o'clock to midnight at least. When the shops closed, it was time to visit friends or for the young men to play football until the last meal of the night, another generous spread timed to finish just before dawn. Then off to bed for a couple of hours of sleep.

This cycle of eating and partying all night was kept up for the whole lunar month of Ramadan. Everyone ate far too much and the grocers reckoned that the fasting month brought them a fifty percent increase in business. And, of course, work suffered. Not only were the working hours shortened but the workers were all short of sleep from being up all night. They came late and left early, doing as little as possible while they were in the office. Government offices, never very efficient, were virtually shut down for the month.

All of this would have been more tolerable if the Tabrizis had maintained their normally placid composure. Instead they were driven by the urge to demonstrate their devoutness by being bad-tempered and obstreperous. Driving during the day was hair-raising as the more holy a driver was, the more he threw all considerations of safety into the lap of Allah and drove like a high speed idiot. Foreigners made a point of keeping off the roads immediately before the evening breakfast; any Tabrizi on the road at that time would be racing back to his family at lethal speed.

The positive side of Ramadan was that the foreigners, working normal hours, were largely left in peace to get on with their work. The Virgin used the quiet afternoons to finish all the paper work projects that had been set aside from earlier in the year. On balance, he preferred Ramadan over the normal run of things.

The Virgin visited RomDril-1 regularly to receive cement from the desert, and to make a start on job planning. Terry was back after being home in Canada for Christmas and New Year. Together they visited the low-pressure manifold on the mud tanks. Terry had been given a Christmas present by RomDril. They had welded a nipple onto the discharge side of the pumps and installed one of MacAllans' four inch butterfly valves and a Weco fitting.

"No more worries now, Greg. We should be able to get you twelve barrels a minute through that. No problem."

"Looks good. I still wish they would do the displacing. That's a lot of barrels to pump and they're better set up for it."

"You guys just don't want to wear your little pumps out, that's all. No - there's not a chance of them being able to do it accurately, so you'll just have to put up with it."

The Virgin left the office early at four o'clock. If Harris called after he had gone, he could always say he was in the market buying some electrical fittings for the villa. Or some pipe fittings. Fixing the electricity or water was a common occupation in Tabriz, so his excuse would be believed. Danka was waiting at the door of the apartment building, dressed in her Sunday best. She picked her way across the mud to the car.

"Boże, Virgin! This place is like shit. Always mud. Is not possible live like this." She lit her cigarette as The Virgin picked his way around the puddles to the road. "Now we will see real communists come to the real church. I think they will not understand. Russians never like to understand Polish. Our church is also not like the Russian church. We are more modern."

The Virgin was smart enough not to respond. He fell back on the weather. "When is this lousy weather going to stop? We should be going to the beach soon."

"The beach? You are crazy! It is too early. It will be cold. First it will be time for mushrooms, then time for beach. In March. After February."

"We were on the beach last year in February. At least once. But you're right. We should be going for mushrooms now. How about Friday?"

Danka clapped her hands. Polish people loved mushrooms. "Yes! We will make barbecue. Wanda will come, and some people from the tannery. Janusz will bring meat. I tell him today. Perhaps Russians will come, if they know about mushrooms."

"I doubt it. They're not allowed to go anywhere, except to church. Maybe later, when the Tabrizis get bored with them. I wonder if they'll be allowed to go to the beach in summer. I wouldn't want to stay all summer locked up like they are and not go to the beach."

"Ah, it is for money they are here, Virgin. Only for money."

It's the same for all of us, thought The Virgin. We're only here for the money, nothing else. Except maybe Eytie Joe. Even he probably came for the money in the early days, but now he's too comfortable, and too uncivilised to go back. They drove on through the empty grey streets. Some shops were open for last minute shopping, but for the most part everyone was at home. The women putting the finishing touches to the evening meal and the men nursing their religious hunger, waiting for the moment of the Ramadan breakfast.

The gate at the tannery stood wide open. The gaffirs had lost their interest in annoying visitors and retired hungry. They would not make trouble again until after they had blown out their stomachs and taken a little nap. The tannery minibus stood outside the accommodation huts, waiting for its driver. It was full of men and the windows were misted. Danka went to them, but The Virgin decided to keep out of the weather. It must be a strange life for the tannery workers, he mused. They worked normal hours, perhaps forty or so hours a week over six days. That left them free for the late afternoon and evenings, and Fridays as well, but there was nothing to do. The tannery was far from town and they had to beg the use of the minibus from the Polish manager. As he was here with his wife and had no car of his own, getting the minibus was very difficult. One shopping trip on Wednesday evenings, and church on Sunday. Practically speaking, those were the only chances of getting out of their confinement. For the rest, they might as well be in prison. There was nothing at all to keep them civilised. Inside their high wall they had the company of their work-mates, enough to eat and too much to drink. They earned their money mostly by sitting and waiting for the end of their contracts. As the old communist saying went - we pretend to work, they pretend to pay us.

Danka got back into the car. "We are waiting for Janusz. Then we will go. The Russians are in the bus. They are wearing ties and are very serious."

Janusz did not keep them long. He came with his hair still uncombed and wearing a disreputable sweater. He had the same bemused expression on his face that The Virgin remembered from the party. Janusz had been deeply drunk then; The Virgin wondered if the two things went together. They drove slowly out through the gate, the minibus following. In the grey of the dusk, the road looked wet and empty.

They were still in the empty kilometres between the tannery and town when they came to a check-point. It was an impromptu army one, with soldiers in sloppy olive-green fatigues wandering around chatting to each other. Some of them had fitted the bayonets to their AK-47s. They stood around two battered oil drums that formed a gateway for the traffic. One of them waved the car down. The Virgin slowed down and groped for his car papers. It was not until he had stopped that he felt that something was wrong. Something aggressive in the manner of the soldiers surrounding the two vehicles. And why were they mounting a check now, when they should be back in barracks eating their breakfast?

He wound the window down. The soldier bent to look inside. The Virgin and Danka found themselves staring into the cold blue eyes of Dov Nagel.

"Where are the Russians?" he asked, showing no sign of recognition.

The Virgin was stunned and could only jerk his head at the following minibus. Dov stood up and waved them on. As The Virgin picked up speed he could see in the mirror that they were opening the side door of the minibus. The memory of Dov and the Palestinian doctor hung over them both. Danka was watching over her shoulder. Then she turned back and sat with a face of stone, staring at nothing in front of them. Janusz must have sensed something because he was asking questions. Danka shut him up sharply and they continued in silence, the minibus following. In the dying light, The Virgin could see tears running down Danka's cheek.

She ran back to the minibus as soon as they parked near the church. The Russians had been taken but the men from the tannery were not worried. To them it was just another inexplicable freak of the Tabrizi system. Danka hurried to the church ahead of them, nearly running in her distress. She had disappeared by the time The Virgin reached the courtyard. He did not go inside but waited there listening to the Mass over the loudspeaker above the church door. He felt sick at heart and wanted to pray.

Several men waited outside with him and the late-comers joined them. All were Polish, and followed the service intently. They sang a little and muttered the responses. When it was the time to kneel, they crouched down on one knee but just kept clear of the wet concrete. The Virgin could not recognise the course of the service and was taken by surprise when the communion bell rang. Most of the people around him filed into the church to take the sacrament. The confirmed devotion of the men, mostly manual workers from their hands and the way they held themselves, was something foreign to The Virgin.

After the service, he waited for Danka to appear. She came out near the end, her face swollen from crying.

"You OK?" he asked.

She looked at him with cold loathing. "You killed them," she whispered in a harsh, unnatural voice and brushed past him. By the time The Virgin reached the street she had disappeared.

He felt lonely at home by himself that night. Having the Russians taken did not really touch him, but the thought that he had lost a friend hurt more than he could have imagined. He called Elena in the morning but she had nothing for him. No invitation to a meeting yet, so they just chattered about the weather and how much they wanted to meet again. He felt glad to hang up the phone and make his way to TAMCO.

Back in the office, it was definitely time to get down to some serious planning for the 9-5/8" casing job. The Virgin should have been rubbing his hands together at the thought of the half million dollars or so the job would make, but his world had clouded over. Taking his pipe data book, he went through the motions of re-calculating the cement quantities required and checked them with the desert. They wanted to have a big surplus of cement on location in case the hole was washed out. Big washouts would mean that large cement volumes would be required, and there would not be time to rush them up to Sabah after Revards had run the calliper log. Better to have the cement ready and waiting, just in case.

He was eating lunch at home alone the next day when the radio surprised him. The BBC World Service headlines announced that two Russian chemical warfare experts had defected from Tabriz to Israel. His lunch forgotten, he waited through the other headlines for the details to come. His blood was racing. Remembering the listening bugs he started to eat automatically to make some noise, then the news came.

The Israeli Government has announced that two Russian experts in chemical warfare have defected from Tabriz and have been offered asylum in Israel. In a press conference in Tel Aviv the two men, Professor Victor Kuryagin and Boris Pulyakov, said they had been employed privately by the Tabrizi Government in a weapons plant at Sabah in Tabriz. They denied that they had been recruited to work on weapons, but had gone to Tabriz thinking they would be working at a military training college. They described the Tabrizi chemical warfare capability as primitive and disorganised. Israeli sources say that the Russian men had been working on a chemical weapons programme that could be very dangerous to peace in the Middle East.

Usually reliable sources report that the two men were snatched from Tabriz by Israeli commandos last week, but there has been no official confirmation of this. The full story of their defection has been sold to an American newspaper and will appear next Sunday.

The news moved on to a story of unrest among French farmers but The Virgin was not listening. He felt a large grin spreading over his face. So Victor had made it. And Boris. And their success would make The Virgin's life much more secure when the shipment arrived. He wondered if he had blind chance to thank, or whether Standford and Crossman were behind it.

He waited impatiently at the office until four o'clock when he was sure that Danka would be in from her duty and took off for Barani. Danka was still in her uniform when she answered the bell. Her face darkened when she saw The Virgin and she started to close the door but The Virgin's smile stopped her.

He held his finger to his lips and bounced into the apartment saying, "Hey! Did you hear about Victor and Boris? They're on the news. They've gone to Israel."

Danka was sure she had not understood. "Again, Virgin?"

"That's right. Israel. It was on the BBC. They said on the news that the Israelis accepted them into Israel. They say they've been working on chemical weapons."

"Virgin – slowly," Danka pleaded. "Why they go to Israel? They are not Jew. They just work in laboratory here."

"I don't know how they got there, but I suppose that if the Israelis granted them asylum, they must have known something useful. Where did they go on Friday after the Army let them go?"

"Virgin, they not come back from Army. No-one sees them after church."

The Virgin gave himself a pause for realism. "Maybe the Army sold them then. I'm sure the Israelis would give a good price if they've been working on chemical weapons. Dollars in Switzerland, no problem."

"Weapons, Virgin?"

"You know - guns, bombs, things like that. Only using poison gas."

"Gas? Boże! Victor is doing this? I do not believe."

Again The Virgin put his finger to his lips, and Danka nodded distractedly to show she had understood. "It's possible, you know. Russia has lots of strange military scientists with no jobs. Are you going to give me coffee?"

"Boże!" mused Danka as they sat over their coffee. "Victor in Israel. What will he do there? Have operation and become Jew?"

"Maybe he doesn't need an operation."

"Is necessary for him," she said with a smile, "But only a small one."

"Are you coming to the rig with me? Let's go and see my friend Terry and perhaps he'll show you round."

Terry, who rarely saw a woman from the beginning of his hitch until the end, was delighted to have a real live one in his trailer. He hurried to tidy up and made the coffee.

"Have your lady sit over here, Greg. You don't want to keep her all for yourself."

Danka looked down at herself. "I think there is enough of me for all people," she said sadly. They laughed with her.

"Terry, you near the tannery here? Danka has friends there."

"Tannery? That's what it is. We get a whiff round here sometimes – never knew what it was. Where is it? We've got some kind of bone-yard over the fence. Dead equipment everywhere. Never saw such a collection of junk. Must have been there forever. If it was back home, you'd have all sorts of collectors rooting through it. Wouldn't surprise me if there wasn't some steam-powered stuff."

"Bone-yard? Oh, I know what that is. That's Eytie-Joe. He's been here for years, and that's all the stuff he's imported since forever. You can't dispose of anything you brought in for construction projects. Once it's done, equipment just has to sit there and rust. You can't sell it."

"Well, it's only worth shipping out for scrap now. Don't know why they don't do it. The Koreans would take it like a flash."

"It'll never happen. It costs so much to bring a ship in here. Then there's all the other rip-offs you'd have to pay – trucking, cranes, Customs… Plus all the co-operatives with their hands out. It'd cost you more than the steel's worth, believe me."

"Hmmm – Tabriz strikes again. Never mind, there's plenty of desert out there they can use as a parking lot. I tell you, I climbed up to the crown the other day. This place is fantastic. In the morning you can see forever. If we were allowed to have binoculars, I swear you could see Crete from up there. And in the other direction – the desert comes right up to the edge of town and then goes on and on and on. You ever get to drive out there? Just head south with a four wheel drive?"

"I wish! But you know what the locals are like. They catch you out there by yourself and they'd make no end of trouble. If you're not sitting at home and drinking tea, you've got to be a security risk. Come to steal their sand or something. I only see the Cape Town Road."

"Know what you mean. Sad, isn't it? They could have tourists all over the place, but who'd want to bother? Now, tell me about the next cement job."

There was a trip to Samida that Friday. The Virgin wondered who to take with him. He suspected the Filipinos would be more fun, but they all went to Mass on Friday morning. He settled for Danka and Wanda. They were waiting for him on the balcony of their flat and hurried out to jump into the car. They lit their cigarettes and The Virgin made for the main road east. The town fell away in scattered villas and empty government factories.

The road was straight and modern, a divided highway built for more traffic than Tabriz could provide. They swept along at 140 kph over the flat and stony coastal plain. The road crossed boring country. No houses, no farms, just rocks and scrubby trees, browsed into umbrella shapes by goats standing on their back legs to remove any greenery they could reach.

The sea lay out of sight of the road. It was there, out of reach behind the low string of dunes that divided the sabhka from the beach. It was an empty beach. For much of the year, it was only accessible by walking along the sand from the few causeways that had been pushed across the sabhka during the war. The Virgin had been there on occasion, and as a beach it had little to recommend it. It was a narrow hundred kilometre strip of sand scattered with dried sea-weed, old plastic and pellets of congealed crude oil. The only break in the monotony was the wreck of the Yugoslav ship from Rijeka that had washed gently onto the beach one night a few years ago and been abandoned in a mounting tide of impossible paperwork.

On the other side of the road, equally distant and equally unchanging, stood the limestone scarp that walled in the coastal plain. The highway they were travelling followed an ancient route. Since men had first walked on two legs, they had passed back and forth along the southern shore of the Mediterranean, and they had all tracked along between the sea and the escarpment. They would have seen the same sand dunes and the same limestone wall. Today, sharp eyes could easily pick up stone arrowheads and tools amongst the pebbles. In a milder climate, the Romans and the Greeks had farmed here and travellers must have found villages and taverns to sustain and shelter them and their animals. Those hamlets were now low mounds of soil built up from their decayed mud walls, and evolving pottery shards counted the centuries that people had lived and loved there.

True, the dryness of the place was relatively new. Arabic colonisation had taken over a land slowly dying of thirst, and their goats had completed the destruction. The only Islamic monuments were the square, standardized Turkish forts built to control the local nomads. Crude and strong, but none of them had survived well in the world war.

At Rommel's Pass the scenery changed. The coastal strip narrowed to a few kilometres and a stream falling from the plateau above had carved a weakness in the limestone wall. The modern highway swept upwards under the forlorn, eyeless stare of an old fort, an ochre stuccoed ruin that had been occupied, attacked and rebuilt for millennia. On top the plateau was green. At this time of the year it was blessed with winter rain and wheat grew. The landscape was dotted with identical Tuscan peasant houses, mostly empty, relics of an Italian settlement scheme for soldiers returning from the Great War. Beside them, identical large modern houses with television antennae and solar hot water marked the Tabrizi government's contribution. People lived normal lives up here and earned their living by working the land.

The road wound this way and that, passing isolated houses and small villages until it passed a small dirt turn-off. An old truck tyre stood at the edge of the highway, with 'Samida' and an arrow painted on it. The Virgin swung off the road and they jolted down through the trees. Samida was famous, well known to classical scholars as an ancient place of pilgrimage. It had been re-discovered in the 19th century and Victorian travellers had sat in the amphitheatre and painted the views. It had been closely studied and between the wars Italian archaeologists had laboured to remove the desert sand and restore the town. They had not finished the job. The war had taken them from their task and their things had been left as they lay. Their narrow railway snaked around the site and the little dump cars sat together in a siding. The old farm house they had used as an office remained, locked and unoccupied, waiting for the diggers to return. The site was Greco-Roman, not Islamic, and the Tabrizi government had no empathy with it. They protected it, but did not care for it. There were no facilities for tourists, only an old man at the gate selling entry tickets for a few dirhams.

The Virgin pulled under the cypress trees to park beside the others. Most of the Hash and a good proportion of the Polish nurses had come. They gathered up their picnic bags and trickled towards the gate.

It always pleased The Virgin to walk through these ruins. He felt history and culture seeping up through the soles of his feet. He was treading worn limestone slabs that had been trodden by sandals two thousand years ago. The man living in that house there might have visited Rome and seen Julius Caesar. If he had travelled east, it could have been into Cleopatra's Egypt. He might have been in Jerusalem during that fateful week. And then, safely home again, his feet would have contributed to the wear and polish of his doorstep. His roof had fallen in now and his walls reached no higher than The Virgin's waist, but the mosaic that graced his dining room floor was still there, revealed and open for northern barbarians to walk on.

His wandering and pondering had left him alone in the upper town. The rest of them had hurried down to the religious centre with its spectacular buildings, the amphitheatre and the sacred pool. The Virgin stayed where he was, soaking up the atmosphere and trying to re-create the hustle of a busy town, living, loving and milking the pilgrims.

The picnic was in full swing when he reached the amphitheatre. Food and drink were spread on the stone seats and in small groups they were laughing and enjoying themselves. The Virgin tucked in with Wanda and Danka, happy but left out of the Polish conversations flowing around him. He sat and let the view carry him. The theatre was small and intimate, set off to the side of the temples and sacred pool. It had been cut into the face of the limestone scarp, using the steep slope to best advantage. There had been a proscenium wall behind the stage, probably destroyed by an earthquake. Now the view over the stage was unobstructed and the audience looked out north, across the plain to the hazy blue of the Mediterranean. It was a magic location, infinitely moving and impossible to photograph.

Rubberdy-Dub picked his way along the seat row towards him. "Hey, Virgin, I want to say thank you. For the belt. It works great."

"You're still going ahead? You've got to be crazy."

"Probably – but yes. I'm getting close. I've got to go soon, before the ghiblis start. But I want it to warm up a little as well."

"I still don't see how you're going to get over all that sand."

"Don't worry. I've got it cracked. It's all a matter of tyre pressure. Get that right and you can roll the cart anywhere. I went for kilometres on the beach last week, and I didn't even get blisters. And I had 50 kilos of water on board."

"50 kilos? Is that enough?"

"Should be – but I'm taking a couple of ground stills along too. Just in case."

"Well, you're a braver man than I, Gunga Din."

Wanda and Danka began to pack. They wanted The Virgin to take photographs of them to send back to their families, and then drive them down to the beach to take some more.

Next morning was busy. Abdul was in at eight o'clock, something unheard of. And he was carrying a packet of documents. "They bring them to my house," he complained. "Make my family frightened." He fanned them out. All the original invoices and certificates of origin for the incoming shipment.

The Virgin did not need to ask whom he was talking about. He quickly scanned the documents. All stamped and signed off, just as they should be. He looked at the dates. Rotterdam had issued them on one day, and they had been legalized in The Hague on the next. The Tabrizi consulate must have been waiting for them and sent them straight on to Major Jamal instead of returning them.

"They say the ship is coming today," ventured Abdul. "Is that right?"

"Jesus – no-one's told me. Can you find out?"

"I try," said Abdul and disappeared to his office.

The Virgin continued scanning the documents. He could not find Major Jamal's container of mustard gas. He guessed the documents for that would have been issued separately in England, and Major Jamal had them right now.

Abdul came in. "The harbour master say the ship comes in today. Discharge at the military wharf."

"Damn! What have we done to deserve that?" The military often indulged in a little private enterprise and unloaded commercial ships. That was no problem – in fact they probably worked better than the normal stevedores – but they had a very inflexible attitude to invoicing. No chance of negotiating discounts with them. Oh well, thought The Virgin, at least this will put an end to the whole business. There was no chance of a second order. Or was there? He shuddered. This one had caused him enough grief, and he did not want to think about what they might order next.

"Well, nothing we can do about it, I suppose. But you'd better lodge something with Customs right away, to keep everything legal. Do you think you could visit the ship?"

"Not possible. I cannot go inside the military wharf. Perhaps I can see it from the Customs office – they have very big windows. What do you want?"

"Nothing, I guess. I just wanted to know if the container for Major Jamal is on board."

"It is," said Abdul complacently. "They tell me last night. First they discharge their container, then they start on everything in the hold for us."

"And the truck pusher is ready?"

"Yes, I see him this morning at his house. He knows, and I will see him again after I go to Customs."

The Virgin got back to arguing with the desert over planning for the cement job, and to typing up the job program ready for Tayfun next day. The work took all his attention and he was still at it when Abdul called to say he had seen the tarpaulin-covered chemical container being swung off the ship and driven away on an army truck. He looked at his watch. It was lunchtime, and Saturday. He had the afternoon off. With a wave of relief he shut down the computer and drove home for lunch.

When he looked back on it, the week following the arrival of Major Jamal's container was very quiet and ordinary. It would be a last island of peace and tranquillity.

Abdul had got the ship discharged with a minimum of aggravation and sent the long chain of trucks straight down to the desert. And he had done it without paying the ridiculous charges mandated in the trucking cooperative's charter. The Virgin blessed his good fortune at having Abdul in the office.

He followed the shipment down to Lima-7. The last of the cement had been discharged twenty-four hours earlier so the road should have been clear, but he was passing trucks all the way south and across the desert. Battered, blunt-nosed Fiats, over-loaded with 1-1/2 ton bags of Class G cement and towing four wheeled trailers, equally over-loaded. He wondered how their drivers kept them going. They had been out of production for years and spare parts must be hard to come by. He guessed that Fiat had deliberately made the trucks tough, basic and easy to repair, and with plenty of power to cope with hauling through soft sand.

Lima-7 was having a busy period, which meant that everyone was out working. Hardly any equipment remained in the yard, and the mess hall was empty. It would be a good month with plenty of revenue. At least he had Florian's time to work through the job plan for the RomDril-1 9-5/8" casing. Florian complained bitterly at the amount of equipment and people that The Virgin had promised to provide. That was normal. He did it every time, but he never complained at the size of the invoices that resulted.

The Virgin decided to take the chance to visit the TAMCO location at Waha. He needed to keep in touch with the people in the field, both TAMCO and MacAllans, and besides, it was an impressive drive. He borrowed a desert Toyota from Florian and set off after breakfast. The track was well marked to start with, heading southeast out of Lima-7, a maze of tyre marks heading away from the hub. Initially it picked its way from one pipeline crossing to the next and the heavy traffic converging on these bottlenecks had corrugated the desert surface. They made for a bone-shaking ride. Once he left the Lima-7 field behind, the vehicle tracks fanned out and it was easy to find freshly blown sand to drive on. The Toyota rode on its balloon tyres like a ship on a lake and The Virgin sailed on, carefully counting the kilometres.

After ninety kilometres the Cape Town Road came into sight as a line of disturbed soil on the horizon. As The Virgin got nearer he could see a truck moving on it, but it had disappeared by the time he bounced onto the asphalt. He was alone in the desert. Flat to the horizon in all directions, and no living thing. He reset his odometer and headed south along the black ribbon. The Russian rig was 135 kilometres away. From a distance it looked active. The substructure and rig floor were in place; the derrick was hooked up and assembled, ready for raising. As you got nearer the signs of its abandonment became more obvious. There was nothing else there, no winch trucks, no accommodation units, no busy people rushing to get ready for the next well. No one knew the story of the rig or why it had been left in the desert. It was certainly Russian. The Virgin had stopped there one day and clambered over the sandblasted steel, marvelling at how similar it was to a Western rig and how everything differed in detail. He had even gone back to his truck for a wrench to scavenge the identification plate from the draw-works, a heavy brass tablet with cast Cyrillic lettering.

He did not stop today. He swung off the blacktop and set his nose southeast again. On the horizon stood the single blip of an oil drum. He headed towards it. As he passed it, another drum came into sight far on the horizon. This was the most difficult stretch of the track at night. The terrain lay absolutely flat and the drums were only visible during the day. At night drivers relied on starting out in the right direction and then using the stars to keep them straight. Not for the first time The Virgin cursed the Tabrizi stupidity that banned the use of GPS navigation on security grounds. They did not want foreigners to have more sophisticated equipment than their own rag-tag army.

Another eighty kilometres and he came to another of the Great Man's white elephants. Crops circles; wheat fields in the central Sahara. Hundreds of metres below the surface lay limitless fresh water. The Great Man had paid a fortune to have water wells drilled and now the 500m long irrigation booms pivoted continuously under the desert sun, irrigating stunted wheat crops. The 'farm' was five kilometres away, looking for all the world like another oilfield camp. He had never been there but had heard that it was well equipped, a hotel in the desert, and full of young educated agriculturists who flew in for two weeks on, two weeks off. Not that there was much to do – a small contingent of Canadian farmers and Sudanese labourers kept the equipment running, and did the ploughing and harvesting as a hobby. The wheat they grew was probably the most expensive in the world as it poured into their silos. When trucking costs back up to the coast were added in, the wheat rated alongside caviar and champagne. The whole set-up rivalled the pyramids in folly.

Still, The Virgin liked to thread his way through the circles and marvel at them. They made for a welcome visual break on the skyline. They also marked the beginning of the heavy sand. Slowly the desert surface became looser, the gravel gave way to fine sand and the Toyota started to labour. The Virgin changed down into low ratio and dithered between second and third gear. Even balloon tyres at 20 psi could not float over this. He drove into the edge of the deep sand desert and its low, rolling dunes. Progress was slow and tedious.

A smudge of smoke on the horizon flagged the Waha field, one of the world's jumbo-sized pools of oil and the major source of the Great Man's money. Pieces of steel junk began to appear in the sand and then the first wells, lone christmas trees linked to gathering stations by four inch pipelines lying on the sand. Here the sand was deeply furrowed and the Toyota needed confidence and power to keep its course. The Virgin pushed the Toyota towards a narrow gap in the line of sand dunes ahead. Lurching from side to side and never letting his momentum drop, he broke through into an open plain with the Waha camp at its centre. Two flares stood to one side, burning continuously and sending a plume of black haze down the wind. Well-heads dotted the plain and black pipelines netted them together. The sun was beginning to touch the dunes. A surreal orange light painted the desert and cast sharp, deep shadows. He swung off the main track and headed for the cluster of small contractor camps.

Snowy the Australian presided over a few hundred square metres of desert, bounded by a low bank of sand thrown up to break the wind. He had an office and two portable dormitory buildings for himself and his Filipino crew. A roofed concrete pad as a workshop, two storage containers for spares and supplies, and four bulk cement silos. He stood in his office door and watched as The Virgin drove into the yard.

"G'day – you timed that right. I was just going to give up on you and go for dinner." Snowy was a tall, thin engineer, middle-aged, who had worked out of the Waha base for as long as anyone could remember. He reached out his hand as The Virgin clambered stiffly from his Toyota. "Leave your stuff. I'll sort your room out later. I've radioed Florian already that you've arrived, so we can go and eat."

Dinner was at the Revard's camp. They had a bigger crew and ran their own mess. It suited them to contract services to other companies, to give the economies of scale and continuity. And it suited MacAllans to pay Revard's merely high fees rather than the astronomical ones that TAMCO demanded for eating at their base. They lined up for their food and sat together to eat.

"So – to what do we owe the honour? The luxuries of Sabah getting you down? Or you're just getting away from the girls?"

"No – neither of those. Just showing my face down here, that's all. And I've been talking sand control to TAMCO – Harris says it's the flavour of the month so we'd better do some or else – and I've got some fliers and technical stuff to hand out. Not that it'll do any good. Even if the TAMCO people down here had an opinion about it, no one would listen to them. But still, we might as well be the good guys."

"Sand control," snorted Snowy. "I wish you luck. They need it, sure enough, but they'd much rather just keep pulling those pumps every nine months. What would they do with half the work-over rigs if they suddenly got efficient?"

"Ours not to reason why. Anyway, I like coming down to visit. It beats working. Found anything good recently?" Snowy's hobby – more like a passion in fact – was the Neolithic culture that had inhibited Waha in more temperate times. He had developed a sharp eye and a feel for what the ancient landscape must have looked like. He had the supernatural knack of finding campsites abandoned 15,000 years ago. Now he never took a trip out of the camp without trying a new path or a different direction. He slowed down for any wind scour and stopped at any scattering of pebbles. He must have found hundreds of kilos of stone tools over the years, and he silently smuggled out a handful on every trip. He had showed The Virgin some of his prizes, delicate leaf-shaped arrow heads, knives, a black flint hand axe still sharp enough to cut your finger. Pierced fragments of ostrich shell and even a whole half-shell, decorated and treasured as a cup. Once on impulse he had taken a bag full of artefacts into the museum for prehistory in Berlin. He never tired of telling how white-coated professors and students had suddenly surrounded him, all handling his treasures and muttering enviously. They had recognized the material immediately and showed him some inferior examples of their own. He had offered to leave his treasures but the museum could not touch material without a legal provenance. They went as far as buying him lunch while they photographed the horde and the senior curator himself had escorted Snowy to the grand front door and reluctantly waved him goodbye.

He had not found anything as exciting recently. He had other things on his mind. "There's a seismic project north of here, did you know that? I've arranged with Florian to look the other way while I go up there and look for the *Lady be Good*."

"*Lady be Good?*"

"Yes – you've heard of it. It was a Yank bomber from the war – a Liberator - flying Naples to Cairo. Somehow got lost over the desert. Ran out of fuel. Put down more or less OK and then they all died of thirst. It got covered by a sand dune and they didn't find the bodies for years. Then it got covered up again, but apparently the dunes are moving and it's in the clear now. I've arranged to go with a couple of the seismic hands. Should be a good trip."

"Yeah – that'd be quite something. Take lots of pics – I'd be interested in them. What's it like out there, anyway? Easy enough to move around?"

"Depends how far east you are. There's a lot of ground up there that's more or less like it is here. Slow going; heavy sand. But you don't have to go far east and you're in big dune country. That's real serious stuff. I bet there's a fortune in oil under there, but it's going to cost a fortune to find it. That'd be a project – putting seismic lines through there. Take forever."

"Friend of mine's planning to walk down here from the coast..."

"What? Jeez, you must have some strange friends. He'll never make it."

"Oh, I don't know. He's got a little cart thing to pull along behind him. Says he can carry all his water in it, and he'll have ground stills with him as well. He says it's only the last 50 klicks or so that are really heavy going."

"Will this be official?"

"Nope. Can you imagine the Tabrizis giving permission for anything like that? It'd blow their little minds. No – he'll just get a lift out of town, and go for it. He's quite confident. He says there's two stretches of sabhka on the way and he should make good time on them."

"You know, he could be right. What's the desert like up nearer the coast?"

"Not bad at all. Pretty flat. Only bits I've seen are gravel. No real topography at all. Not like over in the West."

"I've seen that sabhka he's talking about. Or at least, I've seen one of them. Wandered a bit far north one day. Florian would shoot me if he ever found out. It's big, that sabhka. Runs a long way east, you know. From by the Cape Town Road right over into Egypt. If your friend was travelling east-west, he'd be in much better shape. Still, the southern side is gravel – pretty much like around Lima-7. You could walk on that, I guess. But Jeez, it would be hard work. How many klicks does he think he'll do in a day? 40? 50?"

"I don't know. He's been training on the beach and says he can do 25 in soft sand. But day after day? I don't know, and I don't think he does either."

"His best bet would be to stay west of the sand for as long as he can. Head down towards the crop circles. But not get too close to them or he'll be arrested for sure. If he can get that far in reasonable shape, he'll have a chance. Tell you what – when I go up to the seismic camp next week I'll get the exact location for you. If he gets into trouble, it might be good to know. But he'll have to go soon – the camp won't be there forever."

They watched a video that night and The Virgin went to bed early. He showed his face in the TAMCO office next day before heading back to Lima-7.

He had just finished his sched with the desert when the phone ran. It was too early for Almadi or for any official Tabrizi office, so he picked it up expecting to hear Florian from the desert. It was Elena.

"Good morning, Greg – are you out of bed yet?"

"What – I'm in the office. What are you doing calling so early?"

"Oh – I couldn't sleep. It's ten past six – not so bad. How are you going? Did you get the parcel I sent you?"

Greg ears stood on end. Word code. Parcel referred to – to the shipment. Why was she asking? She must know it had arrived by now.

"Parcel? Yes – it came last week. No problem."

"Oh good. Did you like it? I sent a calendar with pictures of England, because you said that pictures of girls would be illegal." She went on to talk about the chance of sharing a few days together in Crete. An attractive thought, but The Virgin's mind was struggling with the implications of her call. How could she possibly not know about the container's arrival? The idea troubled him for the rest of the day.

Next day brought other things to worry about. The Virgin drove out to RomDril-1 to talk about job planning. As he started down the location road towards the rig he could see nothing much was happening. The kelly was down and no drillpipe stood in the derrick. Must all be drilling ahead, he thought. Then, as more of the location came into view, he realised that the flare pit was burning. Flames were playing fiercely over the pit walls and black smoke rushed away in the wind. There was no one on the floor or even anywhere around the rig. He pulled up at Terry's door. It was not locked and Terry sat writing at his desk.

"Hello stranger. Come to join in the fun?"

"You hit something?"

"You'd better believe it. Didn't you notice how quiet everything is? H_2S. Lots of it. Nearly wiped out the village last night."

The Virgin was stunned. "What happened?"

"We just got there early, I guess. That's the trouble with exploration. Drilling along happily and suddenly we lost everything. Tried to move but we'd stuck fast. Most of the mud on location's gone. You should have been here! I was running around like an idiot shutting everything in and getting the choke manifold on line. And you know what? There's no chokes on location. Not one."

"No chokes? How -?"

"Don't ask. We've got the choke valve – we know that's old and cut out. What I didn't know was RomDril 1 and 2 only have one lousy choke nipple each – but it's got no bean in it. There's only one choke between them. Can you believe that? Only one choke and that's on RomDril-2 at the moment. We're hot-shotting a bunch of them up from the desert just now. And the kelly cock's leaking. The annular preventer closed more or less but we were kelly down so I can't use the pipe rams. And the kill line valve – they tried to use it as a choke and – guess what? It cut out – surprise, surprise. Boy, am I glad I got a fire going in the flare pit. There was nothing holding it all back for a while there. There's not much holding it back now, to be honest."

The Virgin thought for a moment. This was dangerous. The well was basically out of control. If they could not shut it in at the surface, and they had been losing mud... This was very bad. "How much H_2S?"

"Oh – not much," Terry joked. "Say 300, 400,000 ppm. But I've only got a mickey-mouse hand held detector. I can't be sure. Gas detection is something that TAMCO feels is a luxury. Unnecessary. Only foreigners need stuff like that. "

"Jesus Christ! And you're just sitting here? You got a Scott pack?"

Terry waved him to shut the door. Behind it stood the cylinders of a breathing set and mask, ready to go. "Mine. My own personal one, bought by me in Canada. Only one on site, so everyone else has left location and gone into town. I'm managing the well all by my little self. No – don't worry. You're OK. The flare's going and anyway, the wind's good for the moment. Did you see anyone around the village? We cleared them all out last night."

The Virgin thought back. He did not recall seeing anyone as he drove up to the location turn-off. "Didn't see anyone. What happens now?"

"We wait. Nothing else to do. And hope the thing kills itself or the reservoir isn't too big. I've got your guys coming up because we'll end up pumping under pressure for sure. And they're sending up a couple of Miller hands from Waha to give me some help – at least I'll have someone who can tell his right hand from his left. They're bringing a lot of gear. The first thing we'll have to do is rig up a choke manifold and get the damn thing shut in. And then we'll see."

The Virgin's mind was still reeling. Hydrogen sulphide gas was the most feared killer in the oilfield. Low concentrations could be lethal. First you would get the rotten egg smell, and then it would anaesthetise your nose and you would not know if it was getting any worse. And then you would be dead. That was at relatively low concentrations of gas. Things happened very much faster with concentrations in the hundreds of thousands of parts per million. He wondered if TAMCO realised just what they had on their hands. They could easily have had dead people everywhere. From here to the sea.

"But you got the flare alight."

"Yes. My nasty suspicious mind. I had the mud man start a fire of cardboard and pallets as soon as it started. Thank God. He was a useless piece of -- never mind. He lit the fire after I'd shouted at him enough, then when the well really started to blow, he fell over. Just like that. He couldn't move. Must have been the shock. One minute he was standing near the pit, and the next he keeled over. I thought the gas had got him but I couldn't smell anything. When I got to him he was babbling, and as weak as a jelly fish. Just couldn't move. His arms and legs all floppy. A couple of his friends dragged him off and drove him away somewhere. Useless prick!"

"Anything I can help you with at the moment?"

"Well, since you ask, I'd like to get a diesel line over to the pit. Just in case it starts puffing and blowing. I'd hate for that fire to go out. I was thinking of going out now, but it'll be that much easier with two of us."

For the next hour they struggled and sweated, laying a make-shift hose from the diesel tank right across the location to the flare pit. It was worse for Terry. He wore the heavy Scott pack. The Virgin had no protection at all and stayed very close to Terry, near enough to make a grab for the spare mouthpiece in emergency.

They were walking back to Terry's office when there was an impact that The Virgin felt through his boots at the same time that it struck his ears. It sounded like a cannon shot followed by the crash and clangour of falling steel. They ran without thought, not looking back but purely sprinting to get out of the reach of the collapsing derrick.

As they rounded the first buildings, The Virgin risked a look over his shoulder. The derrick was still standing. He stopped and peered around the building trying to make out what had given way. The drilling line was swinging in wild swathes between the legs of the A-frame. It took a moment before he could recognize what he was looking at. The well was blowing up into the derrick, a single thick column of gassy mud that reached up to the crown of the derrick and beyond. Through the spray he could make out the kelly, propped in the derrick and bending beneath the weight of the block jammed crazily on top of it.

He tried to understand what had happened. The kelly should have been in the hole. They were kelly down when he had arrived on location, and now the whole forty foot or more of the Kelly was out of the well, connected to – connected to nothing. The string had parted. Just below the kelly he guessed, because that had been blown clear. They had felt the shock as hundreds of tonnes of tension released like a rubber band snapping. The kelly and the block, weighing tonnes between them had been thrown up into the derrick and now the well was open and blowing.

The Virgin looked for Terry. He was fumbling with his face mask, concentrating on getting it fitted over his head. The Virgin grabbed his arm and pulled him into the open. "The string's broken!" he shouted. "Close the rams!"

Terry stared for a moment at the mess in front of him. He settled the mask around his face and started out for the remote BOP panel. He walked heavily. The Virgin watched as he pushed the levers across, releasing the stored nitrogen from the Koomey unit to activate the three sets of rams and close the blow-out preventer. The spout of mud stopped immediately. The flames in the flare pit hissed and leapt higher as pressure was diverted back to them.

Terry was smiling as he returned. "Oh well. It had to happen. At least there's nothing else much that can go wrong now."

The Virgin thought about the parted drill string corkscrewed in the hole like a piece of wet spaghetti. Now they had no way of circulating to the bottom of the hole. Even when the equipment came up from the desert, they would not be able to kill the well. Not until they had run in and managed to fish the broken stub of drill pipe. And even then, the crap that was right now settling around the bottom of the drill pipe would block any chance of circulation of the hole. They would have to shoot some holes in the pipe further up to get circulation. He shook his head. Hitting a gas pocket was enough trouble under normal circumstances; hitting one with a RomDril rig was a nightmare.

"Right," said Terry. "Nothing else we can do at the moment. How about pissing off and getting me some lunch? I haven't eaten since yesterday. And then if you don't mind sitting here, I'll get my head down for a few hours. I think this one's going to go on and on and on."

The Virgin spent the next 36 hours on location. Help slowly arrived from the desert. TAMCO had done a whip around of the service companies to get enough Scott packs on site. The two Millers hands had brought up a pick-up load of goodies and together the four of them had strung together a choke manifold. That brought the well more or less under control; they could shut it off at any time but it was better to allow it to continue burning and monitor the pressure.

On the second day more supplies came in. Gel and barite to mix more mud. More hoses and pipe work. The MacAllans unit and crew. Discussions with the Romanians brought the crew back to work and they were getting ready to start fishing when The Virgin finally left for home. He was tired, dirty and hungry.

Saturday and he was late out of bed next morning, and late arriving at the office. Abdul had already opened up and Rabka was at her desk. Sitting in his office were Mostyn and Stanford. Stanford was wearing an old fashioned tropical suit in off-white linen. He looked creased, but relaxed and happy. Mostyn jumped up and started to speak quickly.

"Greg – how are you? Surprised to see us? Here, meet my boss, Mr Houghton, Export Manager for Karelia."

They were shaking hands and willing The Virgin to get over his confusion.

"What are you doing here?" he asked. "I mean, back so soon?"

"Oh, perhaps Mr Houghton doesn't trust me out by myself. No, seriously, I had a good time here after I left you. I think I did some real good in Almadi. I had no idea what Tabriz was like... Things look very hopeful, so Mr Houghton has come to see for himself. I've got an appointment for him to see Joe this morning – for some background – and we'll take it from there. I think I'm going to be a hero after this trip is finished."

The Virgin left them alone while he made the coffee. His mind raced over what had happened. First the phone call from Elena asking if the container had arrived, and now Stanford was here. Himself; in person. In hostile territory. That must be a significant risk, so why had he come? He carried in their cups and went back for the sugar and powdered milk.

Stanford was not going to discuss anything important within reach of potential bugs, but he did ask whether Greg had been happy with the chemical delivery, and whether the container had been in good shape. The Virgin took him through to meet Abdul; at least he had seen the container being unloaded even if only from the window of the Customs building. As they left Mostyn asked about the Hash; could Greg pick them up for the run?

Stanford was in the back seat as Greg drove up to Barani. The Virgin introduced him as 'a real English gentleman' which made him fair game for the Polish girls. Danka and Wanda packed in on either side and he sat uncomfortably between them with his hands on his knees. He seemed out of his depth. The run that day was at 19.2 km – a patch of scrubby trees on the way out of town. Stanford was still bemused as the pack set out across the muddy ground, ducking under tree branches and calling out to each other.

It was good country for a covert meeting. The Virgin padded along behind Stanford until he felt safe and slowed to a walk. "Strange life you live, Greg," he said. "I never imagined Tabriz would be like this."

"Cold and muddy, you mean?"

"Well, that too. But so many foreigners – and just running about freely. I'd pictured it as more confined, I suppose. You know, guards on every corner and suspicious figures following you."

"That sort of thing's too much trouble for them. And I think they know there's not much worth protecting anyway. Who really cares about Tabriz?"

"I do, for one. The Great Man might not be doing much at the moment, but he's got a history of crazy ideas. That's why he's so frightening. You just never know what piece of idiocy he'll dream up next."

"So – why are you here? Anything to do with me? Oh, look out. They're coming back." The pack had run a false trail and were straggling back through the bushes looking for the real one. The Virgin and Stanford stood aside to let them past and followed in their wake.

"Greg, you must be crazy. I can't remember doing anything like this since I was in short trousers. And I didn't volunteer for it then. Now, let's talk while we've got the chance. We've lost the container."

"What? Lost it? But it's arrived; everything's fine."

"No it's not. We want to know where it's gone. We've had a cock-up, I'm afraid. A complete cock-up. We put satellite tracking on the container, but we didn't anticipate you would cover it with a tarpaulin."

"I'm sorry…" The Virgin did not understand.

"There's a transceiver hidden on it. In the carrying frame. With batteries recharged by a couple of square centimetres of solar panel. But your ship's crew wrapped the whole thing up in a tarpaulin and it looks as if the batteries have gone flat. Stupid, isn't it? A whole operation nearly ruined because of a flat battery. You'd think the technical people would be a bit smarter. So we don't know where the container was taken. We saw it on the ship. It was right up in the bows and the satellite could see it clearly. But the satellite was over the horizon when the damn thing was unloaded and we didn't see where it was taken. We've got to find it and set it off when it will do the most damage."

"Oh Jesus! So it's still sitting out there. And some-one's going to open it one day…"

"Well, at least the Russians have gone, so you don't have to worry about them opening it. Help us find it, and we'll blow it straight away."

The Virgin's stomach sank to his shoes. His fingernails, his whole future, depended on no one discovering what was in the container. Oh shit! Now he was in trouble.

The Bash that night was at the Cypriot camp, a construction camp staffed by Bangladeshi workers and lots of horny young Greek engineers called Georgio. Noddy was in fine form, the beer was not too undrinkable and the girls showed signs of wanting to dance later. Mostyn scored a compulsory drink for being stupid enough to return to Tabriz, and a second one for being stupid enough to bring his boss with him. Stanford was blessed with a drink as an introduction to the Hash and given the name San Francisco as a reference either to his saintly appearance or to Stanford University. Or possibly both. He took the ceremonies in his stride and did not complain too loudly about the beer.

Thinking about it afterwards, The Virgin decided that Stanford had taken a big chance coming into Tabriz as a representative of Karelia. If the container was unmasked while he was in the country, he would be a sitting duck. And now it had to be found. The satellite could not see it; the whole town had been searched inch by inch and the container was not out in the open. The camp behind the tannery was still the most likely place it had gone, but it must be under cover. Somehow, he would have to get a look inside the camp.

He had little time to work on the problem. The well at RomDril-1 had slowly killed itself. The flow of gas had steadily slowed as the well manufactured its own mud from reservoir liquids and debris. After a couple of days the only gas reaching the surface came from the degassing of the mud column. The fates had been kind to them and the hydrogen sulphide had probably come from a small pocket of reservoir rock, no more. They had stripped in and fished for the broken drill pipe, an easy job as fishing operations go because the stub was high in the well and resting against the inside of the casing. As expected, the drill pipe was plugged with debris high above the bit and Revard's ran in with a cutting charge to part the pipe and allow circulation to resume. Within two days the mud was in good shape again and no more gas was coming back to surface. TAMCO decided to set a cement plug in the hole and follow that up by setting the 9-5/8" casing early, before drilling ahead again. The Virgin was tied up with the job planning and it was several days after Mostyn and Stanford had left before he decided to act.

He started by picking Danka up after her shift at the hospital and taking her for a walk on the beach at Cape Horn. The autumn night when Dov Nagel had come into their life was far behind them now. Spring was coming to the Mediterranean and they could stroll on the sand wearing no more than light sweaters. Days were longer now and the wind had lost its bite. They struggled past the low dunes where they had sat and watched the soldiers clambering into their boats and disappearing into the darkness. The narrow strip of beach was clean, swept of its debris by the winter storms and ready for the summer visitors who would soon be coming.

"Was good night, no Virgin?" chuckled Danka.

"Yes – yes, I suppose it was," he answered. "The start of a lot of trouble. For me, anyway."

"You have problem, Virgin?" They were both breathing heavily as they struggled with the soft sand.

"Yes, I have. And I'm not sure what to do about it."

"First you tell me," she said.

"Right. I think I'll have to." He had thought hard about Danka and how much he should tell her. The trouble was that the smallest glimpse of the picture would put her at risk. There was no way of avoiding it. He did not see why she should ever be questioned about what she knew, but if she ever was… Then again, he reflected, if she was ever tied to Dov and the death of the little Palestinian doctor, she would be finished anyway. Not to mention the disappearance of the two Russians, when she just happened to be along for the ride.

"Do you know why the Russians were really here?" he started.

"Of course, Virgin. They make chemical bombs for Mr Kowalski."

Kowalski. The Polish equivalent of Mr Smith. That was how the Polish staff referred to the Great Man between themselves. They did not want to be overheard saying anything disrespectful about him. "But you got that from the radio, right?" he asked.

"No – is true. Everyone know. Victor talk too much."

"Right – well, that makes it a little easier. Look, I'll tell you the problem but just don't ask any questions about why or how or anything like that. I'm looking for a big container of chemical that was coming for Victor. It should have been delivered to him last week, but now I don't know where it is."

She thought for a moment. "Big? How big?"

"Oh – six metres long – like a shipping container. Probably covered in a green tarpaulin."

"What is tarpaulin, Virgin?"

"A waterproof cover. Made of heavy sheet. Like tent material."

"And you think it goes inside the camp for Victor?"

"Yes."

"But it is too difficult for me to go inside…" He could see she was trying to think of a way of getting in herself.

"No – not you. May be one of the men could look over the wall. How about Janusz?"

"Ah – Janusz. This is better. Janusz can go inside. He makes work like electrician. What is time? Is after work. Come on, we go to Janusz."

They arrived at the tannery soon after work had finished for the day. Janusz, cheerful as ever, was talkative and still sober. They sat in his small cell and drank. The Virgin clutched a glass of neat flash and let the Polish conversation pass over him. He supposed that Danka had been clever enough not to bring up the question directly.

She patted him on the leg. "Hey, Virgin, wake up. Janusz like to make big barbecue on the beach."

"Oh yes?"

"But he got no meat. He talk with the Tabriz people next door, and they have too much meat. Good meat. From Bulgaria. But they like he fix the lights for play tennis."

Janusz got up and rummaged in the drawer next to his bed. He returned with a small halogen tube. It was misty and one end was broken. He tried to talk directly to The Virgin but Danka translated. "He like to have six the same like this one. You can find for him. He say you can buy in souk."

Why not, he thought, and took the old tube. Danka continued, "Tomorrow is shopping day for the men here. If you bring to my flat tomorrow after work, he will come to Barani."

Next day The Virgin took time out from the office to dive into the souk and buy the halogen tubes. He swung past Barani to have a coffee with Danka and leave the tubes with her. Then it was off to the rig to go over the 9-5/8" casing design with Terry. He would need to start ordering cement and chemicals from the desert in the next day or two and he still had to get the design basics past Tayfun.

As he drove out to the rig he was thinking of Stanford – Mr Houghton as he had now become. Why had he bothered coming all the way out to Tabriz? Apparently he knew Major Jamal, and there must be a chance that Major Jamal or one of his colleagues would recognize him. Was the missing shipment important enough to justify the risk? Or was Stanford just tired of sitting in London? Of course, there might be other reasons for his trip. You had to hope that Stanford had a contact or two in Almadi as well. Perhaps there were matters of high policy that inspired his trip and The Virgin's concerns were just a sideshow. The Virgin hoped so. He definitely did not want to be the centre of attention.

He was the centre of attention when he pulled onto location. Terry and Rene De Groot were standing outside the office, deep in discussion.

"Here he is!" Terry greeted him. "The answer to a maiden's prayer."

"Hi Rene, Terry. No maidens that I can see."

"Never mind that. We were just scratching our heads, but now you're here. You need to be at the police post on the Cape Town Road at three o'clock. Can you do that?"

"What? Why?"

"We need a cross-over," said Rene. "RomDril don't have anything with a 1501 thread on it so we can't get onto the drill-pipe."

"But…"

"No time for that," said Terry. "Get your ass back in your car and off you go. We'll need it back up here at six this evening, so you've just got time."

"Florian's sending a pick-up as far as the police post," said Rene. "We were just wondering how we would get some-one to meet it. Wait a minute, and I'll get you some invoices to go down to Florian."

The Virgin drove south in a mood of resignation. It was a boring drive at the best of times, but being forced to do it because RomDril did not have a normal complement of cross-overs on their rig – well, that made it worse. And the drive gave him plenty of time to worry about the missing container.

He did not see Danka again until the next Hash. Her news was not good. "Is not present, Virgin. Nothing. Janusz look everywhere, but not present. He say that there is one place at the back where he cannot see. The Army keep old trucks there, and possible it is there. Janusz cannot go there but he say that if you come up from behind, you can see everything, if you want." He thanked her and acted as if it did not matter.

In the office next morning he mulled over the problem. Should he call Elena and give her the bad news, or should he wait until he could go and look for himself? That was the question. And then he had an inkling of an idea. He left the office as soon as he could and went home to change into coveralls.

He went to the rig. It was a beautiful day to be outside, clear spring weather with only a hint of the oppressive summer heat waiting ahead. March was ghibli season, when dry dust storms from the desert could blanket everything for days at a time and shut down all movement in the oil fields, but today the wind blew cool and fresh, straight from the sea. Without the missing container on his mind, The Virgin would have been happy to be out visiting the rig. Terry was busy with a novel, reading with his feet up on the desk, ignoring the rig slowly drilling out the cement plug that Rene had set the night before.

"Hey man! Bored with the office?"

"How d'you guess? Hey look – mind if I climb the mast? Should be a good view today."

Terry thought about it for a second then put his paperback face down on the table. "Why not? Sounds like a good thing to do before lunch. Think I'll come with you. Let's go inspect your gear first, and then we'll go up."

There was a short section of safety cage around the beginning of the ladder to the monkey board. Higher up the cage had been wiped off during some long-ago rig move and never replaced. The safety harness must have gone the same way, and the two men climbed free, the old-fashioned way. The Virgin was glad it was an A-frame derrick and the ladder leaned in a little. A single mast would have had a truly vertical ladder.

They stepped out onto the monkey board. It was empty. All the drill pipe was in the hole, bar a few stands swaying gently with the rhythm of the rig. The wind was stronger here and The Virgin felt uneasy at the way the floor danced beneath his feet.

Terry was breathing heavily. "Damn – I've got to give up those cigarettes. I used to run up and down here like nothing when I worked for a living."

"Old age, Terry, old age. Your lady's going to trade you in for new model one of these days."

"Some chance of that! She's about the same shape as I am. Or even fatter. Come on, let's keep going before I change my mind."

They were already thirty metres above the drill floor, say thirty-five above the ground. They stepped out onto the next ladder and carried on climbing the remaining twenty-five metres or so up to the crown. The Virgin felt gravity dragging at his mind. He did not look down, and gripped the steel ladder rungs fiercely.

The crown platform was filthy. In the centre of the platform sat the black mass of the crown block, its multiple pulleys carrying the heavy drilling line. Grease spatter from the drill line coated everything. The Virgin crept cautiously along the narrow walkway around the sheaves of the crown block, touching nothing, hand held centimetres above the railing just in case. The mud pumps and the vibrations of the turntable made the world dance under him. He looked down. The ground looked a long way away. Sixty metres – say two hundred feet in the old money. Terry looked out contentedly over the sea, the wind flapping his shirt. The blue-grey, ageless Mediterranean – far from wine-dark – stretched to the sharp line of the horizon.

The Virgin turned and searched inland. Eyetie Joe's camp was below, a scatter of rickety accommodation units set in tall weeds, with a bone-yard of derelict construction equipment and tanks behind them. The tannery lay beyond, a modern industrial complex ready to equip all the neighbouring countries with the finest tanned leather. He tried to pick out the Army camp attached to it. It was a small spread of buildings at the back, set around a tennis court with floodlights. They must be the ones that Janusz had worked on. Behind the buildings, on the side towards the rig, was another bone-yard. It was much smaller than Eyetie Joe's and contained smaller items of dead equipment. The Virgin scanned it carefully. No container in sight, but a low corrugated iron building ran along the fence, with its back towards the rig. It had a single pitched roof sloped out to the fence. The Virgin guessed that it was covered parking for trucks and large vehicles, and that it was open on the other side. It could be hiding the container. He would need to look at it from the front. If he could follow the rough track that ran through the stones and weeds of the surrounding waste land, he would skirt the Army camp and the tannery. He would be able to peep under that roof.

"Crappy sort of place, ain't it?" Terry was standing beside him.

"Wouldn't win any prizes. Rubbish everywhere. If only you could sell all that gear for scrap. You could fill ships…"

"Yeah. Never understood why they don't do it. Just let everything rust away. Remind me why I love this country. You ready for down?"

The Virgin had an opportunity to look more closely for the container that Saturday. That week the post-run Bash would be held at Eyetie Joe's. He skipped the Hash and went straight to Eyetie Joe's, arriving twenty minutes before dusk and long before the Hashers were due. Parking his car beside the empty mess-hall, he stripped to his jogging clothes and took an evening run for exercise.

He soon found the track he had seen from the rig. It must have been a regular path for Eyetie Joe's workers at one time because there was a hole in the rusted fence to give easy access. He dipped through the hole and started to jog up the rough track. It took very little traffic to keep a path open in this dry and dusty land, and he was able to run freely out into the empty space behind Eyetie Joe's. There was little to see; dust, stones and the occasional camel-thorn. He jogged on, trying to orient himself and pick up the fence-line of the tannery.

It was not far away. The path headed straight for the tannery, evidence that at some time there was a lot of contact between the inmates of the two camps. Perhaps in the high old days when all the contractors were busy, the Italians and the Poles had got together to party. Now the Italians had all gone home, but their path remained. The Virgin jogged on, breathing heavily. He was being taken to the nearest corner of the tannery camp, just at the junction with the Army camp behind it. The Virgin avoided staring at the Army camp and looked straight ahead.

This was when he might get stopped. Not very likely in the slack and laid-back atmosphere of Sabah, but you never could tell when some crazy young bully with a Kalashnikov might decide to play the revolutionary. As he drew nearer he was aware of a figure behind the wire. A lightly built man in a white djellabiyah and turban. He had an old man's stoop. He watched The Virgin intently as he approached.

The Virgin forced himself to relax. This figure did not look military even by the casual standards of Tabriz. There was no Kalashnikov for a start. Then The Virgin made out goats foraging behind him; he was a goatherd, nothing more.

When he was close enough to see the old man's straggly white moustache, The Virgin waved.

"Salaam Aleikum," called the man. "Marhaba!" He was still rapt by the sight of an adult running.

"Salaam," The Virgin called back and speeded up a little. The man's goats were grazing in the Army bone-yard. Beyond them he could look under the long roof he had seen from the rig. It was nearly empty. Two deceased trucks and a trailer stood in the shade. The weeds the goats were exploring had not been disturbed in a long time. He continued on his way, not looking back. He would run around in a loop and head back to Eyetie Joe's. With a bit of luck he would get back before the Hashers arrived and no one would see him. He was already due for a compulsory drink for the offence of Bashing and not Hashing. If no one saw him return, he would avoid being given an additional one for secret jogging.

Next day he sent Abdul to the Post Office to search for a missing parcel sent by Elena, and pretended disappointment when he returned empty handed. He called and gave Elena the bad news. She seemed resigned and he got no hint of what would happen next. He decided to put his troubles behind him and go looking for a game of volleyball with the Filipino nurses.

The Virgin returned to the office from a design meeting with Tayfun to find a fax from Karelia curling out of the machine. He tore it off and read. A short letter from Houghton.

Dear Mr Cartwright,

Thank you for your hospitality during our recent visit. Please find the time to visit us in Poole on your next trip to England, and I will be happy to return your kindness.

I have a favour to ask. There has been a request from our insurance company for the return of the insurance certificate for the chemical shipping container. Unfortunately we cannot locate this certificate and we believe that it may have been sent – by mistake – with the container itself. Perhaps your client has it. I wonder if you would be kind enough to ask him to check? If he has not yet found it, it should be located with the other documents relating to the container in a waterproof envelope on the inside of the security cover for the tank valves. This cover is on the front right-hand side of the tank and is secured with a small padlock. The key to the padlock was sent with the shipping invoice and certificate of origin, and your client should already have it.

I am sorry to trouble you and your client with such a simple bureaucratic matter, but your help would certainly be appreciated,

Yours sincerely,

R.T. Houghton
Export Sales Manager

The Virgin re-read the letter and wondered what Stanford was up to. London must have some kind of surveillance on Major Jamal's office. Perhaps they were counting on watching cars and seeing where they went to retrieve the certificate. Perhaps the surveillance would be from a satellite. He went to the window and looked up. The sky was cloudless. Good weather for satellites, he supposed but that was no guarantee of success. Even if Major Jamal or Captain Zella were inclined to help, they were quite capable of putting things off until tonight. Then again, he mused, did satellites rely on old-fashioned cameras nowadays? Didn't they have things like infrared sensors and special cloud penetrating radar? Thinking about it, he had even heard of ground penetrating radar. He gave up thinking and called Major Jamal. He offered to fax him a copy of the letter but Major Jamal did not seem to think it was necessary. He probably had a copy anyway.

He was in Tayfun's office later that morning looking at cement lab reports spread over the desk when they were both surprised by a heavy rumble of thunder. That was unusual in Sabah at any time but unheard of in the dry months. They stopped reading and went to the window. The sky was still cloudless but the thunder rumbled again, longer and louder this time.

They looked at each other. "Thunder?" asked Tayfun. The noise came again, this time sharp enough to make the windows rattle.

"Must be blasting," said The Virgin. "I wonder what they're up to."

As they watched, a dark grey cloud rose above the houses in the distance. The explosions were clear and frequent now. A massive blast threw debris high into the sky. An instant later they felt it shudder through their feet.

"My God – it must be an ammunition dump," said Tayfun as some sort of missile corkscrewed a trail of smoke up into the air. A whistling rush from behind the TAMCO building ended in a powerful blast. They stood stunned for a moment and listened to a cascade of falling glass.

"I'm getting out of here," said The Virgin and dashed for the corridor. It was full of men running for the stairs. He joined the rush.

Think, think, think, he told himself as he ran. The wide marble staircase down to the lobby was a mass of shouting, panicking men. Tayfun threw himself into the crush but The Virgin held back and waited. Someone fell and suddenly he was looking down at a tumbling mass of humanity on the lower flight. For a moment men were rolling and crawling over their friends until they could get to their feet. As quickly as it had happened, the blockage cleared and the rush was on again.

The Virgin watched in disbelief as the flood of men cleared and the staircase emptied leaving only two bodies, one moving feebly. It was un-naturally quiet in the lobby. He walked slowly down. As he turned onto the last flight of steps he saw that the large plate glass windows surrounding the main door had dissolved into heaps of shards. There was another whistling rush and he threw himself to the ground, covering his head in a reflex as an explosion split the air.

Beside him was the body that was lying still. He was looking into the staring eyes of a bald man. His glasses were crushed between his head and the white marble step. The Virgin took in the twist in his neck and realized that the man was dead. Reluctantly he reached out to feel for a pulse, knowing it was useless. The touch felt repulsive and he made no real effort to find the vital spot.

A moan came from the other man, and muttering in Arabic. The Virgin got to his feet and moved to help him. He had broken his lower leg; that much was obvious. His leg lay along the step and the ugly angle in it was clear. He looked young. Slim, bearded, with a mass of disordered hair. He was in pain; his face was white and beaded in sweat, a dribble of blood coming from the corner of his mouth. Another crash came from outside.

The Virgin knew he had to get under cover. Without thinking, he scooped the man up in his arms. The man screamed and fainted. The Virgin carried the body down to the lobby floor and turned sharply to hide under the steps. He laid the man out on the floor beneath the sloping concrete ceiling. They should be safe enough. He cowered and listened nervously.

God bless the Tabrizi Army, he thought. I wonder what piece of stupidity caused this? He had heard of something similar in Islamabad, an ammunition dump exploding and showering part of the city with unexploded shells and live mortar bombs. MacAllans had the corner torn off a pump unit by the force of an unprimed 150mm shell hurtling down out of the blue. He had spoken with the engineer who had been there that day. He had rushed to join all the other MacAllans hands that were cowering in the vehicle maintenance pit in the workshop, but the thought of a shell coming through the roof and into the pit had put him off. He had taken refuge under a large Cat generator. The Virgin remembered that bombardment had lasted for hours.

The man beside him started to come round again. He was trying to focus his eyes and make sense of his situation. The Virgin patted his shoulder by way of re-assurance but the man just moaned. He wondered if he could find the man some water. There was a coffee machine on the floor above; that had paper cups, but it was a long way away. As if to confirm The Virgin's decision to stay under cover, the ground shook again with another thunderclap.

He looked back on the following hour as one of the worst of his life. There was nothing he could do for the man with the broken leg. They just had to wait until it was safe to go outside. All the man could do was wait and suffer, but he had decided not to do it in silence. He started to cry out, sometimes in hysterical chanting and sometimes letting his voice rise to a penetrating shriek. The Virgin quickly gave up trying to comfort him and just tried to shut out the noise.

It was the shrieking that eventually brought help. The large explosions tailed off until nothing but the distant crackle of exploding small arms ammunition could be heard. A face peeped under the stairs and soon a crowd of shouting, officious volunteers surrounded the injured man. The Virgin left them ordering each other to do something and crept away.

Outside the world appeared more or less normal. The explosion that had broken the windows at the front of the TAMCO building had come from something hitting the ornamental fountain outside. It was wrecked and water gurgled in the gutter. Apart from that, he could see no damage. His car looked safe and he gingerly drove into town.

Abdul and Rabka were waiting for him, glad he was safe. "It was the Americans," said Abdul. "My brother says before the explosion he saw a big plane flying high up, and the Israelis only have small planes. So it must have been the Americans."

"How are your families?" asked The Virgin. "Do you want to go home?"

"Yes – we are going," said Rabka. "We have telephoned and they are safe but my mother is crying. We were only waiting to see you first."

"I think you should go home too," said Abdul. "After this the Army will be stopping all the roads. And make sure you have your desert pass and TAMCO pass and your badaka with you all the time, or you will have trouble."

The Virgin toyed with the idea of going to Barani to sit around with Danka for company, but he did not want to sleep there, and he definitely did not want drive around after dark. He gave Florian a quick call and locked up the office.

Next morning the traffic flowed normally as he left home. In the centre of the first roundabout sat two Toyota pick-ups with twin light antiaircraft guns mounted in their trays. Their crews, wearing an assortment of military clothes, headscarves and sandals, were seated around a small cooking fire. The Virgin continued into town and passed soldiers at every intersection. At the traffic lights near his office a larger group was sitting by two Russian APCs. The traffic lights had been switched off and two young soldiers were extending the chaos by their efforts to control the crossing.

Abdul was full of news. "The television says that Israeli terrorists are inside Sabah but the Army will find them. Today there will be soldiers all around the town … you will have trouble to go to the rig, I think. And TAMCO is closed for the funerals."

"Funerals?"

"Yes, one man was dead inside TAMCO and another one died in the mosque. He had a heart problem, I think. So TAMCO is closed."

"So - the television thinks it was the Israelis and not the Americans. I'm surprised they didn't decide it was both."

"But they did! They say the American Number 6 Fleet brought the terrorists to Sabah in the night and then Jewish terrorists from Egypt took them in taxis to attack the ammunition store. It's true, I know it. My brother was in the souk the night before and he was in one shop and look what happens. He is inside the shop when one man comes. Every one is saying 'Salaam, salaam' but the man says by surprise 'shalom', like the Israelis say. Then he ran away. I know the Israelis are in Sabah all the time."

Hmmm – maybe, thought The Virgin, knowing better than to argue. "But the Army is going to surround Sabah? Perhaps you'd better come with me to the rig. You can talk our way through. Have you got time for that?"

With Abdul beside him, The Virgin pushed his way into the traffic stream and steered onto the wide processional way that ran in front of the People's Hotel.

"There's soldiers everywhere, Abdul. I didn't realize the Great Man had so many around here. But has he got enough to surround the town?"

"He is sending them from Almadi. They are coming to the airport this morning. There will be enough, you will see. Tabriz is very strong in its soldiers."

"They look very dangerous to me," said The Virgin diplomatically.

"Oh yes – very dangerous. If we find the Israelis they will have no chance."

From somewhere ahead of them came a burst of firing. The Virgin looked behind him and started to pull over, but the rest of the traffic stream continued as normal. "I think no problem," said Abdul.

"Sounded like a problem to me," but none of the other cars seemed to pay any attention. He drove on. Beside the road sat an APC, with its crew sheltering behind it. The turret-mounted machinegun on the APC was firing short bursts into a neighbouring apartment block. The smoke drifted across the road.

"Jesus! Let's get out of here!" He steered wide, avoiding the cars slowing down to watch the fun. "What the hell are they doing? A gun like that can fire straight through a building. God knows what damage they're doing on the other side."

"Perhaps they find the Israelis…" but even Abdul could not sound hopeful.

They crossed the Army line at the edge of town. A new road block had been set up and The Virgin handed his papers to Abdul. Uniformed police were checking papers and staring into the cars, but today soldiers were standing behind them. As the car crept forward he could see a single line of soldiers stretching out across the rough ground on either side of the road. One man every ten metres, just standing there with his Kalashnikov, looking very bored. The Great Man had surrounded the town, just as he had promised. The check on car and papers was cursory, as if everyone knew the whole exercise was a waste of time. Israelis were known to be too clever to be caught.

On the rig, all Terry could talk about was the explosion. How it had been felt on the rig, how he had climbed the mast to get a better look at the distant cloud. He guessed it had happened somewhere near the airport. That squared with what The Virgin had seen as well, but he was not going anywhere near it. He was sure the Tabrizis would be far too sensitive for the next week or so. Terry had been listening to the BBC who confirmed an ammunition dump explosion, and that many people were believed to have been killed. The Tabrizi government had admitted to nothing so far. Then Terry remembered he had a message for The Virgin; two truckloads of cement were waiting at the road block on the other side of town. Someone would have to go and assure the police that they were not a threat to national security and could be allowed through. That was a job for Abdul and The Virgin drove him back into town to pick up his car.

After he closed the office that afternoon The Virgin drove to Barani to see what news Danka had from the hospital. She came to the door in her night dress, bleary eyed and tousle haired. "Boże, Virgin, you wake me up. Never mind. I make coffee. And lunch. But quiet please – Wanda is sleeping."

The Virgin settled in the tiny kitchen and watched Danka making sandwiches while the kettle boiled. Under her boring nightdress she wobbled delightfully as she sawed at the bread. "So – what's happening at the hospital? The explosion must have been quite near to you."

"True, Virgin, very true. Was like the war. Explosions, broken windows. And all the time the floor is shaking. We are all hiding on the floor - doctors, patients, nurses, all crying. There is no electricity now. No lights, no hot water." She settled her fat bottom onto the stool on the other side of the table and sipped her coffee. "Virgin, I tell you, I never have fear like this before. I am shaking all over. And then the people start coming. So many people. I think the houses fall down, so people have many broken bones, skull fracture, internal injury. Some burns. Terrible. We want blood too much but the blood bank is empty. Everyone must give blood and use immediately. No testing – very dangerous but what can you do? I work all night – come back for breakfast. We all work all night."

Wanda appeared in the doorway, also in her nightdress, and The Virgin moved his stool along to let her squeeze in. She shared his plate. She was feeling depressed. "I go back to Poland, Virgin. I have enough. This place is crazy. And dangerous. Very bad. And for what do we stay? A little money? Is not enough. I go back. I have my children, my husband. Good food – sausage – friends – sex..."

"Oh Wanda, you can't leave us. What would we do without you?" teased The Virgin.

"I care for that?" she asked, reaching for a cigarette packet and the empty sardine tin from the shelf. "If you love us so much, take us to live in your big villa. Not this shitty place."

"Yes, Virgin, we come and live with you," said Danka. "Cook, clean. Even sex sometimes – if you are polite."

"Sex as well? I'll have to think about that. Would it be both together or one at a time?"

Wanda pretended to slap him. "Both together! We are good Polish girls, Virgin. We are not like this."

"Maybe not – but I am. One beautiful Polish nurse is very good, but two would be even better."

Wanda stubbed out her cigarette in disgust. "Beautiful? Boże, Virgin, you are crazy. Like this country."

The Virgin was sitting alone in his office next morning when the door creaked open and Evelina looked in. He jumped up. "Wow – Evelina. You are a surprise. What would you like? Coffee?"

She sat and sipped her sweet coffee while The Virgin watched from the other side of the desk. She still looked pretty to him. Slim and black haired. And deep, deep eyes. But sexless. What a shame.

"How did you do with the explosion then? No-one hurt I hope."

She grimaced. "No, thank God. Everyone's safe. Most of us have lost our windows but that's all. We've covered them with cardboard, and the electricity came on again quickly – because of the hospital, I suppose. But there were so many patients. We lost some…"

"Must have been terrible. Danka was telling me."

"Yes – we all had to work hard to treat them. But it's better now. Most of them have gone home again. If they have homes to go to. The apartment blocks out that way are still standing, but with a lot of damage. The private houses have really suffered. Not so well built, I suppose, and many of them just collapsed. And you? You survived…"

"Oh, I was alright. I was visiting TAMCO at the time and I just hid under the stairs until it was all over."

"You know why I came? Captain Zella's been talking about you again."

The Virgin's ears stood up. "Me? What does he want with me?"

"I don't think he likes you. He asked me if I knew you, and then he told me he was going to make real trouble for you. I just thought I'd tell you."

The Virgin thought for a while. He did not think Zella could do too much by himself, especially with Major Jamal looking over his shoulder, but he could still make life difficult. And it was quite difficult enough in normal times. He was willing to bet that Harris had lodged his passport with the tax department again, and if Zella ever got his hands on that he could cause endless delays. Perhaps he had better say something for the benefit of the bugs. He guessed that any private conversation with a girl would be judged salacious enough to pass on to Major Jamal. "Has he caused you any more trouble?"

"No – he's not too bad at the moment. Mind you, I'll never let myself get caught alone with him again. I'll never forgive him for what he did."

"Never mind. Put it behind you and forget about it. You can't let someone like that influence your life."

"Easy for you to say, Virgin, easy for you. I still know what happened, and so does everyone else. I feel very ashamed about it."

"That's silly! There's lots of girls around who have done it for real and no one minds them. No one cares."

"But I care, Virgin. I care. One day I will want to marry and what will I tell my husband? Tell him about Captain Zella? How can I say that?"

"Don't worry about it. It won't be a problem. And if it is, well, come and marry me instead. I don't mind at all."

She smiled at him. "But you have Polish girls, Virgin, and your girl-friend in London too."

"I'd give them all up for you, Evelina. Just say the word and they're history."

After she had left, he sat and thought for a long time about Captain Zella and his potential for mischief. That put him in mind of Major Jamal and the insurance certificate. He telephoned and asked for Major Jamal.

He waited, listening to voices in the background. The phone was picked up. "Mr Cartwright. It is Captain Zella here. What do you want?"

The bastard himself. Oh well – no harm in being polite. "Good morning, Captain Zella. How are you this fine morning?"

"Well, Mr Cartwright, well. You wanted to speak to Major Jamal? I am sorry but he does not work here anymore. What did you want from him?"

The Virgin was shocked and disappointed. "Oh – I didn't know. He was looking for an insurance certificate for me. A certificate from the chemical container we sent you."

"I saw the fax," said Zella smoothly. "What does this certificate look like?"

"I really don't know. I suppose it will have the number of the container on it. And Karelia's name, of course. But the letterhead will be from an insurance company. Please don't worry about it too much. If Karelia have made a mistake, well, they'll just have to sort it out at their end. It's their problem."

"We will see, Mr Cartwright. If it is here, we will see."

The Virgin put the phone down with a shudder. If Major Jamal was out of the picture, Zella might get to be much more of a problem. Well, there was nothing that could be done about it. He waited until Rabka and Abdul came into work and left for the rig. At least the problems out there were real and could be dealt with. And the military cordon had already degenerated to small groups of soldiers camping out in the bushes and sleeping around the clock.

He spent the rest of the morning yarning with Terry but did not stay for his chicken lunch. Rabka had a surprise for him when he returned. "Captain Zella came looking for you. About eleven o'clock. Is he your friend?"

The Virgin thought about the bugs before answering. "No – I wouldn't call him a friend exactly. I know him from here, that's all."

"You must be careful with people like that in Tabriz. They can make a lot of trouble for you if they don't like you, you know. He had your passport with him. He showed it to me. He seemed cross that you weren't here."

Oh shit! How had he done that again? Or why had he done it? Did that mean he wanted another shipment of gas? Or worse? Or perhaps he just wanted something for himself – a visit to Amsterdam, for instance. Amsterdam was always popular with young Tabrizi clients. Zella would certainly find the chance of a trip with unlimited sex and alcohol enticing.

"Oh well," he told Rabka, "He should have called first. I suppose I'd better tell Harris about it all. If he wants me to go anywhere, he'd better allow extra time to recover the passport."

"Plenty of time," said Rabka. "If Captain Zella has it personally and he's not available when you want it…"

The Virgin found the thought of Captain Zella weighing on his mind that afternoon and he shut up the office early and went looking for Danka. He met her from the shuttle bus that brought the nurses back from the hospital and she led him upstairs. He stopped her on the stairs and asked her about Zella. Yes, she had seen him in the last couple of days, but he had not spoken to her. She had heard nothing. She took him to her apartment for coffee and in return The Virgin took her shopping down town.

The 9-5/8" cement job came on the next day. The casing was on bottom in the evening and The Virgin spent the rest of the night with Rene and the guys mixing and pumping cement for the first stage of the job. He helped as they cemented only the lower half of the hole because the formation would never support the weight of a full column of liquid cement. The job was successful and he drove back home just before dawn. Rene would be able to get his head down for a few hours before the rig was ready for the second stage, but that was an easier job and The Virgin felt justified in staying away. It was Friday after all.

Captain Zella caught him in his office later in the week. He came with a silent assistant carrying a brief case and they sat down without waiting for The Virgin to offer them chairs. Captain Zella refused a coffee and came straight to business. "Now, Mr Cartwright, tell me about this insurance certificate. Why is it needed?"

"I don't know. There was a fax from Karelia – that's all I know."

"Ah yes. The fax." He reached for his assistant to place a copy in his hand. "You are talking about this one?" He handed it over.

"Yes – that's the one. That's all I know about it."

"Who is this Mr Houghton?"

"Their Export Sales Manager, I suppose. He was here a couple of weeks ago. Seemed quite a nice man. You should visit him next time you're in England. I'm sure he'll be glad to take you around a little."

"Maybe. And what did he talk about when he was here?"

"Not much really. He asked if you were happy with the chemical and whether you'd want any more. That was all, I think. He was with one of his salesmen and they were going to visit some other people here and in Almadi. Mostly in Almadi, I think."

"So who did he visit here?"

"They spoke about Italco but I think that was just social. I don't think Italco buy anything, but they do know a lot of people. I don't think they talked about anyone else." *Listen to your own surveillance tapes, you little creep* was what he really wanted to say.

"What did he say about the insurance certificate?"

"Nothing. Never mentioned it. Reading his fax, I don't think he knew anything about it then. Look, do you want me to call him? I'll ask him to give you a call, if you like."

Zella was unfazed. "I don't think it is necessary. We will look to see if the document is in our files." He got to his feet and his assistant jumped up behind him. "Do not try to go anywhere, Mr Cartwright. Do not forget I have your passport, and I will want to ask you more questions."

It riled The Virgin to have to put up with this sort of bullying but he was in Tabriz. You expected a Tabrizi bureaucrat to abuse his power if he had the chance to control a foreigner. He decided to take it all in his stride but he asked Zella anyway. "I'm scheduled to go out for a training course in a couple of months. I guess you will have finished with my passport by then?"

"That will not be possible, Mr Cartwright. You must go for your course another time."

"Really? How long do you think you'll want to keep my passport?"

"We will see, Mr Cartwright. Perhaps next year it will be possible."

The Virgin fought to control his face and escorted Zella out of the office. As he stepped out into the corridor, Zella made his mind up about something. "You see, Mr Cartwright, Major Jamal is dead. He was going to find your insurance certificate and was involved in an accident. You call him and now he is dead. I will think about this very carefully."

The Virgin shut the door behind him very gently. He then forced himself to sit quietly in his office and think about what he had heard. Major Jamal was dead. The Virgin had sent him to find the insurance certificate on the container and he was dead – in an accident. Major Jamal had gone to the container, and there had been a massive explosion at the Army's munitions depot. And Major Jamal had died in 'an accident'.

The Virgin felt sick. Stanford had used him to kill Major Jamal, and anyone else who happened to be within range of the exploding munitions depot. They must have rigged the container to explode if anyone opened the cover for the valves. Probably an explosion big enough to destroy the tank and its contents, and anything nearby. It was just unfortunate that the Tabrizis had stored the tank in a munitions depot.

The Virgin realised he was in very deep trouble. He forced himself to think rationally. Captain Zella had said that the insurance certificate and Major Jamal's death were connected. He did not really think that. The Virgin was sure he did not suspect anything. If The

Virgin were under suspicion, he would have been taken away immediately.

Zella had not made the connection – yet. Perhaps he never would. And if he did? The Virgin was just an innocent salesman. Even a paranoid like Zella would have to admit that he could not have had anything to do with loading the container. On the other hand, The Virgin might just know something about it, and it would be worth a few fingernails to find out exactly what he did know. The Virgin would have to get out immediately. He could not risk being questioned. It was time to send a distress signal.

Elena was at home when he called, cooking lunch.

"Hey, Greg, I'm cooking Greek shrimps wrapped in bacon. Do you want to come?"

"I wish I could. I've just had some really bad news. They've impounded my passport. It looks like I won't be able to leave the country for ages, maybe not until next year or even later."

"No! What happened? Can they do that?"

"They can do what they want. Foreigners are on their own out here. A friend of mine died in an accident and they want to keep me here for questioning. As some sort of witness, I suppose."

"Greg, that's terrible. What friend? What sort of accident?"

"It was a Tabrizi friend, an important man called Major Jamal. He was a nice old man. I liked him but he's had an accident and I don't even know what sort of accident. I think the man holding my passport is just doing it to upset me. What could I know about any accident anyway? Or perhaps he's going to ask me to do something for him."

"Do something for him? Like what? Money?"

"Oh no – I shouldn't think so. I don't know. Perhaps it's business. I wish he'd just come straight out and ask me for whatever it is he wants. He should know that if he puts enough pressure on MacAllans, they can do quite a lot for him. He doesn't need to screw me around."

"But I was planning to go to Crete with you…"

"I guess you'll have to cancel that idea."

"What about Christmas?"

"I don't know. I just don't know. Perhaps he'll ask for something and we can get it all sorted out quickly. I hope. On the other hand…"

"But you must come for Christmas! That's ages away. Surely they'll give you back your passport by then. Or can you just leave without it?"

"Without it? Not a chance. You've got to have a passport with an exit visa to cross the border and here's one foreigner who's not playing any games crossing borders illegally. Don't worry, I'll get there for Christmas even if I have to put all your presents in a wheelbarrow and push it from here to Almadi." There – he had sent up the distress rocket. Elena took it in her stride.

"Oh Greg, I hope it won't come to that. You've spoilt my lunch now."

"Yeah – mine's not going to taste very good either."

The Virgin had to get out of the office. It was lunch time and the streets were empty. He drove aimlessly. There was nothing to do except brood and waste time until Danka would be free. He could not stop himself re-living Zella's visit and his hatred of the pencil moustache grew in his mind. He could see it wriggle up and down, semaphoring its owner's unique mix of vindictiveness and narrow stupidity. He shook off his mood and started to drive home. Then he realized that he should be checking if he was being followed. On the quiet road approaching his house he stopped the car as if he had changed his mind and turned back to go to the vegetable shop. The road was empty. No hint of a shifty glance or a following car caught by surprise. He bought fruit and vegetables, and carried on to the street of butchers. He parked again, this time under the rows of sheep's heads hanging over the shop doorways. Still no hint of a tail. He bought a kilo of camel steak and carried on.

It was still too early for Danka. He drove out of town on the coast road. Now he was sure that he was not being tailed. No one could follow him on that empty modern highway without being obvious. He went on to leave some oranges with Terry and drove cautiously back into town.

Danka's building was busy with people popping in and out, and he did not have to wait for entry. Danka was happy to see him, and even happier with the steak and vegetables. She did not want to walk on the beach but caught the urgency of The Virgin's mouthed message and changed her mind. He did not let her talk until they reached the beach.

"What is it, Virgin? You find the container?"

"No. Not that. I've got to leave. Urgently. I've got to get out, and Security have my passport. I'm in trouble, Danka."

"Boże, Virgin, what can I do?"

"Listen, you told me once the guys from the tannery go down to the desert for a picnic sometimes. I've got to get down to the desert. Secretly."

"But you can go to the desert. Go to your company."

He had thought about that. If the worst came to the worst, he would get down to Florian somehow and beg him to help. But there was not much a foreign organization could do when it came to crossing Tabrizi borders. "That's no good. That's the first place they'll look for me, and you can't hide in the camps. Too many Tabrizis around. Look, it's Wednesday today. Any chance we could talk a group of the guys into going down on Friday?"

"But what will you do, Virgin? You cannot live in the desert…"

"Don't ask, Danka. Just get me down the Cape Town Road, and I'll manage. Do you think you can do it?"

Once again The Virgin was sitting in Janusz's cell, sipping at his flash. Danka talking urgently with Janusz. They got up to go. "Wait, Virgin," she said as she left. "We do something, I think."

They returned with a stocky man with a greying walrus moustache. "Is Pawel, Virgin. He is manager now. The real manager goes to Warsaw."

Pawel held out a farmer's hand to shake. "Witajcie, Wirgin," he rumbled, and still holding The Virgin's hand said something to Danka.

"He says you're welcome and they will do their best to help. They can lend you a desert pass and badaka from a man who left last month. But we must be careful. No talking."

"Please tell him thank you. I'll need to drop some things here tomorrow after work."

"It is not a problem, Virgin. I tell him tomorrow we come with the meat for the picnic, and Pepsi, and your things. Then you come and sleep with me, and on the tomorrow they will take us from Barani. Good, no?" and Janusz was filling glasses all around to toast their fortune.

The Virgin dropped Danka off at Barani and drove into the packed suburbs of Sabah. He was looking for Rubberdy-Dub's villa. He lived with four other computer operators in a drab pile with a genuine Swedish sauna on the roof. The only one in the whole of Tabriz. Imported by a Scandinavian company back in the days when money flowed freely and new infrastructure projects were coming off the drawing boards every week. Times had changed and the elegant blonde Scandinavians working on a prestige project had been replaced by down-at-heel Brits and Canadians working for a Greek body shop that rented them out to TAMCO as filing clerks. And the sauna had been converted into an English pub bar.

The Virgin pulled Rubberdy out of the bar and took him down to his apartment. "Look, Rubberdy, I'm in deep shit and I need help."

Rubberdy did not know how to respond. "You mean, you need some money?" he asked.

"No, no – nothing like that. I mean real trouble. With Security. I think they want to arrest me."

Now he was shocked and frightened, but he understood. At heart everyone was frightened of Tabriz. "But help? What can I do…?"

"You're going to give me your little cart to take down to the desert for an engineering check."

"My cart? But – but it's OK – it doesn't…"

"Rubberdy, we're talking about my arse here. Seriously. And I promise it'll never come back on you. No one will ever know. Not even the foreigners, unless you tell them yourself."

Rubberdy looked at him dumbly. "I suppose… But where are you going?"

"Don't ask. Really, don't ask. I've come around for a drink and you're going to ask me to take the cart down to our desert workshop for checking. I'll back my car into your yard, we'll load it up, and I'm out of town on Friday. That's all you want to know, OK?"

"OK, I suppose." There was really nothing else he could say. Then he cheered up. "Do you want me to show you how it all works? It's really good." The cart was standing against a wall behind the villa. Its aluminium mesh body hung between two bicycle wheels. Rubberdy had imported a carbon fibre pack to make the two elegant shafts that stretched out in front of it. Together they dismantled it, Rubberdy showing off all the features he had built into his baby over the last year. The Virgin backed his car into the yard and they packed it into the boot. The shafts fitted diagonally over the back seats.

Back home, The Virgin spread Rubberdy's map on his table. It was a section of the international aviation map, confidently displaying all the official airstrips around the oilfields, and less confidently shading in the topographic relief and sand dunes. His father's generation had fought battles back and forth across this desert. Nearer the coast some of the prominent features still had their wartime names. Rubberdy had marked his route out in red ink. South from Sabah crossing low hills and a small sabkha, and then further south coming to the Al Ha'il Depression, a really big sabkha. Al Ha'il stretched from near the Cape Town Road all the way east to the Egyptian border and beyond.

He rose early from a sleepless night and packed a small bag. He knew he was playing for time and that every moment that his departure could be hidden would be a moment gained. He left his bed unmade as normal and tried to leave no suggestion that he was departing for good. If Zella thought he was coming back, perhaps he would not start looking for him too seriously. Socks, Bandaid and his walking boots. A thick sweater against the desert cold. Just for luck he rolled Elena's panties up into a small ball and hid them in one of his boots. Toothbrush, razor. He took two double sheets from his linen cupboard. They would be his shelter and camouflage. There was still enough room in the car boot for his bag and the sheets. He threw his straw hat onto the back shelf of the car and went back to lock the door. He clicked the garden door closed. Whatever happened, he would never see this house again. Excited and a little sad, he drove into town.

Time dragged in the office. He called Elena. He sensed she wanted to sound cheerful. "Have you packed your little wheel barrow?" she asked. "You'd better start pushing it now if you want to get here by Christmas." It was not comforting, but what else could she say? No one in London could help him now.

He told Abdul and Rabka that he might have to go to Almadi. He thought he might drive down on Friday, and take in some of the sights on the way. The highway to the west passed two beautiful Roman towns and the ridge of the Jabal Al Dun was only a short diversion into the edge of the desert.

On the rig he told Rene a different story. He was going on a trip east to the war cemeteries at Hell-fire Hill and might be away for a day or two. Could he please pass that on to Florian by radio as the telephone was giving trouble?

After leaving the rig he still had time to kill. He drove to Cape Horn and sat in the sun, watching the tireless Mediterranean lap at the rocks and thinking that Crete was only a short boat ride away. Not far, but out of reach.

His watch was moving in treacle, but at last he could pick up Danka and buy the meat and the Pepsi for the picnic. As he followed Danka along the crowded pavements, he was moving in a daze and he tried to resist the urge to hurry. Apparently Danka did not feel the pressure. She chattered with the shopkeepers normally and bargained unsuccessfully for cheaper prices. The Virgin felt glad when at last they could load the car and drive to the tannery. Janusz was waiting for them and helped them unload the cart. He promised to put everything onto the bus and to fill the water containers.

The sun was dipping in the sky as they drove back towards town. Now they would have to get rid of the car. They joined the evening procession into town and wound slowly around to the Egyptian souk. It was an informal island of tolerated enterprise on one of the flat empty lots that surrounded the town centre. They wove between the puddles to the high wall of the souk, ignoring offers from Sudanese waifs to wash the car. Hiring a car washer meant you had an informal guard for your car, something he definitely did not need tonight. He hoped he was talking naturally to Danka as they got out and he slammed the door with the key still in the ignition and the window slightly open. The car would not survive the evening.

They picked their way into the souk, avoiding porters and puddles and diving into the narrow lanes of stalls selling the produce of Egypt. Here everything was available. Watches, radios, shoes, sports clothes, all very cheap, and of very poor quality. He followed Danka as she patiently pushed her way through the crowds to the far corner of the souk. They stepped out into a mass of parked cars and strolled out towards the road and Barani. Ten minutes later they were fumbling their way up the stairs in the dark.

Wanda was waiting for them with food ready to cook. The Virgin sat in the front room sipping flash and Pepsi. The girls busied themselves in the kitchen. He flicked through an old woman's magazine in Polish; they had nothing to read in English. He thought of the hours he had wasted sitting in this room with his thoughts, not listening to the Polish conversation flowing over him, content to have company as he sat alone. Tonight was different. The girls had taken him in even though they knew he was trouble. These were real friends, ones that he could count on even when life itself might be at stake.

Dinner was breaded camel steak and mashed potatoes, with ketchup as a vegetable. The meat looked oily and he ate out of duty rather than hunger. After eating, he sat in silence as the girls enjoyed their cigarettes and flash.

Danka carried in a large saucepan of hot water from the kitchen. "Come, Virgin. You can have shower in Barani." She led him into the bathroom. It was basic but clean. "Good – now, you must use this tap for cold water. The shower is not good – only cold." She passed him a plastic jug and showed him how to half-fill it with cold water and dip a little hot water from the pan to take the edge off it. Oh well, thought The Virgin, it will be my last shower for a while, so I had better enjoy it.

He went to Danka's bedroom cold and only a little cleaner. It was a narrow cell with a single mattress on the floor. The Health Department provided only theoretical furniture so Danka's bedside table was a small wooden box covered with a hand-sewn cloth. A cheap reading lamp gave soft red light. Danka was sitting on the mattress waiting for him.

"You go into bed, Virgin. I make my shower, and come later." She opened the covers for him and waited. There was nothing for it but to strip off, leave his clothes in a pile in the corner and dive into bed. The sheets felt good on his skin and he shivered. Danka smiled and stroked his hair. "You wait, Virgin, I come and make you warm."

She came to him in a rush, shivering under her thread-bare bathrobe. She threw it aside and jumped into bed. In the red light The Virgin caught a glimpse of her generous white body. He wriggled over to put his back against the wall and give her space to lie. She felt cold and moist from her shower. He put an arm over her and pulled her close to share his warmth. She burrowed her face into him and he felt her warm breath on his shoulder.

His warmth was reaching her and she started to relax. He propped himself up on one elbow to look at her. The magic of love had transformed her and she looked beautiful. Her eyes, always pretty, were watching him curiously and the soft light gave her plain face radiance. He bent to kiss her. She tasted fresh, of toothpaste and smoke. She wrapped her arms around him and pulled him over her.

Later, she lay on her back with a smile on her face. "Was good, Virgin. Very good. We must do this before; it would be better. You like also?"

He poked her in the ribs. "Of course. Wonderful. Fantastic."

"Ha! You say to all the girls. I know." but she was still smiling. She pushed the pillow over for him to share. "Now, we sleep. Tomorrow will be very busy."

Danka had a shift worker's ability to sleep on command and her breathing soon became regular. The Virgin was uncomfortable.

Trapped between Danka and the wall, and with her wispy hair in his face, he lay awake and thought.

Most of all, he wanted to be out in the desert. Free from Zella, free from MacAllans, just alone and independent. The desert did not frighten him. He knew about the desert and what it could do. What it would definitely do to the unwary or unprepared. But at least the desert had its own laws and it never deviated from them. The worst it would throw at him would be a ghibli and even that would not be too bad. It might throw his compass off but at least it would hide him, and only the very thickest ghibli would stop him locating the sun and navigating that way.

He had only to get into the desert and he would be safe. That was the difficulty. There would be the five regular checkpoints to negotiate – they would not be a problem if the police were their normal sleepy selves. And then there was the main customs and police post on the Cape Town Road. Would anyone remember him from his trip down there to collect the cross-over for the rig? He had waited for at least twenty minutes before the pick-up from Lima-5 had met him. When was that? Last week? The week before? Would they recognize him at all? He had been driving a car then; this time he would be just another passenger in a Polish minibus.

He did not know how long he had been lying there awake when he heard a soft knocking at the apartment door. Strange, he thought, why don't they ring the bell? The knocking persisted and without waking Danka he crawled out of bed and tiptoed to the door. The peep hole was useless; there was no light in the corridor. As quietly as he could, he unlatched the door and opened it.

Major Jamal stood there. Not wearing his tweed suit but a plain white djellabiyah. He did not look well. He was hunched, thin and pale, and his hair blew in sparse wisps over his crown. His eyes were intense and bloodshot. The Virgin stared at him. He was talking, his white moustache moved, but no sound came. Still in shock, he looked over Major Jamal's shoulder at Stanford, who was giggling insanely and pointing at The Virgin's nakedness.

He woke with a rush, heart pounding, and remembered where he was. He could see grey between the slats of the shutters but he knew that it was far from dawn. His arm was cramped beneath him and he tried to get comfortable by rolling his face into the wall and lying on the other side for a change.

Next time he woke he had Danka curled up behind him. Her breathing tickled his back. There was light in the room now. His mind started to race again and he knew there would be no more sleep for him. He climbed out of bed and left Danka sleeping.

He was clean, shaved and boiling water for coffee when Danka appeared in her bathrobe. "Boże, Virgin, I'm tired," she complained. "I want to sleep again."

"You can sleep in the bus. What do you want for breakfast?"

"Just wait. I wake Wanda and make breakfast." The Virgin made three cups of coffee.

They had a quiet and thoughtful meal with little said. Afterwards The Virgin sat alone in the main room. Danka stood on the balcony watching for the minibus, while Wanda made sandwiches. He hated the waiting. Eventually Wanda brought her picnic bag and came to wait beside him.

"They are here, Virgin," called Danka. "We go now. Quickly."

With a sense of relief, The Virgin hurried down the stairs. Danka held him at the door and stepped out alone. The minibus was waiting with its sliding door open. There was no one else around. It was too early and the neighbouring apartment blocks were still asleep. Danka waved him in and he slipped out of the building and took the empty seat waiting for him at the back of the bus. The mesh body of his cart was in the aisle beside him, full of blankets and picnic bags. His neighbours looked at him curiously. They were working men with lined faces and cheap tee shirts. He nodded smiles at them and they smiled shyly back. Then Janusz, tousled as ever, reached over the seat to shake his hand. "Good, Wirgin, good to come!" The Virgin felt a glow of welcome and safety.

And then they were off, lurching over the rough ground towards the road. Sabah was waking sluggishly to another Friday and there was very little traffic around. Once they got onto the modern roads around the old town centre, the driver put his foot down and they sailed over the empty concrete fly-overs. Beside him, the town still slept. The Virgin craned around to get a last look at Sabah.

The highway ran out of town between a jumble of villas and the walled compounds of the rich. The road had trees beside it here, tough eucalypts throwing striped shadows across the road. The driver slowed for the police post at the edge of town. It, too, was sleeping. They slowed to a crawl as they approached the transportable building beside the road. Outside a young policeman sat on a metal chair. He was hatless and had yet to put his shoes on. He looked at them without curiosity and casually flapped a hand to wave them through. Good, thought The Virgin, let them all be like that and we will be fine.

They started on the serious driving. Flat, stony ground on either side of the divided highway. The red-gold disc of the sun shouldered its way up out of a grey dust haze. There must have been some wind across the desert in the last few days. Perhaps The Virgin would have his wish and be blessed with a small ghibli or two to hide in. He looked out over the featureless landscape. He would not miss this, he decided, not for a minute. He closed his eyes and tried to sleep.

They were stopped at the next checkpoint. Two soldiers idly waving cars through wanted a closer look at Danka and Wanda in the front seat. One of them held his hand out for papers. The driver had a wallet of car and company documentation ready, and his badaka and driving licence on top. The soldiers were holding the documents but staring at the girls. Danka said something abrupt in Arabic and they straightened up. The men handed back the papers and they were through. Danka cranked herself round in her seat to give him a wave and a smile. The Virgin closed his eyes again.

They did not have a serious delay until the first check point on the Cape Town Road. They were stuck behind a battered Volvo truck. Its load was piled high and covered in tarpaulins. Strings of empty plastic containers were tied to the outside of the load and several white-turbaned Sudanese sat on top. The driver had got down and was arguing listlessly with the police about his documents. The minibus driver switched off the engine and they waited. The passengers slid open their windows and lit cigarettes. Patience, The Virgin told himself, patience. This is normal. He closed his eyes and tried to relax.

They must have waited for fifteen minutes or more when there was hooting from behind. The Virgin looked back. A black Mercedes limousine was passing the substantial queue on the wrong side of the road. It pulled up opposite the police post. A fat, balding man leant out of the window, shouting and gesturing emphatically with one arm. He accelerated away without waiting for approval. Lethargically, the police sent the truck driver back to his cab and moments later he was jolting off down the road. The police waived the queue of vehicles through without checking.

They were at the edge of the true desert now. No more vegetation, just a wide brown nothing stretching to the horizon in every direction. And there was only one more check to go. Now The Virgin would see if anyone remembered him. He wished he had cut his hair short and shaved his beard right off. Too late now, and he peered forward waiting for the dot on the road that would turn into the last checkpoint.

Two more desert trucks waited beside the road, complete with empty plastic containers and forlorn Sudanese passengers. Their faces were expressionless as they awaited their fate. The black Mercedes had parked next to the police post and the fat man was laughing and smiling with the policemen crowded around him.

They rolled to a halt. Once there had been a ceremonial arch here, built out of steel and bearing green placards with slogans in white Arabic lettering. There had been an accident and only one lonely upright remained. The span of the arch, with its stirring slogans intact, lay propped up beside the road on oil drums. All around the sand of the desert was littered with the rubbish of people who had been held up here, perhaps for days, while they waited for their paperwork.

The minibus driver waited patiently for someone to notice them. At last one of the policemen took his attention from the fat man and gave them a cursory wave. The driver let in the clutch and they jolted slowly over the ship's cable that lay across the road as a speed bump. They picked up speed and headed south. A load fell from The Virgin's shoulders.

He was asleep when they slowed down and turned off the highway. A short, hard-packed road led to a brine pit at the edge of the Al Ha'il sabkha. They must have used this brine to lay dust during the road construction. A narrow track wound past the sump and along the edge of the sabkha. They climbed stiffly out of the minibus and stretched themselves. They were out of sight of the highway here. To either side layered brown dirt had been cut into badlands by ancient rains flooding down to the sabkha. In front of them stretched Al Ha'il. Flat, white salt, a lake made solid.

It was not yet mid-day. The Virgin had plenty of time to waste so he helped putting up the beach umbrellas and getting the barbecue ready. In the shade beneath the umbrellas the weather was fine. The sun had not hammered winter out of the desert yet and the air temperature felt comfortable. A dry wind was blowing, not enough to stir the dust but enough to cool the skin. He spread a blanket under one of the umbrellas and stretched out. Now he could sleep.

Danka shook him awake. "Eating, Virgin! Come and eat." He joined the crowd around the barbecue. They were laughing and chattering, plastic cups of flash and Pepsi in their hands. They had set a grill up between three stones and steaks were sizzling and dripping over the coals. The Virgin was suddenly hungry and the meat smelt good. Following the girls, he carried off a steak sandwiched between two slices of white bread.

They settled back on the blanket. Danka poured him a Pepsi. "For you, no flash today. We have flash," and she poured big slugs into the cups for herself and Wanda. She raised her cup. "Good luck, Virgin!"

He was beginning to feel restless and took Danka for a walk after they had eaten. "This place was like the sea before, Virgin? How much before?"

He thought. "Not long, I think. I bet there was still water here twenty thousand years ago. But salty water. And if you look in the rocks over there, you can find shark's teeth from dinosaur times. Big ones too. Anyway, I expect that a million years ago or more, it was like the sea here. Perhaps even connected to the sea."

Danka shrugged her shoulders. "Twenty thousand year is long time to me, Virgin."

He smiled. "But not to a geologist. That's not even yesterday. More like – just before lunch. But this is a very historic place, you know. Come on, I'll show you something."

They walked on along the edge of the sabkha until they came to a place where a small promontory jutted out into the salt bed. The ground was rough and disturbed and black rocks were lying scattered in the sand. "Look, the caravans used to stop here. They used these stones around their fires."

Danka looked at him in disbelief. "How do you know, Virgin?"

"Just look – you'll find things." He searched for a moment and then turned over a stone with his foot. "There – now what do you think?" It was a thick shard of rough pottery, probably from a storage jar of some sort.

Danka picked it up. "Heavy," she said. "You think they come here by camel?"

"No other way, except walking. And I wouldn't want to walk with a pot like that on my back. Keep looking. I expect you'll find some bigger pieces. I think they used them as plates after the jars had been broken."

Danka started to search. The Virgin had often promised himself he would bring a metal detector here one day, but now it was too late. Something caught his eye. "Look – recognize this? It's a gun-flint. You know, from the old rifles they used to have. Or perhaps from a fire lighter – it's all the same."

They walked back to the others, Danka clutching a large pottery fragment. "You've got to imagine that people have always walked around this end of the sabkha. They didn't want to cross it with their camels – it's bad for their feet – so they came around the end. And later on, when Europeans came, they just followed the caravan routes. There's even an old Italian fort about five kilometres that way. That must have been a God-awful posting for those poor guys. Sitting in the middle of the Sahara, playing soldiers and watching for passing camels. Even today trucks can't drive over the sabkha, so the Cape Town Road goes through here as well. Just the same way."

The guys were relaxing when they got back, sleeping or smoking in the shade. The Virgin went to the back of the minibus to unload the cart. Slowly and with care he started to assemble it. Rubberdy had done a good job. It was the Ferrari of carts, a sleek, shiny aluminium speedster. Empty, it moved with the lightest touch. He started to weigh it down with water containers. This would be his life's blood. He loaded the cart so it almost balanced over its axle. Just a slight weight on the shafts, Rubberdy had said.

The sun was beginning to shine under the umbrellas and take away their shade. He got Danka to stir up the men. Complaining, they followed Pawel out onto the salt and started to play football. They threw long shadows on the ground as they ran back and forth, stirring up the surface. The Virgin watched for a while and then went back to his packing. He clipped the MacAllans safety belt around his waist and adjusted the shoulder straps. It was comfortable enough.

"You are ready, Virgin?" asked Danka standing beside him.

"As ready as I'll ever be, I guess."

"Come on – before you start, first you must sit with us. It is tradition." They joined Wanda on the blanket. Danka offered him a Pepsi bottle. "Drink, Virgin, drink."

He smiled at her concern. "I'm not a camel, you know. I can't store up Pepsi for three weeks of travel. If I drink too much, I'll just piss it away."

"No problem. But drink anyway." Then she was silent for a while. "Virgin – you must tell us. Why is your name Virgin?"

"That? Oh – it's just a Hash name. They say I look like Richard Bransome."

"Like who?"

"Like Richard Bransome. You know, the guy who owns Virgin Records and Virgin Atlantic. The businessman. Always flying around the world in a balloon and doing crazy things like that."

"Virgin, this is stupid!" She did not approve. "When do you go?"

He looked around him. "About half an hour, I guess. You can still see too much just now."

"I am cold," she complained and snuggled up to him. Wanda snuggled up to the other side and they waited in silence.

Pawel and Janusz came to help him. The three of them lifted the cart off the ground and carried it out through the football players. The football players were dribbling and feinting over their tracks. Danka and Wanda took another route out to join them.

The Virgin looked back. Already the minibus was far away, nearly invisible in the dusk. This would have to do. They set the cart on the ground. Pawel picked up the shafts and gave an experimental push. It rode easily. He said something to Danka.

"He says it is very good," she said with a defiant note in her voice.

"I know," said The Virgin. "Tell him and the guys thank you for everything."

Pawel gave a long answer. "He says it is nothing. We are Polish. Always we have trouble with Germans or Russians or Austrians. And then with Communists. For us this is normal. And he says – Good Luck."

The Virgin slipped the ends of the shafts through his belt loops and clipped the towing strap into the large eye at the back. He shook hands with Pawel and Janusz. A hug for Wanda and another longer one for Danka. She was crying. "Virgin – you go to where the sun wakes up – keep going and you will make it. I see you in Cairo."

He waved to the footballers, faced the sabkha and started to walk. The cart came freely, the salt making a light crunching sound beneath the tyres. Yes, he thought, I'll keep walking to where the sun wakes up *and I'll make it.*

Other titles by Jacqueline George

The Prince and the Nun
Foreign Affairs
Her Master's Voice
Light o'Love
How to make Wild, Passionate Love to your Man
Falling into Queensland
Where Gold Lies

www.jacquelinegeorgewriter.com

Printed in Great Britain
by Amazon